To Harry.

THERE IS A PLACE

CATHY M. DONNELLY

Best wishes.
Cathy Donnelly

ISBN-13: 978-1519344205

ISBN-10: 1519344201

DEDICATION

For my dear friend
Heather Cook

ACKNOWLEDGMENTS

I am grateful to **Wilma and Cliff McKinnon**, my sister and brother-in-law, who kindly agreed to be included in the novel and also willingly and honestly gave their opinion when I needed it.

My thanks to **Val and Bill Pollock** for reading an early draft of the novel. Their input was invaluable. Their knowledge of Scottish history is impressive and Bill's collection of books is a joy to behold. I would also like to thank **Colleen Dooley** and **Suzi Sterel** for their valued input.

When I visited Inchmahome, **Lynne Gardiner** was very kind in sharing her knowledge of the island. **Malcolm** ferried visitors to and from the island and I kept my promise to mention the *enigmatic boatman* in this novel. **Joyce Reekie** is an expert on Alloa Tower and was most helpful on my visit there.

We are taught that God made our planet in six days.

Some know of an ancient story which tells that although He was well pleased with His work, God decided His world needed a special touch of magic.

So, on the seventh day, God created Scotland.

Cathy M. Donnelly

Chapter 1

Flodden Field, September 1513

Light invaded the darkness. The pain pulsed to the beat of the drum inside his head. The outside world tried to force itself upon him but he resisted. He tried to drift back to the place of oblivion but it was not to be. He sniffed the air. What was that smell? Blood? His stomach heaved at its sourness. The noise in his head was outranked by other sounds. Screaming. Moans of pain and despair.

Michael opened his eyes slowly. The sun hung in front of him. The ground beneath him was hard and uneven. He could no longer embrace the emptiness. Michael flexed his limbs and was surprised to find no pain. That came in an engulfing wave as he pushed himself to a sitting position, forcing him to snap shut his eyes and cling to the earth with unsteady hands. He waited until it subsided and the world again assaulted his senses. He could once more smell the blood and hear the cries of agony. He felt a sticky cold liquid beneath his hands and forced his eyes open.

The man before him appeared to be kneeling in prayer, his head bowed in perfect stillness. As he focused, Michael saw the hilt of a sword over the man's shoulder, the rest of it having sliced through his body with the point pinning him to the ground. Michael jerked backwards. He lifted his hands to wipe his eyes. They were covered in blood.

Then Michael remembered. A terrible, profound, grief overwhelmed him. Robbie was dead. Sadness erupted from his heart and overflowed in hot blinding tears. Still he sat there, without will or need to move, such was the weight of his sorrow.

The cries stirred him from his hell and he focused again on the world around him. For a moment he hoped it was but a dream, a nightmare, and that it would soon be over. He knew it was not. He stood up and slowly wiped his hands against his legs as he stared at the scene before him. Bodies lay as far as the eye could see, among a jumble of swords and shields. He had to find Robbie. He would not leave him in this field of death. He would find him and take him home.

Panic gripped Michael when he realized this was not the place he had last seen his brother and held him as he died. Robbie had managed a brief smile, despite the pain of the awful wound to his gut, and then he was gone. Michael tried to shut out the memories of what followed but the images of what he had done came flooding back. He took a few steps forward, sank to his knees and vomited.

When the nausea passed, he set about finding Robbie's body. He stepped over the dead, the almost dead, as he searched. There were so many. They lay crumpled on the ground, body upon body. He saw others walking among them. Perhaps they had seen Robbie. He made his way to the man walking away from him. He shouted out but the man kept going. He raced after him, stepping over, on, bodies and slipping on the blood. When Michael at last reached the man, he put his hand on his shoulder. The man stopped and slowly turned. Michael froze, his breath trapped in his lungs. An axe was lodged in the man's stomach. His guts had slithered out of his body and dangled to his thighs. Michael forced himself to look at the man's face. Dried blood and dirt were caked on his skin and his unblinking eyes stared straight ahead. When they came to rest on Michael the man held out his hands. His silent mouthing of the words "help me" tore at Michael's heart. He could not help this man. He was already dead. Michael continued to stare at the walking corpse. How could this be? How could this dead man be on his feet?

Michael turned and ran, stumbling and then getting up and running again. When he eventually stopped, he looked back at the way he had come. From the distance he could see many men roaming among the bodies. Were they ghosts also? He thought they must be. A wave of shock hit him. Was he dead too?

Chapter 2

Michael's attention was drawn to a still figure on a nearby hill. He rubbed his eyes and in that moment the figure appeared at his side. Michael stepped back quickly, his eyes searching for a weapon, despite the fact that the man was dressed in the black woollen habit of a monk.

'That will not be necessary, my son. I mean you no harm.'

The man pushed back his cowl. His hair was long and white, his skin pale and wrinkled. His sparkling blue eyes belied his obvious age and his smile seemed kind. 'My name is Maurice. I have come to help you, Michael.'

'You know me?'

'We have never met but I hope we will become friends.'

'Then I am not dead?'

'No. You are very much alive.'

Michael's relief lasted but a moment. 'I cannot find my brother. And I can see...' His eyes returned to the battlefield. The monk placed his hand on Michael's arm. Instantly his panic subsided.

'Let us find a place to sit and talk.'

Michael followed the monk to a slight rise in the ground and they both sat on a large boulder. 'Can you help me find my brother's body? I need to take him home.'

'He is already home, Michael. He is long gone. Not like the others you see wandering over there.'

'You see them too?'

'I do.'

'Who are you?'

'I am an ordained priest of the Order of St. Augustine. We are often called the Black Canons. I am here to help the dead move on.'

'What!'

'Those men you see wandering among the bodies have not accepted they are dead and their spirits refuse to leave.'

'They do not know they are dead?'

'Perhaps some do but just refuse to go. It often happens when a life is brought to an abrupt, unexpected end.'

'How can this be?'

'The body dies, Michael, but the spirit is eternal. It too needs to move on from this world. I help them to accept the death of their body and show their spirit the way to the light of God.'

'You can see the light of God?'

'I come from that light.'

Michael stood up and stepped back. He realized he must have hit his head harder than he thought.

'No, Michael, you are not imagining this. St. Augustine once said that faith is to believe what you do not yet see. The reward for this faith is to see what you believe. Please sit down and I will tell you a story.'

Reluctantly, and more because he could not think what to do next, Michael did as he was asked.

'I was once Prior of my order on an island called Inchmahome. I was happy there, administering to the people around Menteith and the monks under my charge. Then I forgot why I became a monk. I grew ambitious. I became chaplain to King Robert the Bruce and his soldiers. I was obsessed with Scotland's right to be a free nation with a Scottish king and I delighted not only in blessing the soldiers before battle, but encouraging them to rid our land of the English. I was present at the battle at Bannockburn in 1314. I gave a rousing speech before the battle and then celebrated the death of our enemies when it was over. It was great day for Scotland. King Robert made us a proud nation again.'

For a moment the monk remained silent, his gaze fixed ahead. Michael watched him and said nothing.

'I forgot my pledge to God, to honour life and serve Him,' Maurice continued. 'But God is merciful. He let me see the error of my ways. As I indulged in the pride of victory, I gradually began to see the spirits of the dead soldiers, just like you did today. I saw them not as enemies of my country but as children of God. When death took them they were not English or Scots. They were just spirits looking for a way home. Some of them could not find it though.

'When I realized these spirits could see me and knew I saw them, it changed my world. I began to see the horror of war, not the glory. But I also realized that I could not stop men killing each other. I had to content myself with doing what I could to help. I lingered after the battle and talked to the spirits. I explained what had happened and encouraged them to move on. Some took heed of my words but there were others who would not accept them and wandered away in search of I know not what. My heart broke to see those lost souls. Afterwards I wanted to return to the sanctuary of Inchmahome, but I realized God had given me a gift. There were many battles to follow, many souls to help. When my own body finally died my greatest desire was to continue my work. I have been doing this now for a very long time.'

Michael wondered if this was real. He was sitting in a horrific battlefield with a dead monk. Weary as he was, he knew in his heart it was true.

'Why do I see the ghosts?'

'It is a gift from God, Michael. A gift you can accept or let go. This has been a bloody battle and many souls are lost. The King is dead and a great many of the nobles and soldiers. As you can see, there are too many to count. I help those I can. You too can help, if you choose.'

'Help! Just because I see them does not mean I can help them. I am only 16. I have just lost my brother and I can barely help myself.'

Maurice gently rested his hand on Michael's shoulder. 'Look out over the field. What do you see?'

Wearily Michael directed his gaze to the devastation. 'I see…I see bodies, crumpled and piled on top of each other. I see a few men, dead men, wandering around in a daze. I see blood, lots of blood. I see carnage.'

'Look harder.'

Michael tried to still his growing panic and held his gaze over the scene. At first he thought it was a mist seeping up from the ground and moving in swirls. The closer he watched he saw that the patches of mist were coming from individual bodies. He focused on one and saw the white mist detach itself and drift upwards. His eyes encompassed the whole scene and he saw many puffs of the white mist.

'You see it, Michael? You see the spirits of the dead leave their bodies and drift away? You are seeing the very essence of a man's soul leaving a body that is no longer functioning and moving towards another existence. What else can you see?'

'Some of the mist is lingering over bodies and I see more men walking around.'

'They are the ones I try to help. Lost souls, who need to accept their death and move on. Without help some of them will continue to wander this earth for a long time, without comfort or peace.'

'You think I can help them like you do?'

'Most certainly. Otherwise God would not have given you the gift to see them, or me.'

Michael looked at the monk. His eyes held only kindness and a comforting warmth radiated from the hand still resting on his shoulder.

'You have other gifts, Michael. I can help you accept them, develop them, and perhaps find peace.'

'What do I need to do?'

'First we will find you water and food. Then you must rest.'

Maurice led him to an upturned supply cart where they found some stale bread and a half jug of ale. Michael softened the bread in the liquid. How did he end up in this place of misery? It was not how he envisaged his life would be.

Robbie, his beloved brother, his hero, had returned from furthering his education in France and Michael thought life would be as it was before he left. But Robbie came back a grown man. They still rode and hunted together but Robbie spent much of his time talking with their father about the politics of Scotland.

Six months after Robbie's return, King Henry VIII of England invaded France. The French King convinced King James to invade England so that Henry would be forced to divert his troops home. Robbie insisted on joining the King's army.

'No, Robbie, I forbid it,' his father had said. 'You have good prospects and can follow any path you choose. Except this.'

'But Father, our King cannot deny the King of France. Think of the alliance. We need the French as much as they need us. King Henry has ambitions and Scotland will be his next target if we fail to show our power.'

'The King made a foolish decision and I will not give up my son as battle fodder.'

'The French are providing arms, ammunition and troops. We can do this and show the English we will not sit around waiting for them to cross our border. I will not be gone long. I want to do this, Father.'

Michael silently listened to the argument. Robbie's determination was infectious but Michael prayed his father would prevail in stopping him.

Their mother eventually joined them, demanding to know what the argument was about.

'Your son wants to fight for the King, my dear. He will not listen to me. You talk to him.'

The colour drained from her face. 'No, Robbie, you are not long returned. You cannot leave again. Do you want to put your mother in an early grave?'

'As I have explained to Father, this will be a skirmish. The English troops are in France. It will be over quickly.'

Robbie's stubbornness eventually won the day. Bile rose in Michael's throat. He stood up and went to Robbie's side.

'Well, Michael, it looks like your brother is leaving us again,' his father said.

'Not without me. I am going with him.'

In the silence that followed, no-one realized that their mother had slipped unconscious from the couch. Once revived, she cried uncontrollably.

'You are going no-where, Michael. You are sixteen. Look what you have done to your mother.'

'Father, if you forbid it I will run away and find Robbie anyway. It would be better if you agreed to let me accompany him. I have never disobeyed you but I will if I have to.'

Robbie's laughter released the tension in the room. He patted Michael heartily on the back. 'He will do it, Father. Best you agree to him coming. I will keep him safe. I give you my word.

In the days that followed, Michael was caught up in Robbie's excitement and looked forward to the adventure they would share.

They bid farewell to their weeping mother and anxious father on a warm August morning and rode to join the Scottish army heading for England.

Michael's memories of that journey and what followed pierced his heart as no dagger could.

Eventually he lay down by the cart, weary to the core, and instantly fell into a dreamless sleep. When he woke, he looked over the battle scene. Complete silence surrounded the many bodies. Not even the birds could find a song in their hearts. Maurice again appeared by his side.

'Are you ready now, Michael?'

'I think so. I still do not know if I can do this.'

'You can.'

Michael took a deep breath and followed Maurice back to the battlefield. There were many more spirits wandering among the bodies. His heart bled again for Robbie but he still felt there was the possibility that he might be one of those lingering between this world and the next, despite what Maurice had said. He might yet get the chance to embrace him one more time and say goodbye.

'Father, who are they?' Michael said, pointing to living people making their way through the bodies.

'Families looking for their kin, or whatever they can take from the dead.'

'They are robbing the dead?'

'Have pity on them, Michael. For some their lives depend on what they can scratch from the earth or find on the bodies. They are weary of the constant fighting and numbed by the death and destruction. Who could blame them? Their lives are hard enough and what they take is of no use to the dead.'

An English soldier approached them. He had a large wound on his skull. The blood had dried like a frozen river down his face and neck. Michael felt anger surge through his body. This could have been the English bastard who killed Robbie. Maurice stood close to the man and laid his hand on his shoulder.

'My name is Maurice, soldier. And yours?'

'George.'

'I know you are lost George. I want to help you.'

'Where am I? I cannot see my friends. They are gone.'

'They are with God now, my son. Like you they fought bravely but were overcome.'

'They are dead? I am dead? What will become of me? I do not know how to get home.'

'Heaven will be your new home now, George. I can help you get there if you let me. You can be with your friends again and find peace.'

George's sadness reached out and touched Michael. His anger disappeared and he felt only compassion for this man.

'Look behind you, George,' Maurice said. 'See that light over there? If you go towards it, it will take you to a better place.'

'I am afraid.'

'Here, take my arm and I will walk with you.'

Maurice slowly led the soldier towards the light. In a blink of an eye, he was gone and Maurice returned to Michael's side.

George was one of many Maurice helped that day. Michael watched and listened but still did not think he could do this.

Later in the day they came across a young Scottish soldier, about Michael's age. He was still holding his sword and held it up as they approached him.

'No need for that, my son,' Maurice said. 'We have come to help you.'

'Where is the King? The battle is not going well. I need to find him.'

'The battle is lost. There will be no more fighting today.'

'Lost! Are you mad? It has only started. The English are gaining on us. We need to get to higher ground. Get away from me, old man. I need to find the others. We have much to do if we are to win.'

Michael recognized his pain and frustration. He stepped forward and gently put his hand on the soldier's arm.

'The battle is indeed lost. My brother is gone too. I know how you feel, but you need to take care of yourself now. I can help you leave this place. Please let me help you.'

He looked down at Michael's hand and then into his eyes. He sighed and then nodded.

'Walk with me a little,' Michael said. 'I will take you home.'

'You did well, my son,' Maurice said when Michael returned to his side. 'Remember it will not always be like this. Some will fight against the fact they are dead. Others may panic or want to hit out. But it will be easier if we both do it. Are you ready?'

'I will try, Father.'

'Call me Maurice.'

Every time Michael helped a spirit to move to the light, there was another. He was sad for the ones who refused to leave but realized he could not force them. Long into the day they worked. He found himself quite a distance from Maurice as the light began to fade. Eventually he could only see one spirit a short distance away. The man did not look harmed but as Michael drew closer he saw that a sword had been plunged into his chest and withdrawn, leaving a gaping wound. His torn clothes had once been costly and finely tailored, his muddied boots expertly crafted. Michael thought he would have been a handsome man before the torment of death engulfed him.

'Who are you?'

'My name is Michael. I can help you.'

'Help me! I am dead. How can you help me?'

'What is your name?'

The man stared at Michael. 'I am Lord Robert Erskine.'

'I am honoured, my Lord.' Michael knew of the Erskine family. They were part of Scotland's history, a noble line that stretched back centuries. They had fought with Robert the Bruce at Bannockburn and with Joan of Arc in France. The family seat at Alloa Tower was on the north bank of the River Forth.

'You need to move on from this place, my Lord.'

'I am going nowhere except home. Can you help me get home?' Lord Erskine's voice held a hint of desperation.

'Not to where you lived before but you can go home. See that light over there. If you go into it all will be well.'

'I see the light, lad, but I am not going yet. There is something I have to do first.'

'Can you tell me what that is?'

Lord Erskine stared at him. 'If you must know, I need to see my son, John.

'But he will not be able to see you.'

'Somehow I need to make him. I want to hold him and tell him I love him. I never did that you know. I never told him how much I cared.' Lord Erskine turned from Michael and stared into the distance. 'I wanted him to be a man, a strong man. My Isabella is a loving mother. I have other children and they all adore John. He needed no affection from me. Or so I thought. I have been wandering around here, thinking of my life, and I need to do this before I go. I need to let John know how much he means to me.'

'Not everyone can see the dead.'

Lord Erskine looked down his body at his wounds and the blood hardened on his clothes. Suddenly he took a step towards Michael and stared into his eyes.

'But you can. You can go to my home at Alloa Tower and speak to him for me.'

'I cannot.'

'Then I will not leave this place.'

Michael looked around for Maurice but he was no-where to be seen. He did not know how to deal with this.

'Will you do it?'

'I will try.'

'No!' Lord Erskine shouted, 'not try. Promise me you will seek John out and give him my message.'

Michael sighed. He just wanted to go home himself. See his parents and grieve with them for Robbie. He could not just turn up at the Erskine home and announce he had a message from a dead man. But what if the situation was reversed? What if the message a stranger carried was from Robbie?

He looked at the man before him. 'If I promise to do this, will you be content?'

'I will do anything you tell me if you give me your word.'

'On my honour, I will find your son and pass on your words. He might not believe me but I will do it. What do you want me to say to him?'

'Remind him of our blood pact.' Lord Erskine smiled and held out the bloodied palm of his left hand. On his wrist a freshly healed thin white scar was visible. 'John came to me a week before I left. He took a knife and cut himself and wanted me to do the same. I was about to admonish him for such foolishness but he stared me straight in the eyes and told me, told me mind you, to cut myself. I took my knife and did as he asked. He grabbed my hand and held our wounds together. He said he had a dream and in it I came to harm. He wanted me to remember that moment and that no matter what happened to me, the scar would remind me of him and was a sign of his love and respect for me. If I faced death then he wanted me to know I was not alone. He said it would be our secret. If you tell him I was remembering that moment as I died, he will believe you come from me. Tell him I love him and I am proud to have him as a son.'

'I will keep my promise.' Michael said.

'I think you will. I am weary now. Where is this light?'

'Right behind you.'

'Thank you,' Robert Erskine said, before turning and walking away.

The sky was tinged with pink as the sun made its way towards the horizon. The smell of decay and blood still hung heavy in the air.

Michael and Maurice stood on a small rise overlooking the battlefield. They had done what they could. Michael was tired to the bone and yet his weariness was tinged with a sense of wonder. They had helped many of the spirits to move on but for those who chose to remain they could do nothing.

People still wandered the darkening landscape. They had brought carts and horses to take away the dead for burial or to dig holes and bury them where they had fallen. Cistercian monks were helping weary soldiers with the bodies.

'They will take as many as they can for burial at their monastery at Coldstream,' Maurice said.

'What will we do now?' Michael asked.

'My work here is done but there are other places my services are needed. You do what you must, Michael.'

'I want to go home. I need to tell my family about Robbie. Grieve with them for a while. But not too long. I have a promise to keep.'

'To Lord Erskine?'

'How did you know?'

'It may not be easy. His family, in their grief, may turn against you. At best they may think you a madman.'

'I will take that risk. I cannot break my promise.'

'Good on you, lad.'

'Will I see you again, Maurice?'

'Doubt it not. We have much work to do together.'

Michael did not go home immediately. He still held the faint hope that one of the bodies would be Robbie. He helped the monks and soldiers take some of them to the monastery. All this was done in silence, for what words could a living person find when surrounded by such butchery?

After washing off the caked blood, dust and indescribable smell of death, Michael ate the food the monks gave him and slept. At dawn he put on his clothes which the monks had cleaned as best they could, and a black cloak they gave him to keep warm. Some of the soldiers who had been helping with the dead let him ride on their cart with two bodies. Michael thought it such a strange journey. No words were necessary; no thoughts shared.

When finally Michael arrived home he found the news of the defeat at Flodden had already reached his family. Having feared the death of both sons, his parents were overjoyed to see their youngest alive. The loss of Robbie would be dealt with later. For a short time they wanted to celebrate a life thought lost. Michael did not tell them of Maurice but only that he had made a promise to a dying Lord Erskine to take a message to his family. He was anxious to keep his word and hopefully give comfort to John Erskine. If it did not go well at least he had done his best. He stayed with his parents for only five days as he was weary and needed time to rest. He wondered at the rate of healing of his cuts and bruises. He must have imagined the severity of some of them because the skin had nearly grown over and there was no infection. His parents did not beg him to stay for they could not fully grieve for their dead son in front of the living one.

Chapter 3

Alloa Tower was an impressive stronghold. It had four levels and soldiers watched from the turreted roof. Michael led his horse to the shade of an old chestnut tree. Now that he was in sight of Lord Erskine's home, his fears returned. To tell a stranger he bore a message from his dead father would not be easy. He had considered saying Lord Erskine asked him to deliver the message before he died. That would indeed be plausible. Somehow he could not bring himself to lie. The truth, no matter how unbelievable, would be told. He tried to rehearse in his mind what he would say but eventually gave up and headed towards the Erskine home.

There were numerous outbuildings and stables on either side of the Tower. Soldiers were everywhere. He pulled up his horse when he saw six men riding towards him.

'What business do you have here?' one of them said. 'The household is in mourning and not accepting visitors.'

'I was at Flodden. I bring a message from Robert Erskine to his son, John.'

The soldier who appeared to be in charge nodded to one of his men who turned his horse and rode back towards the Tower.

'Do you carry a weapon?'

'There is a knife in the saddlebag.' Michael stayed still while two soldiers checked him and his horse. They removed the knife.

Soldiers with drawn swords were waiting outside the Tower. He sensed their alertness and dismounted slowly.

'Come with me,' a soldier said.

Michael followed him through the large ornate entrance and up the stone stairway. He could not help but admire this fortified home. The walls were adorned with colourful tapestries and the area he could see was beautifully furnished. He instantly felt that this was a place of tranquillity and love—a family home. The soldier opened a door and Michael stepped through into a large room. Three men stood facing him. One of them was Lord Erskine's son for the resemblance was unmistakable. He had the same long face, thin nose, high brow and dark eyes. His beard was shorter but redder than his father's. Four dogs were lying on the floor near a roaring fire. They pricked up their ears for a moment, looked over at Michael and then lay down again.

'I am John Erskine. You have a message for me?'

'I was to deliver it only to you.'

'What is your name?'

'Michael Craig.'

John Erskine turned to the other two men. 'Leave us.'

Once alone, John Erskine indicated for Michael to sit on one of the embroidered armchairs positioned around the fire. Light flooded through the windows and gave an almost yellow glow to the room.

'Here.' Lord Erskine handed him a large goblet and sat on the chair opposite him. Michael drank deeply.

'How old are you?'

'Sixteen.'

'Where is your home, your family?'

'My father was a professor of law at Glasgow University. He is retired now. Our home is at my mother's family's estate outside of Edinburgh.'

'You are not a common soldier then?'

'I went with my brother, Robbie. He was lost.'

'My father's body was brought home three days ago. We buried him with honour.' John Erskine stared at the flames. When he was ready he would ask about the message. Suddenly he rose and fetched the wine from the table. He refilled both their goblets, took two large mouthfuls and returned his gaze to the fire. Michael watched him. He looked to be quite a few years his senior. Perhaps he sensed Michael's scrutiny, or the time was right, for he turned and looked Michael straight in the eyes.

'You were at the battle?'

'Aye,' Michael said. The memories came flooding back. He shivered.

'Were you injured?'

'I was fortunate. Only cuts and bruises. But the others. I will remember the carnage for the rest of my life.' He took another mouthful of wine, hoping it would steady his shaking hands. 'I have never been in battle and hope never to be again.'

'My uncle and his two sons were also lost. My wife Margaret's father too. So many of our kin—dead. You were with my father during the battle?'

'No. I met him when it was lost.'

'His injuries were severe. He would not have survived long with them. You were with him when he died then?'

'No.'

'Why are you here? You said you had a message from him.'

The time had come. Michael felt strangely calm. 'So that you know I come here at the request of your father, he told me of your dream. He showed me the scar on his wrist and told me how you had cut yourself and made him do the same. How you asked him to remember that moment and know he was not alone and that you loved him.'

John Erskine stared at Michael, his face devoid of colour. He opened the palm of his hand and rubbed the scar on his wrist.

'He wanted to come home to you, tell you he loved you, something he said he never did, to his great regret.'

'He must have trusted you to tell you this. But you say you were not with him in the battle, nor were you with him when he died. When did he tell you of my dream and our conversation?'

Michael paused but for a moment. It was too late to turn back now. He looked John Erskine directly in the eye. 'We spoke after he died.'

John Erskine stood up and stared at Michael. 'What foolishness is this? Are you demented, man? Are you playing a game on people deep in grief? Does this give you pleasure?' John was now pacing back and forth in front of the fire.

Slowly, without emotion, Michael told John Erskine his story. When he finished he realized he was again seated opposite him, his head in his hands. He looked up slowly.

'You can see the dead?' he whispered.

For a long time they held each other's gaze. John finally rose and refilled the goblets. When he sat down, he raised his drink to Michael.

'Thank you for coming here, Michael Craig. You are obviously a man of integrity, for not all would keep a promise to a dead man and face ridicule. I believe what you say. My heart tells me it is the truth. I did have a dream before my father left to join the King. It felt so real and when I awoke I knew he would not return.'

Michael sighed. The tension left his body.

'We will keep this between us,' John Erskine said. 'I do not think my family will understand. They will doubt you, I think. Perhaps one day I will tell my mother, but not now. I would probably have died too but for my father's insistence that I guard our family, our home and the King's son.'

'My father told me your family are guardians of royal children.'

'Aye. It now falls to me. The Queen Mother is grieving, or so she would have us believe, and is with child, so I thought it best to guard his Grace here for a time. There is much intrigue at court.'

'It is a great responsibility.'

'One which the Erskines have always shouldered with pride. I have some business to attend to now but you will join us for dinner and I will tell the servants to ready a room for you.'

As Michael sat alone by the fire, the dogs having left with their master, he thought how strange it was that John Erskine believed him. If roles were reversed he might not have been so receptive.

The Erskine family was welcoming despite their obvious grief. John's wife, Margaret, was a beautiful woman. Her dark eyes held only kindness. His mother, Isabella, was frail, but perhaps it was her sorrow that made her seem so. John Erskine would no doubt have told them the reason for his visit but they did not discuss it. The women excused themselves early to attend to the children.

John and Michael moved to the armchairs beside the fire while the servants cleared the table. Eventually they were alone, except for the dogs, who settled themselves by their master's feet.

'They like their comfort,' Michael said. 'Our dogs are the same. My father tries to discipline them but my mother spoils them.'

'Mine may seem placid but believe me, they would defend me with their lives. I was surprised they barely gave you a glance when you first came into the room. It was the only reason I saw you alone. I trust their instincts. So what will you do now, Michael? You are welcome to stay as long as you wish.'

'Thank you, my Lord, but I do not know what I want, or need, to do.'

'My name is John. We will be friends you and I. I feel it.'

'I do not think I have come to terms with what happened to me at Flodden. Part of me still cannot believe it is real. Maurice said it is a gift.'

'God must have given it to you for a reason. It is a strange gift indeed, but a gift nonetheless.'

'But what do I do with it? Go looking for dead people to help?' He looked at John. 'I apologize. I did not mean to…'

'I know, but you coming here, passing on my father's message, means a great deal to me. Now I know how much he cared for me, and despite my grief I am content. I cannot tell you what you should do. I believe our destiny is shaped by the choices we make. I do not envy you yours.'

'It feels like I have lived a whole lifetime in just a few weeks.'

'You do not have to make a decision now. Take time to heal, to grieve. You will always be welcome in my home and will have my protection and guidance.'

They both watched the flames in silence. Michael contemplated on how they came to be here together and wondered if John was doing the same. One thing Michael was sure of was that whatever path he took, he could count of this man's friendship.

Eventually they bid each other goodnight. Fiona, one of the servant girls, showed him to a comfortable room in one of the outbuildings. Michael fell into a deep, dreamless sleep the moment his head touched the pillow.

When he woke he realized half the morning had passed. He washed himself in the water left for him and dressed. Just as he was finishing there was a knock on the door. Fiona told him when he was ready his Lordship wished to see him. She showed him to a room on the ground floor.

John Erskine was seated at a desk. 'Good morning, Michael. You slept well, I hope?'

'I did, but late I see.'

'You needed the rest. Sit by the fire. There is food laid out for you. I will finish this while you eat and then show you my home.'

Michael ate heartily of the fish, cheese and oatcakes set before him. It was a peaceful the room, just the gentle sound of John's quill scratching on parchment and the crackling of the wood on the fire.

'You have a beautiful home,' Michael said.

'It keeps my family safe and it is always a joy for me to return here. We have the advantage of seeing much of the surrounding area so it will be difficult for any enemies to catch us unprepared, and the well in the Great Hall ensures we will always have water in the event of a siege.

Michael followed John up the staircase. Many portraits hung on the walls. On one of the landings, Michael suddenly stopped. 'Your father,' he said.

'You recognize him?'

'When I saw him his beard was thicker and his frame heavier.'

'This was painted 10 years ago.'

On the third level was the library. Michael was mesmerized by the shelves of manuscripts and books. The room had the smell of leather. Comfortable chairs surrounded a table by the window and others were positioned near the unlit fire.

'Some of these documents go back centuries,' John said. 'The history of my family. My father loved this room. He said it filled him with a sense of belonging to this great kingdom. Our private rooms are on the fourth level. Let us visit the nursery. I would like you to meet his grandchildren.'

Margaret was sitting on a rocking chair, a child asleep in her arms.

'I brought Michael to meet the children, my dear.'

'This is Janet,' she said. 'Always active and wanting attention. She gently kissed the child on the head.

'She is beautiful,' Michael said.

'Margaret says she has a liking to me.'

Both men laughed and Margaret shook her head, a smile touching her lips.

'Your mother took Katherine to the garden,' she said. 'It was such a pleasant day and I thought it good for her to have something else to think about other than your father.'

'And over here in the crib is his Grace, King James V of Scotland,' John said proudly. 'The beauty beside him is our daughter, Margaret.' The child King's hand rested across the body of the baby girl. 'They will be friends I think. The preparations are in place for his crowning on the 21st at Stirling Castle. We go in a few days.

'Who will rule Scotland for him?' Michael asked.

'His mother is Regent. It is the wish of the late King. God help us—King Henry's sister. It would be better for Scotland to have one of our own to rule until the child is of age but for my part I will do what I can to protect him.'

Suddenly the boy opened his eyes and cried. He looked to baby Margaret beside him and returned to his dreams.

Michael bid farewell to Margaret and followed John up the narrow staircase to the roof. From the rampart he could see the surrounding countryside and the River Forth, a short distance away. Stirling Castle stood out against the horizon.

'It all looks so peaceful out there,' Michael said.

'Indeed. From here we look at the beauty of God's work. It is only when we look closer that we see the destructive nature of man. We blight the earth with our petty differences and the blood of our people. For what? I often thought it was power but I sometimes wonder if there is just something evil in man.'

'You think men are evil by nature?'

'I am not sure what I believe any more, Michael. The death of my father has left a melancholy in my heart. I see the world through sadness. That will pass, I hope.'

'I wonder if it will ever change, all this fighting,' Michael said. 'How do we get out of this cycle of destruction and live in peace with each other and our neighbours.'

'I do not know the answer to that. I wish I did. It saddens me to think my children will continue to do their duty and stay loyal to our kings but still not attain the peace our land deserves.' John turned to Michael and smiled. 'Enough of this morbid talk. As I said, we leave in a few days for Stirling Castle. Will you come with me to the coronation?'

'Me! You are inviting me to the crowning of the King?'

'Only if you wish. With your gift, perhaps you may be of assistance.'

'But I only see the dead.'

'Believe me, there are dead men who would wish to harm our King. Perhaps seeing the dead is not your only gift. Did you not wonder why I accepted your story so easily?'

'I was not expecting that.'

'I had a nursemaid, Ellie, when I was a child. She told me she could look at someone and tell if their heart was good. She also sensed danger. One day, after a great storm, we were playing in the garden. James and I were chasing each other around a tree when suddenly Ellie rushed up to us, grabbed each of us and ran back to where my mother stood near the house. Just as we reached her, the tree crashed to the ground. We could have been killed. My mother always kept Ellie close after that. She died when I was 12. Mother took us to her room to say goodbye and she seemed to be laughing and talking to herself. She had a beautiful smile on her face at the end. I have often wondered what it was she saw that we could not. I have never forgotten her. I was thinking that you may also have the gift of sensing danger. You have done me a great service by coming here and I expect no more of you. I would like you to consider working for me. You do not have to make a decision now but at least come to the coronation.'

The next afternoon Michael accompanied John Erskine and some of his men for a ride in the countryside. John said he needed to clear his head for what lay ahead. Michael enjoyed the company and the fresh air and his heartache eased for that short time. They returned before the evening meal. The Erskine family was already seated by the time they washed and changed clothes.

'We are happy you decided to stay, Michael,' Margaret Erskine said as she indicated for him to sit down.

Michael was still a little overwhelmed by the depth of hospitality he received in this house.

'Has Kate arrived yet? John asked.

'Just after you left,' Margaret said. 'I did call her but she is in the library as usual, her head deep in one of your manuscripts.'

'Kate is the daughter of Margaret's cousin,' John said. 'She visits us regularly. Her mother died some years ago and her father has remarried. She is a great help to Margaret and my mother, and the family is very fond of her. I have never known a girl to read so much though. I am sure her aim is to read every manuscript I have.'

All heads turned as the door was thrown open.

'John, forgive me. I was so absorbed I forgot about dinner.'

'It is of no import. Come, meet our guest. Michael, may I present Kate. Kate, this Michael Craig.'

John's voice seemed far away. Michael's focus was on the vision of beauty who was quickly making her way to the table. She took the seat opposite him. He had never seen such a perfect creature. Her long red hair was tied back in a green ribbon and hung over her shoulders. Her oval face glowed and was a perfect pallet for her full red lips, green eyes and long dark lashes.

She smiled. 'I am pleased to make your acquaintance, Michael Craig.'

He stood up and bowed. 'And I you, Kate.'

'And what brings you to Alloa Tower?' Her voice was soft and sweet.

'Michael was at Flodden, Kate. He spoke with my husband before he...'

'Oh, Aunt Isabella.' Tears came instantly to Kate's eyes.

'His dying thoughts were of me and his family. I could ask no more.'

There was no more talk of battles and grief during the meal. Instead they talked of the forthcoming coronation and the intrigues of court. Michael tried to pay attention but his eyes kept wandering to Kate. Sometimes when he looked at her she was already looking at him.

Michael stood silently on the roof of Alloa Tower. The moonlight bathed the land as far as the eye could see. The air was crisp but still. The sounds that came from the soldiers on guard faded into the background. He felt an agitation of spirit and a yearning, for what he did not know. He turned quickly at the movement behind him.

'Michael. I am sorry to disturb you.' Kate was wrapped in a green cloak, her face partially obscured by her hood. She came to stand beside him. She threw back her hood and smiled at him. A beautiful smile that set his heart racing.

'I often come here at night before the guards come on duty,' she said. 'In the silence I can almost believe all is well with the world. There are no battles to take men from their families, no hungry children because of it. Up here there are no enemies, no kings.'

'No kings?'

'Are you shocked? I mean no harm to the King. He is but a child and yet many will die for him so that he may grow and become like his father—someone whose life may be cut short at the hand of his enemy. It is the cycle of our country. In all my life I have never felt the peace that ought to come from people living in harmony, working and bringing up their children. Perhaps I will die without experiencing it.'

'Do not say that.'

'Forgive me for my ramblings. Sometimes I get sad for what might be. I was sitting with Aunt Isabella earlier and saw the pain in her eyes and heard the grief in her words. The man she loved since she was a young woman, whose children she bore, whose life she shared, is gone. For what? It is said that many thousands were lost. I would hate to love a man with all my heart and lose him to such a cruel end.' She sighed and looked again into the distance.

Michael did not know what to say. Her words voiced his own feelings of helplessness. There had been no glory in Robbie's death. He died too young.

'Oh Michael, forgive me. John told me of your brother's death. I have only made you sadder I think. You loved him very much?'

'I did. He taught me how to fish and climb trees. He took me on adventures and we would laugh till we cried. He was my friend and my hero. He was always taking care of me. Robbie was the brave one. He was four years older. When he was 18 my father sent him to France to further his education. When he came back my father wanted to send him to the University but Robbie wanted to go fight for the King. I insisted on going with him. Father said I was too young and forbade it but he eventually gave his permission.

'It did not take me long to realize there is no glory in war. There is hunger and cold and blood and death. Then we fought with the King at Flodden. I could not save Robbie. The pain of his loss will never go away. Perhaps you are right, Kate, there is no point to all this fighting. What is it to fight for your country when there is no peace at the end of it? There is only death and sorrow.'

'We are a strange species,' she said. 'I wonder why God bothers with us.' She looked at him and he was sure she could see his soul. 'I should not have disturbed you.'

'For tonight, let us be sad together, Kate.'

She put her hand gently on his arm and in silence they grieved.

Chapter 4

Michael tried to stay out of the way as much as possible as the preparations were made to move the King to Stirling. Such a small bundle, who was unaware of the intense activity going on around him. Eventually they made their way to Stirling Castle. He had hoped Kate would be accompanying them but she stayed to help Isabella Erskine with the children.

The ancient castle dominated the land as it rose from its high rock. The procession made its way up the steep hill and entered through the large ornate gateway into the courtyard. Michael helped the men with the horses and John and Margaret Erskine went with the baby King to be greeted by the Dowager Queen, Margaret Tudor.

That evening Michael accompanied John and Margaret to a feast in the magnificent Great Hall. At one end was a dais where Margaret Tudor sat with her advisers. Heat radiated from the five fireplaces and the light of many candles was reflected on the tall windows. Minstrels played in the galleries but the mood was not festive. Too many of those present had lost family and friends at Flodden.

Michael stayed by John's side as he had requested. Almost immediately he saw that not all the guests were alive.

'You were right, John. There are hostile souls around.'

'You see them.'

'Some seem just curious but not them all. What do you want me to do?'

'There is not much you can do with everyone else here. Stay with me.'

Michael was surprised that he could easily distinguish between words spoken in truth and those which held lies or concealment. But as the evening progressed, the noise increased and he began to feel overwhelmed by it all. His heart beat so fast he thought it would burst. He was disorientated, as if he stood in two places, and was not able to discern reality from illusion. The ghosts mingled with the living and it seemed as if the room was spinning around him. John saw his discomfort and took him out onto the ramparts. Michael breathed deeply and the cool night air calmed him.

'This is too much for you?' John said. 'Perhaps I should not have asked you to do this.'

'I must learn to concentrate and stop it all coming to me at once. You go back. I will stay out here for a while and then find you.'

John Erskine patted him on the back and smiled. 'Take as much time as you need.'

Michael continued to breathe deeply. He closed his eyes and felt the cool air on his face. He did not know if he could endure what was happening to him. How could his world have changed so much so quickly?

'It is your time, Michael,' a voice behind him said.

He turned to find Maurice smiling at him. 'I did not expect to see you again so soon.'

'I said I would be around to help you.'

'It is happening too quickly. I cannot tell if the voices are in my head or real. There are so many at the same time I cannot hear what they say. I feel I am going mad.'

'Not mad, Michael.' Maurice walked to his side. He looked out over the ramparts at the surrounding land. 'Ah, it has been a long time since I stood here and watched Stirling in the moonlight.'

'You have been here before?'

'King Robert and I stood on this very spot and talked many times. But those were the days when I thought I had an answer for every question; when my ego far outweighed my wisdom.'

'I do not think I can do this, Maurice.'

'You did not believe you could help the dead but look what you did at Flodden. You made a difference. You helped those lost souls move on and then instead of walking away from a promise to one of those dead men, you kept it. Now here you stand, befriended by a great man who accepts your gifts, and you are to attend the coronation of a king. Everything is changing for you.'

'How can I stop this confusion in my head?'

'What you said to Lord Erskine is correct. You need to concentrate. You are in control. It will take time but you will learn to shut all else out but what you want to hear and see. Come, I will stand with you tonight.'

With Maurice beside him, the voices seemed subdued. Michael stayed by John's side while he was in conversation with Lord Maxwell.'

'Breathe, Michael,' Maurice said. 'He said he would support and protect the new King. Feel the emotions behind the words. Do you feel passion with his commitment? Take your time.'

Michael did as he was instructed. He tried to put all else from his mind and just feel.'

'Well, Michael,' John said as he moved on to speak to another of the nobles. 'How did you do?'

'He is telling the truth. I can only go with my feelings and I believe him.'

'You did well. Lord Maxwell is one of my trusted friends but things change and I had to be sure.'

Michael stayed close by while John spoke to many others. At the end of the evening they again went out onto the ramparts.

'I am grateful, Michael. You confirmed my suspicions about some of those here and I can be careful around them. Others were a surprise.'

'I had help. Maurice was with me.'

The coronation took place in the Chapel Royal. The baby King was to stay at Stirling Castle with his pregnant mother, Scotland's Regent.

The following week Michael returned home to see his parents and collect some belongings. They were distraught he would be not be staying but pleased he had a place in the household of such a prestigious and respected family.

Margaret Tudor gave birth to her dead husband's son, Alexander, a brother for young James. In August of 1514 Margaret married Archibald Douglas, Earl of Angus, who would rather see the Scots aligned with the English than the French. The marriage nullified Margaret Tudor's regency. John Stewart, Duke of Albany, was appointed the new Regent. Albany's father was a son of King James II, making him third in line to the throne after James and Alexander. Tensions at court were high as the nobles competed for positions of power.

Michael lived at Alloa Tower and became part of John's circle of confidantes. They formed a deep and respectful friendship. He always accompanied John when he left the Tower to meet with other nobles or attend the Regent at Stirling. Michael enjoyed the activity and intrigue of the royal court. He was able to develop his intuitive skills and his ability to read a person by their words and actions. John trusted Michael's gifts completely and thus was able to play the game of politics more effectively. Many lost spirits sought Michael out and he did what he could to help them.

His nightmares of Flodden still haunted him and his visions sometimes confused him but he accepted it was how his life would be. He was happiest when Kate came to visit. Being with her brought balance to his world.

Late in 1515, John asked Michael to accompany him to France.

'I am to attend the christening of the daughter of the Count of Guise,' John said. 'Claude and I have known each other since we were children and our families have been friends for centuries. The Guise family is one of the most powerful in France.'

'You think I will bc useful there?'

John laughed. 'No, Michael, I am inviting you because I enjoy your company and would like you to meet them. Hopefully any ghosts you meet will be friendly ones and will not interfere with our pleasure.'

Michael was pleased. He was employed by John and made to feel like a member of the family but this invitation made him realize that John truly regarded him as a friend.

Kate came for a visit the week before they were due to leave. They would often go riding together when she stayed. On this day the sky was intensely blue and it was unusually mild for the time of year. They dismounted by the edge of the Forth and led their horses to the water.

'John tells me you are going to France with him,' Kate said. 'Will this be your first visit?'

'Aye. I am not sure about the sea crossing though. Robbie took me fishing on a boat when I was younger and it did not agree with my stomach.' When he was with Kate, mentioning his brother brought back only good memories of the times they spent together.

'I hear the Guise family has a magnificent home so there will be much to do there. And I am told French ladies are very beautiful.'

Michael noticed her cheeks colour before she looked away. 'I heard that also,' he said. He could not bear to see the hurt on her face as she quickly glanced at him and then turned her head.

'But of course, they cannot be as beautiful as a Scots lass, especially one with red hair.'

Kate laughed. How he liked to hear that sound. In fact he liked every moment he was in her company. When they played cards with the family, he could never concentrate as he was too busy watching her and listening to her every word. If she was at the dining table he hardly tasted his food. He missed her when she returned to her family home and looked forward to her next visit. She was never far from his thoughts.

Joinville, the home of the Guise family, was a magnificent country estate and Michael received a warm welcome. The christening was a grand affair. The French ladies were indeed beautiful and many smiled in his direction or tried to engage him in conversation. Michael was gracious and polite to them all, but he kept wishing Kate was by his side.

Michael was invited to attend a gathering of the immediate family members before he and John were due to depart for home. After the meal, the Count's wife, Antionette, brought baby Marie to the room and asked Michael if he cared to hold her. A strange thing happened as he cradled the baby in his arms. The world around him faded and he was standing by a bell tower on an island, the infant in his arms. The baby was covered in a white cloth with a red cross. Michael wrapped the cloth closer around the child and she smiled at him. There was trust in that smile.

The vision disappeared and he was left with a premonition that this was not the last time he would see Marie de Guise. He told John and saw surprise in his expression at the mention of the white cloth with the red cross.

Michael liked Claude and Antoinette very much. They were an obvious love match. He caught them exchanging many tender smiles, especially when in the presence of baby Marie. He noticed the same shared look between John and Margaret Erskine whose family continued to grow. This turned to a longing to have what they shared. He thought of Kate and knew he had been in love with her from the moment he laid eyes on her.

At night the demons were kept at bay by dreams of her. He could see her smile clearly, the way her eyes crinkled when she laughed and her long red hair flowing over her shoulders. In one dream he saw their wedding day. She was so beautiful, her gown enhancing her slim body and flowers adorning her hair. His parents were there, smiling proudly, side by side with John and Margaret Erskine. The dream moved on and they were sharing a home filled with love and laughter. He saw them reading quietly by the fire, every now and then looking up at each other and smiling. They strolled in their garden in the evenings, talking and touching as they walked. They looked up at the star they had picked for their very own. In the moonlight he took her in his arms and kissed her tenderly.

Sometimes the dream would move even further ahead and he could see Kate nursing their child at her breast. A girl. Most men would prefer their first born to be a boy, but he wanted a daughter—a tiny version of Kate. A son would come later.

In reality they did not talk of love or the future. Sometimes Michael sensed Kate's impatience with him. He did not respond to the gentle way she laid her hand on his arm, and when they gazed into each other's eyes he was always the first to look away. Michael knew she was waiting for him to declare his love but he could not. She did not know what he was capable of. She did not see the dark side to who he was and he was afraid to let her see that other world.

But how long could he endure seeing the disappointment in her eyes? The trip to France made him realize that he must speak to

John about his feelings. One night not long after their return from France, as they stood on the battlements of Stirling Castle, Michael found the courage to speak.

'John, do you know if a marriage has been arranged for Kate? She is after all from a wealthy and noble family. It is usual for such things to be conducted in this way, it is not?'

'It is.' John smiled. 'I asked Margaret to find out from Kate's father if such an agreement was in place.'

'You did? Why?'

'Oh Michael, it is obvious you and Kate have feelings for each other. Margaret and I discussed it and decided we should find out sooner than later.'

'And?'

'Colin did have someone in mind for her.'

'Oh.'

'Nothing has been finalized. I told him as far as I was concerned you are part of my family and I would consider it a favour indeed if he gave due consideration to the possibility of a union between you and Kate.'

Michael was speechless. Although his own family was reasonably wealthy and his mother of noble stock, he did not consider himself of such standing to marry Kate.

'You did that for me?'

'You are my friend and we all have a great affection for you. It is no lie. We do consider you family. If you and Kate wish to consider a life together, and I can see she feels the same way about you, then no-one will stand in your way. You will have my blessing and my support. I also would consider it an honour if you would both make your home with us for as long as it takes for you to find your own home. We hope it will not be too far away.'

'John, I do not know what to say. I did not expect this.'

'You do love her, do you not?'

'With all my heart.'

'Then let it play out, Michael. When you wish to proceed I will go with you to see Colin.'

'I would be glad of that. If I proceed.'

'You have doubts?'

'Not about my love for Kate. But John, she does not know what I am. It may frighten her and she might find it abhorrent. I will not hide it from her.'

'If she loves you she will accept you as you are.'

'I will tell her. I have to.'

'Good luck, my friend.'

Michael was withdrawn at dinner. Kate had been looking at him strangely all evening, obviously hurt by his detachment. When the servants came to clear the table, the women made to move to the seats by the window and leave the men to talk. Michael stood up quickly, knocking the chair to the floor. The dogs stirred by the fire and Michael's face grew red.

'Kate, would you join me on the roof. There is something I wish to discuss with you.'

Isabella and Margaret both smiled. 'Take your cloak, Kate,' Margaret said. 'It is cold tonight.'

Michael nervously waited while Kate fetched her cloak. John said nothing but gave him an encouraging smile as he walked away.

It was indeed chilly on the roof despite there being no wind. The stars sparkled in the sky and the smell of burning wood permeated the air. Kate wrapped her dark green cloak tightly around her body as they walked to the parapet. They both looked out into the darkness.

'You seem distracted tonight, Michael. Are you unwell? Are you leaving us?'

'No.'

'Tell me what you are thinking for I am imagining all sorts of bad things.'

'You and I are friends I think, Kate. I have a great fondness for you. My feelings for you are deep. I love you, Kate. I think I have loved you from the moment I saw you.'

'Oh Michael.' She turned to him and put her hand on his arm. 'I too...'

'Please, Kate, you need to listen to me before you say anything. There are things about me you do not know; things you may not be able to accept about me.'

Without looking at her he told her about Flodden, Maurice, and seeing the dead. He shared his inner-most fears, the nightmares, his struggle to control the onslaught of spirits who sought him out. He also told her about the way he helped John Erskine. He left nothing out for he knew he could have no secrets from the woman he loved.

'No-one else knows these things about me, except John of course, and no-one else can. But I need you to know, not because I want to frighten you but because I love you and want to marry you. I will understand if you cannot.'

Suddenly Kate threw her arms around his neck and looked straight into his eyes. 'Michael Craig, I love you. I love you with all my heart and if I have to share you with ghosts then I will.'

'Kate, you are certain?'

'Whatever the future holds, we will face it together.'

He kissed her then, so tenderly and with a joy that shook his very being. She held on to him as if she would never let him go. They stood there for a long time, cradled in each other's arms.

'Are you afraid of what you can do? Do the ghosts harm you?'

'No. Only my fear can do that.'

'And are you afraid often?'

'No, my love. I am taken by surprise sometimes though.'

'Are there ghosts here now?' she asked, looking around.

'Not tonight. They would not dare approach me when I have the woman I love in my arms. You are sure this does not frighten you?'

'Not when I have you beside me. I know you would not let any harm befall me.'

'I promise to love and protect you all the days of my life.' Holding her close, Michael felt a peace that had eluded him for a long time. With Kate's love he could face whatever life threw at him.

The Erskine family was delighted at the news. Two days later, John and Michael accompanied Kate to her family home in Argyll. Colin Campbell was gracious although Michael sensed he thought his daughter could make a better match. He gave his consent to the marriage and to the couple making their home at Alloa Tower. Colin's wife of four years was with child and so the arrangement suited all.

John negotiated the generous dowry. It was agreed that the marriage would take place in July, six months hence, and would be held at Colin Campbell's home. John and Michael then visited his parents who were both delighted with the news. Michael saw in his mother's eyes a future filled with grandchildren.

There was much to be done in the kingdom that winter and Michael spent long periods away with John. Kate was pleased at the thought of beginning their married life at the Tower. John and Margaret overwhelmed them with a wedding gift of land not far from the Tower where they could build their own home. Work would start after the wedding and there was much talk of how they would both like it to be. Seamstresses were employed to make the new gowns for the wedding and the Tower was a hive of activity.

When the Guise family heard of the wedding they extended an invitation to Michael to visit with his new wife. Kate was very excited and the flurry of dressmaking increased to feverish pitch. After all, a Scottish lady must look her best when visiting the nobility of France.

Michael's feelings for Kate grew daily. The Erskines thoughtfully allowed them time together and the joy of their love was a beauty to all. His happiness seemed to banish his nightmares and instead of remembering the pain of the past, he was looking forward to a future with the love of his life.

Chapter 5

Three weeks before the wedding, Michael went with John and his men to Stirling Castle. His duties as governor of the castle were varied and complex and took up a great deal of his time. He not only had to ensure the safety of the King but now that Margaret Tudor had been forced to flee to England by the Duke of Albany, the situation between the factions at court was uneasy.

They took the journey slowly on the way home, enjoying the peace and quiet. Wild flowers were in abundance, the air warm and still.'

'Well, Michael, not long now,' John said. 'Are you nervous?'

'A little. I just want it to be over and for Kate to be my wife.'

'Patience, my friend. I am sure the ladies have at least six more gowns to make before then.'

Both men laughed.

'Are you pleased with the plans for your new home?'

'We are. Although Kate keeps changing her mind about how many rooms, but we will be ready for the building to start in a month or two. Again I must thank you for your generosity. I will feel better knowing Kate is close to the Tower while we are away.'

'My mother and Margaret adore Kate. It will be a very suitable arrangement for us all. I remember the first day you appeared at the gate. You looked so young and afraid, wrapped in that old cloak. I did not know then that one day I would consider you such a friend and now you will truly be part of my family.'

'It does seem God has a plan for us all, John. I am very content with the one He has chosen for me.'

'You love her very much, do you not?'

'More than I could ever put into words, even to her. I will love her forever. She is part of me.'

'And so it should be, my friend.'

The sun was lowering in the sky as Michael and John reached Alloa Tower. Michael was aching to see Kate. Each time he went away the missing became greater, as did his love for her. John joked about it on the ride back but admitted how much he missed Margaret and the children when affairs took him from them.

Margaret Erskine greeted them warmly. 'Well, how are the weary travellers?'

'Glad to be home, my dear,' John said, embracing her.

'I will organize some food. Do you want to refresh yourselves first?'

'Indeed. It was a dusty road.'

'Where is Kate?' Michael asked.

'She went out riding. Said it was too beautiful a day to stay inside and we were not expecting you back until tomorrow. She also wanted to look again at where your new home will be. I sent a couple of the men with her before she could protest. You know I do not like her riding alone. She should be home soon.' Margaret exchanged a smile with her husband. 'It will not be long until you are man and wife.'

After he washed and changed his clothes, Michael wandered up to the roof. He wanted to be alone to enjoy the feeling of anticipation at seeing Kate.

He looked to the east to see if he could spot her returning. He heard a movement behind him and turned to see her smiling at him. She was wearing her favourite green cloak and her hair was loose around her shoulders.

He rushed to take her in his arms.

'I missed you so,' she said, burying her head into his shoulder.

He held her tightly, savouring the smell of her, the feel of her. 'I missed you too, my love.'

She offered her lips to him and he tenderly kissed her. When she pulled away he saw a tear run down her cheek.

'What is wrong, Kate?'

'I just love you so much.' She took his hands in hers. 'Do you remember the first time we stood here together?'

'Of course. It was right on this very spot, although you were a little further away from me than this.' He gently ran a finger down her cheek. 'I remember thinking you were the most beautiful lass I had ever seen. You were wearing that green cloak and your eyes sparkled in the moonlight. Even then I wanted to take you in my arms.'

'Did you, Michael, that first time?'

'I did.'

She gently lifted his hands to her lips and kissed both of them, slowly, without taking her eyes from his. 'You do know I love you?'

'I know it.'

'You will be in my heart forever, Michael, forever.'

'Kate, what is wrong. You sound sad. Tell me. I will make it better. I hate to see you sad.'

'Oh Michael, if only we had more time.'

'Time for what? You are frightening me, Kate. What has happened?'

She released his hands and took a step back. 'Michael, it was no-one's fault. I should have taken more care. I was so excited, standing where our home will be and imagining what it will look like. On the way back I raced away from the men. I shouted for them to catch up with me. I was looking back at them. I did not see the branch.' Tears streamed down her face.

In that instant he knew the truth.

'I am sorry, Michael. I am so sorry. I was foolish. I love you with all my heart. I do not want to leave you but I must. I had to hold you one more time. Do not forget me, Michael.'

And then she was gone.

Michael stood perfectly still. He did not want to think. He felt nothing and he wanted to stay like that. But that is not the way of grief. Such pain engulfed him but still he stood there. He only turned when the door to the roof opened.

It was not until John Erskine walked over to stand in front of him that he realized Michael already knew the grave news he brought.

A sombre weight hung over the Tower in the days following Kate's death. The grief that emanated from the family permeated every corner of the place. Kate had been liked by all and loved by many. The men were subdued and the servants spoke in whispers. Michael often went riding or would stand alone on the roof, gazing out over the countryside. Only John Erskine knew that Michael was searching for another glimpse of Kate's spirit.

The day came that was to be their wedding. Michael left at dawn and did not return until dark. John sensed he wanted to talk so he followed him to the roof.

'Margaret is worried about you, Michael. We all are.'

'I only knew Kate for a short time and your family has known her all her life. I understand that you too must be grieving.'

'You were both in love. It is a different kind of bond. We loved her dearly and miss her. We can only imagine the pain you must be feeling.'

'I do not know what to do, John. I feel myself slipping into a dark place and it is harder each time to pull myself back. What if I am to blame for this? Is God punishing me for what I did at Flodden—the lives I took? At night the dark shadows come. I know they are preying on my pain but I seem unable to send them away.'

'You need time to heal. There is a place, Michael. It is called Inchmahome? It is a monastery on an island on the Loch of Menteith.'

'Inchmahome! That is where Maurice was a prior.'

'The monks will welcome you. Some time there, in the midst of the beauty and peace, may help lift the darkness. Perhaps Maurice will find you there. Stay as long as you wish and come home when you are ready. I will give you a letter to Father Joseph who takes care of the day to day business.'

Michael saw the concern on his friend's face. He knew that he was only adding to the family's sadness. 'Perhaps it will be for the best.'

At dinner that night, John told his family that Michael was leaving.

'Where are you headed, back to your family?' Isabella Erskine asked.

'Michael expressed an interest in seeing Inchmahome, Mother.'

'Ah, well worth a visit. I have been there on occasions with my h...my late husband. We went in the summer. It was so peaceful and beautiful that I did not want to leave.'

'I have a friend who used to be a monk there,' Michael said. 'He said for him it was the most beautiful place he had ever seen.'

'He may be right. There is something special about it, something not of this earth.' Isabella Erskine smiled. 'I am being fanciful I think, but you may find peace there, Michael.'

The decision was made and so on a warm summer morning, his heart filled with sorrow, Michael bid farewell to his friends and rode away from Alloa Tower.

Chapter 6

Willie, one of the stable boys, accompanied Michael to bring back his horse. He was not one for talking so the journey through the countryside around Stirling was a time for much needed solitude for Michael. They eventually reached a small hamlet and were greeted with a friendly smile from an old woman who was sunning herself outside her tiny cottage. She told them they had arrived at the Port of Menteith and directed them to the stables and the boatman's house.

They dismounted and walked the horses down the pathway towards the loch. Michael could clearly see Inchmahome Island. It far exceeded the description given to him by Maurice and Isabella Erskine. He could see the bell tower through the trees and make out some of the other buildings. The hills on the mainland seemed to cradle the island in a protective glow. Ripples of water gently caressed the shoreline. He caught sight of an osprey high in the sky. He watched it as it made a dive to the loch's surface and then gracefully take flight towards the heavens, a large fish protruding from its mouth. Michael smiled as he watched it soar.

There was a stone house not far from the water's edge, surrounded by a neat garden. The stables were at the back and he could see some cows, sheep and goats not far away. There was also a large henhouse and small outbuildings. As they reached the cottage a girl about his own age came out of the door, dusting flour from her hands as she walked. She was pretty with rosy cheeks and long dark hair tied back with a red ribbon.

'Good day to you, sirs. Would you be wanting to go to the island?'

'Aye. My name is Michael Craig. Willie here will be taking my horse back.'

'I am Moira McKenzie. My Niall does the rowing but he is off getting grain for the monks. He will not be back for a while. If you ring the bell over there one of the monks will come for you. They will not be long if they are not at prayers. There is water and some feed over there for the horses. Come to the house when you are done for something to drink. You better have some food before you head off, Willie.'

Moira had some poached fish and bread waiting for them. The house was spacious and neat as a pin. Michael felt at ease in the welcoming atmosphere.

'Thank you,' 'Michael said. 'This is kind of you. Have you lived here long?'

'Since I married my Niall two years ago. He has been here since he was a lad.'

'And he works on the island?'

'He helps out in the orchards and does some of the heavier work for the monks. That and the farm make us a good living. We also look after the horses for any visitors to the island as well. You will be staying a while?'

'I do not know.'

While they sipped the milk, Moira told them a little about the area and the people in the village. Laughter came easy to her and Michael liked her very much.

Willie headed off and Michael bid farewell to Moira. He pulled on the rope attached to the bell by the jetty and was surprised to hear its sound echo around the hills. He sat down on an old log and waited. It was not long before he spotted a small boat heading his way. The monk brought the boat alongside the small jetty and threw a circle of rope to Michael who looped it over the short wooden pole.

'Greetings, greetings,' the monk said as he threw back his hood to reveal a tonsure of red hair. 'I am Father Andrew.'

'Michael Craig. I have a letter of introduction from Lord Erskine.'

'He and his family, they are well?'

'They are.'

'Good. But you need no letter to be welcome at our priory. Come aboard.'

Father Andrew refused assistance with the oars so Michael took the opportunity to scrutinize the Black Canon. He had a pale complexion, slim build and his long fingers grasped the oars tightly. His smile crinkled the edge of his green eyes. He was perhaps 20 years older than Michael and a head shorter. Michael realized that he too was being watched.

'Do you have business here, or are you in need of sanctuary?'

'Sanctuary.'

'We ask no questions here. You may stay as long as you wish. All we ask is that you help with the work. In exchange you will have a bed, food and time to heal whatever ails you. But if you need to talk, please seek me out.'

'Thank you, Father, I will remember that.'

The rest of the short journey was in silence. Michael revelled not only in the beauty of this place but the growing feeling inside him that he would find the way forward here.

He stepped off the boat onto lush green grass. While he waited for Father Andrew to tie up the boat, he looked around. There seemed to be many different species of trees, and the colourful wild flowers, swaying gently in the breeze, blanketed large areas. The buildings of the priory loomed high above, giving a sense of strength and protection.

Michael was given a room allocated for visitors on the ground floor of the west range. The monks' dormitory ran along the east range of the building and was accessed by stairs from the cloisters. Father Andrew showed him around the other parts of the priory, introducing him briefly to some of the monks. The cloisters were enclosed along the east and west sides of the buildings and in the centre was a garden. Also on the east side were the infirmary, the warming room and kitchen with its large double fireplace. When they came to the chapter house, Father Andrew explained this was where the monks met each morning. Seating was a stone bench which ran all the way around the room.

The bell rang. Michael declined Father Andrew's offer to join them for prayers. He watched the monks make their way to the church and then went to sit on a fallen log by the water.

It was not until the first three days had almost passed that Michael realized he had hardly spoken a word. In a way the silence helped him grieve. There were no distractions, no putting off the process of remembering, smiling at the memory and then allowing the pain to overwhelm him. He did not stand in its way although at times he felt he would die from it.

He chopped wood, cleaned rooms, and helped Moira's husband in the orchards. Niall was a tall, strong man with an easy smile. He seemed to sense Michael's pain and did not engage him in unnecessary conversation.

On the fourth day Michael found himself following the Canons to one of their many calls to prayer. He sat in the nave allocated to guests and parishioners. The Canons sat on the wooden seats of the choir. Father Andrew was at the front of the high altar and the two other monks assisting him were seated in cubicles carved out of the wall. Light flooded through the large windows, enhancing the vivid colours of the tapestries and other wall hangings, and was reflected on the polished wooden seats of the choir. But there was no peace for Michael as he listened to the chanting and the prayers. After that day he spent many hours in the church seeking release but it did not come. There were times when his thoughts stilled and he felt devoid of feeling or emotion but this did not last. He searched for God in this place of worship but could not find Him. Instead he became restless and angry. The monks saw his pain and left him alone. Michael ignored the shadowy spirit figures that followed him and they, perhaps sensing his anger, kept their distance.

One day the rain fell so fiercely that no work could be done outside. Michael made his way to the scriptorium where he found some of the monks in deep concentration on the delicate work of copying and illustrating manuscripts. He watched with fascination at their skills and stayed behind when they left for prayers. He browsed the books on the shelves then carefully took one from its place and sat down with it at the table. The work of the beautifully illustrated Books of Hours was exquisite. He sat there for a long time, taking in the smells of the inks and the parchment.

Michael gradually developed an easy friendship with the monks. Father Joseph took care of priory business and set out the tasks for the day. His bushy dark eyebrows and full red lips were a sharp contrast to his pure white hair and pale skin. His ears seemed to have outgrown his head. He had a gentle manner. Father Joseph also tried to find as much time as possible to travel to the other churches in the area that came under the guardianship of the monks of Inchmahome. He regarded the duties of a priest above all else. 'Administration can wait,' he would say, 'but the needs of the people cannot.'

Father Malcolm was the infirmarian and looked after the health of the other monks. He grew medicinal plants and herbs in the priory garden, the properties of which he willingly explained to Michael. He was a small, thin man with a wide smile.

Father Bernard was in charge of the scriptorium. He had a pronounced birthmark on the left side of his face and walked with a limp. He suffered from stiffness in his joints but thankfully his hands had not been affected.

Father David was a head shorter than Michael but strong and sturdy with big hands and feet. He took care of the gardens and orchards and was helped by Father Donald who had only been on the island for a few years. Father Donald was a jovial man, whose permanent grin displayed the space where his front teeth should have been. Father Callum had taken holy orders early in his life and was happy to be in charge of the kitchen.

Father Colin and Father Daniel were two elderly monks whose health was gradually declining, especially in the winter months. They attended prayer when they could and helped in the gardens when they felt well enough. Father Colin tended to forget things and repeated himself endlessly but the other monks never spoke of this. They listened to his stories as if for the first time. Father Daniel had lost his hearing and rarely spoke but he always had a smile for everyone.

Michael spent time more with Father Andrew who became his confessor. He was a caring soul, quick to laughter. Michael eventually shared what had happened to him at Flodden. To Michael's surprise Father Andrew accepted the story without question. 'God works in mysterious ways,' he said. He did however caution Michael not to tell others for they were devout men who might see Michael's gift as coming from the devil.

Winter that year came early and the edges of the loch froze. After Christmas it began to thaw. Michael thought perhaps he should go home but something kept him there. Eventually the routine became a way of life for him. It somehow numbed his pain and for the most part kept his demons at bay. He realized he wanted to find God, to speak to him. He did not expect it to be easy or quick but he hoped that one day he would come to know His forgiveness and perhaps find the peace for which his soul yearned. He spent many hours by the edge of the loch, pondering on his future, and trying to listen to what his heart wanted.

When the earth was once again renewed with spring, John Erskine came to the island. 'You have been gone a long time, Michael. Are you well?'

'I am, John. You were right. This is a place of healing.'

'Have you decided what you want to do now? You know you are welcome to return with me. There will always be a home for you at Alloa Tower.'

'I have thought much on this, John, and I have decided to become a monk.'

'What! This is a serious decision, Michael. I would not have thought this would be your choice.'

'It is the right one for me. I know I will never love another woman as I love Kate. Becoming a monk is not an escape from life but an embracing of the future. I need to find God's love and also His forgiveness. I will accept the gifts I have been given and use them where I can. I know this means I will have to hide them, but I feel this is the way for me.'

'If that is your decision then you have my support. In fact I have friends in Rome. You can train there if you wish. There would be much for you to learn in the Holy City.'

'Thank you, John.'

'I will make the arrangements. Will you come back with me until you leave? The family misses you and I would greatly enjoy your company again.'

Michael bid farewell to the monks who seemed sorry to see him leave. He confided in Father Andrew about his plans and he seemed genuinely pleased.

Michael first visited his parents. They were surprised and confused by his decision but in the end they accepted his choice and gave their blessing. His mother's widowed niece and her young family were living at the family home. Laughter again rang through the rooms. The new family situation would ensure his parents' later years would not be lonely.

Michael was glad of the chance to again spend time at Alloa Tower with the Erskine family. He and John had long discussions by the fire. He knew he would miss his friend but it did not deter him from the path he had chosen. Before retiring each evening, he spent time on the roof, engulfing himself in memories of Kate.

When the day came for him to leave, he and John embraced each other with sadness.

'We will meet again, Michael, I am sure of it. When the time is right, come home.'

Chapter 7

Rome was a revelation to Michael. The history of the place was apparent in its many churches and ancient buildings. He settled in well at the Order's priory and was eager to learn. He was friendly to everyone but only formed a close bond with Father Martin, a fellow Scot.

The first time Michael was introduced to Father Martin he clearly saw the shimmering light that surrounded him. It was Father Martin who first showed him around the city. In the Sistine Chapel, the beauty of the ceiling, which Michelangelo had only completed a few years previously, deeply moved him as did the weight of the centuries of praying that hung heavy in the air. They both knelt before the altar in prayer for almost an hour. As they made to leave Michael asked Father Martin who the Bishop was seated on the elaborate chair beside the altar.

Father Martin stopped walking and stared at Michael. 'That is the Holy Father's chair. There is no-one there, Michael.'

That night after prayers, Michael told Father Martin of his unusual abilities. He did not, however, tell him of the terrible deed that ignited them. 'You think it strange I want to become a priest?'

'I have seen much in my life, Michael, and studied some of the ancient texts in the Vatican archives. There are many aspects to spirituality that the Church has hidden from all but a few, including references to those who could see beyond the veil of this existence to the world of spirits and demons. But I have ultimate faith that God has a reason for everything.'

Michael learned many things from Father Martin in his years in Rome. He studied hard and became fluent in Latin, Spanish and French. The only thing he struggled with was the routine of prayer.

'I sometimes find I have no words for God and often wonder if God cares one way or the other,' he told Father Martin.

'You must keep trying, Michael. God is with you.'

'You have probably noticed my hair is falling out?' Michael said. 'I wonder if God is giving me a message that the life of a monk is not for me.'

'And here was me thinking you were pulling it out because you did not like our tonsure.'

Michael laughed. 'I will keep trying, Father, I promise.'

By the time Michael was ordained a priest when he was 25 years old, he was completely bald.

After his ordination, the Prior arranged for him to spend time at Serrabone Priory in the Languedoc region of France. He reminded Michael that the world of a canon was to get out into the world. It was with great sadness that Michael bid farewell to Father Martin but looked forward to this new adventure.

Michael spent most of the sea journey by the edge of the ship. His stomach heaved with every wave and he sighed with relief when they finally docked at Marseille. He was fortunate to be offered a ride from a merchant going to Perpignan. His journey from there was slow but it gave him a chance to absorb the beauty of the Pyrenees.

Serrabone Priory was located in the heart of a magnificent oak forest in the Aspres mountain range. Michael's first view of the priory was against a sky tinged with pink in the fading light. He received a warm welcome from Prior Armand. Weary, Michael joined the monks for Compline but they were kind enough not to awaken him until the first Mass of the day. Father Armand showed him around the building and told him the history of the 11th century priory.

From the outside it appeared austere but inside was truly beautiful. In some ways it reminded Michael of Scotland's Rosslyn Chapel, built in 1446, which he had visited with John Erskine. The pillars in the cloistered hall of Serrabone Priory were intricately carved with animals and plants. The pink marble of the indoor cloisters glowed in the candlelight. For the first few days, when not at prayer or work, Michael stood at the south facing cloisters, looking over the dense display of trees that carpeted the hillside. Michael spent many hours in Father Armand's company for he was a wise man with a natural gift of healing. With his help Michael learned how to use herbs and plants to treat the sick, and how to channel God's healing energy. Michael often accompanied the other monks to the nearby villages and found great joy in saying Mass in Spanish. He also enjoyed the physical work in the fields and the orchards.

Despite the beauty and peace of the place, Michael's demons again found him. In his dreams he returned to the nightmare of Flodden. He wandered among the dying and the dead. He could smell the blood and the rotting flesh. He held Robbie in his arms, looked into his lifeless eyes and again felt the agony of his brother's loss. The pain of losing Kate was still deep. In unexpected moments he remembered her smile and felt her in his arms. When he woke from these dreams, loneliness engulfed him. Even awake, he felt despair edge its way into his reality and he fought to keep it at bay.

'Will you go home when you leave here?' Father Armand asked one beautiful evening as they walked in the grounds.

'I do not know.'

'What holds you back?'

'If I return to Scotland I may struggle harder to fight off my demons.'

'We all have demons, Michael.'

'Mine are of my own making. Part of me does not want to let them go. I cannot banish them for I deserve to be haunted by them. I have not been punished enough for my deeds.'

'Oh Michael, those are the worst demons of all. The ones we cling to. Can you tell me why you need them?'

Michael looked at the old monk. The terrible secret he held in his heart was known only to a few. Despite the pain it would cause him to again speak of that time, he would do so for such a man as this.

'I killed men at Flodden.'

'That battle cost your people dearly. But you thought your cause just. Many people have killed in battle.'

Michael's heart beat faster. The bile rose in his throat as it always did when he remembered what he had done. The pain of losing Robbie and Kate was still raw but his actions at Flodden would forever be a festering sore from which he found no relief. He could never forgive himself and nor did he expect God to either.

'I did not kill those men in battle, Father. Perhaps I could live with that. I slaughtered them. I ended their lives out of anger, revenge, hatred. My pain and fury at my brother's death was uncontrollable. I turned from him and slashed out at every man in my path. I stepped over their bloodied bodies. Some had not yet died and were groaning in agony. Those around me saw the madness in me for they tried to get away. I chased them. I struck them from behind. They did not want to die by my hand but I would not let them escape. I killed or maimed many men that day. I only stopped when I was struck from behind. Sometimes I think it is gone but then a fleeting thought arouses it. I am consumed by the guilt of what I did. I live in the hope that God will forgive me but I know it will haunt me to the day I die.'

'But God must have forgiven you or he would not have given you the gift to help lost souls. He would not have sent your Maurice to help you.'

'But what if it is not a gift that I now can see the dead as Maurice said, but a punishment for taking lives in anger. Even though I can help them move on, God is reminding me that I took from others the time they were allotted on this earth. I denied souls the chance at life.'

'Is it God who does this to you or your choice to cling to your guilt?'

'I weary from thinking of it. I will never know.'

'There is something that may help you.'

'What is that, Father?'

'There is a journey that pilgrims have taken for over 700 years. Many say it is a journey of the spirit. I myself made it as a young man and am one who sees it this way. It is called the Way of St James. Some just call it the Camino. St Francis of Assisi himself walked the Camino in 1214. The journey begins at the foot of the Pyrenees and crosses the mountains into Spain. You walk on a path across the northern part of that beautiful country. It finishes at the church in Santiago de Compostela which holds the relics of St James the Apostle.'

'How will going to Santiago help me?'

'It is not just the destination that is important, Michael, it is the journey itself. Many meet their demons on the road to the Field of Stars and travel a while with them. Some encounter new demons. It is a time to be alone with God, to let Him share your burden and to carry you when you are weary. I have never felt closer to my God than when I walked with Him on that journey.'

'Could I do this?'

'I think the Camino is waiting for you, Michael.'

Chapter 8

A week later Michael began his journey. Father Armand gave him a sturdy staff and a rough map of the towns and villages on the Camino. He eventually arrived late one afternoon at the small French town of St Jean, the starting point of his journey across the Pyrenees. The town was surrounded by sandstone walls and nestled at the foot of the mountains. He wearily made his way to the well to refresh himself.

Two monks had already drawn up the bucket.

'Good day to you,' the older one said, offering his cup.

'Thank you. Walking is thirsty work,' Michael said, sipping the cool liquid.

'I am Brother Francis, and this young lad is Brother Pedro. We are Benedictines. You are an Augustinian, I think, and from Scotland.'

'Father Michael.'

'We are pleased to meet you, Father.'

Brother Pedro refilled Michael's cup. He looked quite a few years younger than Michael and his wide smile was infectious.

Brother Francis was an old man, his skin wrinkled and brown, but with eyes that sparkled. 'I never visited your country but I heard it is beautiful. I came to Spain from the south coast of England many decades ago.'

Michael accompanied them to Mass at the Gothic church and then after their meagre meal at the hospice, they walked around the town.

'Is this your first visit?' Michael asked Brother Francis.

'Oh no. I came on this pilgrimage when I was a young monk. I accompanied one of our older brothers. Now, as I face leaving this earth, I felt in my heart I wanted to do it again. As was my part as a youth, our Prior has sent Pedro to keep me out of trouble on my journey.'

Brother Pedro smiled broadly and patted Brother Francis affectionately on the shoulder. 'Tees pleezure to do dis.'

Standing on a little stone bridge over the River Nive, both listened eagerly as Brother Francis told them a little of the history of the pilgrimage to Santiago de Compostela.

'St James travelled to preach in Spain after the death of Jesus. He eventually returned to Jerusalem and was martyred in 44 AD but his remains were taken to Spain. When they were uncovered in the early 9th century, the King of Spain built a church over the tomb and in different forms there has always been a church to house his bones. When the original town was razed to the ground in the 12th century by the army of Richard the Lionheart, the King of Navarre rebuilt the town on its present site. There are many reasons to walk the Camino. It is regarded as a form of penance, to gain forgiveness for our sins. For me, I travel it now to cleanse myself for my meeting with God. It is a hard journey, Father Michael, but one to embrace. There will be times when you will travel alone or with fellow pilgrims, but the main thing is to walk with God as your companion. That is all that matters.'

Michael left alone at dawn the next day. Crossing the mountain range was hard on his body so he stopped often to rest and admire the views. Silence embraced him and he was left with only his inner thoughts. Memories of Robbie and Kate were his only companions.

By the time Michael reached Roncesvalles, the first Spanish town on the other side of the Pyrenees, he was weary and suffered greatly from blisters. The monks there gave him salve to ease his discomfort, a bed for the night and food for his journey.

Michael walked on paths through forests and often lay on a carpet of leaves to rest. He passed through many villages and towns on the journey and the kindness of the people humbled him. They were all eager to share the history of the area and what food they could spare.

As the days passed, Michael realized that for long periods of time he did not think at all. The beauty of the countryside with its green fields, bubbling streams, and array of wild flowers, often took his breath away. Sometimes he would stand on one of the stone bridges over a gentle flowing river and just listen to the birds. At night he slept without dreams and awoke with anticipation of the day ahead.

Father Armand told him that many pilgrims carried a stone of sorrow with them which represented their sins. This was to be laid at one of the many crosses on the journey with a prayer to God to forgive them. Michael looked around and was drawn to a stone that although grey in colour had sparkles of crimson. He picked it up. It felt warm from the sun. He carried it with him and although he passed many crosses he did not leave it there. Then one day he saw a stone cross standing in the middle of a field. Butterflies surrounded him as he walked towards it. They stayed with him until he sat down at the base of the cross and then they floated away. Michael thought of his life and the pain he held deep in his heart, much heavier than that of the stone he carried. Was he doomed to live a life without forgiveness? He hoped not. He gently laid his stone beside the others at the foot of the cross and again asked God to forgive him.

The walled city of Burgos was rich with ancient churches, almost white against the blue sky. The local priest, Father Juan, offered Michael food and a bed for the night. After Mass they walked around the cloisters in the cool evening air.

'You have a beautiful city, Father,' Michael said. 'It appears to have been here a very long time.'

'Many people have ruled this area—Romans, Visigoths, Arabs and Christians. It has seen much of the passing of man's earthly journey. One of Spain's most famous heroes was born here in the 11th century—a noble named Rodrigo Díaz de Vivar. He was a great military and political leader in a time of great hostility between the Christians and Moors. He treated the Moors as equals and they showed their respect for him by giving him a title of honour. They called him El Cid.'

Father Juan insisted on giving Michael provisions for what he said would be a long journey across the Meseta. There were steep climbs those first few days and then the road stretched out before him. It seemed an endless landscape, flat and devoid of grass. The sight of the odd single tree here and there filled him with a sense of isolation and loneliness. Michael missed the sight of the mountains and the greenery of the forests on the earlier part of the journey. He was grateful to encounter the odd farmhouse where he was able to get some food and water. He offered to do some work in return for this but it seemed that payment was not deemed necessary for a pilgrim. He sometimes slept in a monastery or a stable and many nights he just slept under the stars. He walked in solitude in days of sunshine or cloud or wind and did not mark the passage of time.

In Leon, Michael visited the Basilica of San Isidoro and the funeral chapel of the Kings of Leon. In Astorga he spent some time exploring the ruins of the Roman baths and the forum.

So far the weather had been on his side but then the rain came. His robe was saturated and it rubbed against the back of his legs as he walked. He ignored the discomfort and the cold and kept moving. The external sights of the journey had kept his mind from going inward. In the constant rain, with no visibility except the ground in front of him, he had nowhere else to go but to his thoughts. The cold and hunger weakened him and in that weakness he felt his demons stir.

As he approached Ponferrada, Michael could clearly see the battlements and turrets of an old castle rising into the darkening sky. Although the rain had stopped a few hours before he was still wet and weary, each step a conscious effort, but he was determined to rest within the castle walls. He sighed with relief as he crossed the archway into its protection. He recalled Father Armand telling him the castle had been built by the Knights Templars to protect the road to Santiago. The Templars were a 12th century order of valiant warrior monks whose history inspired many. On the 13th October

1307 they were treacherously destroyed by Pope Clement V and King Philip VI of France. Father Armand told him that many a weary pilgrim still sought sanctuary here on their long journey. Michael made his way to a sheltered corner and settled himself against a wall. There was both beauty and loneliness about the sight of the birds, black against the crimson tinged sky, as they flew high above the castle. Were they wandering like him or did they have a destination? To the birds it did not matter for they had the ultimate freedom—no rules, no commitments, no sorrow or demons. They lived in the moment and found their place there.

Michael tensed at the sound of footsteps and saw a dark figure approaching. He dragged himself to his feet. The tall man wore a white cloak emblazoned with a red cross on top of a similarly marked white tunic over chain mail. Michael knew that Templars had survived the attempt to wipe them out and that the Order still existed in secret. Perhaps this man was one of them and was visiting the Order's old castle. He had a long sword strapped to the belt around his waist. His hair and beard were long and white although the top of his head was bald. Michael thought him very advanced in years.

'Do not be afraid. I come in peace. 'My name is Jacques. And your name, Priest?'

'Michael.'

'Well, Michael, the night grows cold. I have a fire and food. You are welcome to join me. Unless of course you seek solitude.'

'I have had much of that lately. I will be pleased to accept your hospitality.'

The fire was glowing brightly and Michael felt its welcoming warmth as he settled himself beside it. He gratefully accepted the flagon of wine from Jacques. It was sweet and refreshing and slid easily down his throat.

'Help yourself to the vegetables and fruit.'

'Thank you.' Michael ate heartily, and was aware of Jacques's constant gaze. The old knight's face was wrinkled and dry and his eyes held a weariness of spirit.

'Here, have more wine. You are a long way from Scotland, Priest. What brings you here? Are you a pilgrim?'

'I am on my way to Santiago. And you?'

'I make no pilgrimage.'

'So what brings you here?'

The light of the fire was reflected in Jacques's dark eyes. 'I do not know.'

'How long have you been here at the castle?'

'Again, I do not know. Time does not exist for me. I often find myself sitting by a fire in some ruined castle or church. I have no recollection of how I got there or where I am.'

'You have been injured perhaps, and your memory has gone?'

'No.' Jacques stood up. 'No. I wish it were so. I would gladly forsake my memories. I have prayed and begged my God to rid me of them but I think He will not. I deserve to be reminded of what I did, for I know my actions are unforgiveable. I think God knows that too. Now I wander this earth without friend or home or purpose.'

Michael watched the outburst in silence. This man was like him.

'My greatest demon is a past that will not let me be,' Jacques said.

'We all have demons.'

Jacques laughed. A bitter laugh. 'Let us compare demons, Priest. You first. Tell me what seeks to destroy you.'

Michael told Jacques of Flodden and the guilt and pain he carried in his heart. Jacques was silent for a long time.

'I am sad for your pain, Priest.' His voice was gentler and his anger seemed to have left him.

'And what of your demons, Jacques?'

Again, a long silence.

'I was wrongly accused of great evil. I was stripped of all dignity. In my pain I weakened and betrayed my people, myself and my God. I told them what they wanted to hear. I did not think I would do that. It mattered not to them that I recanted. The torture did not stop. They nailed my hands and feet to a door and left me to die. I prayed for death but it would not come. They took me down and laid me on a table. They covered me with a white cloth and my wounds bled through it. They kept me in darkness for seven years.

'Then they let you go?'

'No. They slowly burned me alive.'

Michael gasped at the horror of his words and realized that this man was a spirit.

'So you see, Priest, I am bound to this earth. I could not live with my betrayal and I cannot die either. My God will not forgive me.'

'God forgives everyone.'

'Ah, the words of a priest. Only words. Your demons still haunt you. What you did at Flodden. If God will not forgive you, why do you expect me to believe He will forgive me?'

Michael could not reply. He stared at the fire. Emotions buffeted his body and his mind was in turmoil. How could he be a priest and not be able to help this man? How could he help anyone? Any glimmer of hope he had that he would find forgiveness for his deeds was gone. He was not able to forgive himself and that guilt would be chained to him for the rest of his life. He felt the tears sting his eyes until they became a torrent he could not stop. Eventually he fell asleep and in the depth of his turmoil he dreamt.

The cold night air unfolded around him, cloaking him in sadness and despair. The fingers of pain grasped every cell in his body and squeezed like a vice. Michael remembered when he had fallen from his horse when he was ten. His whole body ached and he cried until he felt sick. He would gladly exchange that pain for what ravaged him now.

His body had healed from the fall as his mother said it would. But he would not recover from this. His thoughts returned to Flodden. The sorrow of the loss of Robbie again gripped his heart. When Robbie had died he did not think to hate God but then God took Kate. For the first time he realized that it was not so much about God forgiving him, but that he could not forgive God.

He closed his eyes and felt Kate's gentle kiss on his cheek. He took a deep breath and caught the scent of the lavender pouch she always had tucked in her dress. He held out his hand and felt the softness of hers. His memories made all this possible. Only the memories, for he knew she would never come to him again as she had done on the roof of Alloa Tower the day she died.

His sorrow turned to anger. Why had he become a priest? He had made a dreadful mistake. Maurice told him his ability to see and help the spirits of the dead was a gift from God and that God would want him to use it well. So God gave him a gift? Well, He could take it back. What benefit would he get from it? Only more sorrow. Let God give him back Kate and he might consider it.

So raged the battle between God and man as it often does in times of sorrow. Someone had to be held responsible and Michael had no-one to blame but God. In the darkness Michael sensed Maurice close by but he offered no words of comfort. There was nothing a spirit could say to a man who was facing the dark night of his soul.

Eventually Michael found himself again on Flodden Field. He knew the place although it had changed greatly from the last time he saw it. The grass had grown long and patches of flowers decorated the sea of green. The warmth of the sun penetrated his body and a calmness overcame him. For a time all his pain and guilt disappeared.

When Michael woke the next morning he found Jacques still by the fire. Michael told him of his dream.

'What do you think it meant?' the old knight asked.

'That God will forgive me and I Him, but I do not know. I feel there is hope for me. I believe my demons will always be with me but I am the one who gives them power. I must learn to control them. Perhaps by the time I leave this earth they will not come with me.'

Jacques smiled. 'You think this is a lesson for me also, Priest?'

'Perhaps it is.'

'I am pleased for you, but I cannot so easily believe God has forgiven me any more than I can forgive myself. But I will ponder on it. I will do that, for I believe you to be a righteous man and I think there is a reason we came together.'

Michael smiled. 'So I cannot help you move on from this world?'

'Not yet. But I have a feeling we will meet again and perhaps then I may be ready to go.'

'I hope so, Jacques. I will remember you in my prayers. Thank you for your kindness.'

'I am grateful for your company, and advice. I think you would have made a good Templar.'

'I am honoured you think so.'

Jacques grasped Michael's hands in his own. 'Non nobis, Domine, non nobis, sed nomini tuo da gloriam.'

As Michael walked away from the castle, he thought of Jacques last words. "Not unto us, o Lord, not unto us, but unto your name grant glory." It saddened Michael that he was unable to help the Templar but perhaps he was right. One day they would meet again.

Michael could see the town ahead of him. He had reached Santiago de Compostela. He stopped and sat under a tree by the side of the road. The journey had been long and hard. At times he had been hungry and thirsty, cold and weary. The blisters on his feet were still raw and his bones ached. Michael expected to feel more elation at his journey's end but instead there was no excitement at all. He let his mind wander back over the time it had taken him to get here. He smiled when he thought of Brother Francis and his young companion, Pedro. Brother Francis was preparing himself to meet his God. Brother Pedro had barely started his journey in life. He was filled with expectation of the future and adventures still to come. Jacques carried with him the weight of regret and self-blame and his refusal to accept that God would ever forgive him. Meeting the

Templar made him realize that there were others who sought to find a way forward from regret and sorrow.

As his memories washed over him, Michael realized Father Armand had been right. The Camino was indeed about the journey. He wearily dragged his body to stand and again set his feet on the road.

When he reached Santiago he made his way to his Order's priory. The Canons gave him food and water and a place to clean the dust of the road from his body. There was no hurry to enter the great Cathedral and Michael spent a dreamless night there. He joined them for Matins and the first meal of the day. He was a monk again and the doubt he once had about choosing this way of life faded. It was with a lighter heart that Michael joined the monks to walk to the Cathedral.

It was as beautiful as Father Armand had described, with its spires reaching to the heavens. At the entrance Michael saw that other pilgrims were making their way to the statute of St James on their knees. Michael knelt and did the same.

The incense hung heavy in the air and gold statues sparkled in the light of many candles. There was a stillness, a sanctity, about this place and it overwhelmed him.

Michael knelt in prayer and thanked God for his life. He followed the others down the steps to where the bones of St James lay in a golden casket. He felt as if a tiny bird was fluttering inside him and when he knelt before the casket and opened his mouth to pray, the bird flew out into the air. A peace he had never known crept over him, drenching him in its exquisiteness, its healing. Tears streamed from his eyes. Michael knew that whatever life held for him, whatever God had planned for him, he would welcome it and be grateful.

At the priory, they took care of his body and helped him get his strength back. On the third day the Prior gave him the news that he would not be returning to Rome. He was going home to Scotland.

Chapter 9

Michael stood under the bright blue sky and watched an eagle fly overhead. It was taking its time, surveying the territory and enjoying the peace of its world. He watched it until it was out of sight before continuing his journey. He deeply inhaled the air. Scottish air. There was nothing like it. It was the smell of home. He had been gone a long time. He had learned many things and a whole new world had opened up to him. There were times when he had doubted the path he had chosen and had struggled with his sanity but the journey and the people he had met changed that. He would store the memories and draw on them for courage and strength.

Michael made his way to Alloa Tower for it was John Erskine's influence that had brought him home. John had been alerted to Michael's approach because he was waiting for him at the entrance.

'You have grown, Michael.' John Erskine shook his head. 'I have thought of you often but never dressed like this. You look very…very holy in your robes. And what happened to your hair? Too much praying perhaps?'

Both men laughed and embraced. It was as if the five years apart had never been.

'Come. Have a wine with me to celebrate your return.'

Margaret Erskine greeted him warmly. She and John had added two more children to their brood while he was away and young Margaret was even more of a beauty than when he last saw her.

John and Michael sat by the fire long after the family retired. John listened intently as Michael told him of the places he had been and the people he had met.

'So, Michael, does the life of a monk suit you?'

'I find it hard sometimes. The routine of prayers and work can be overwhelming but we can go out into the world. I enjoy this part of my life immensely. The balance is good and I have come to terms with my choice.'

'Did the Prior in Rome show you my letter?'

'No. He just said you requested I return to Scotland which I was happy to do. Where will I go?'

'Inchmahome will be your home. I know how fond you are of it. But I have asked that you be the spiritual adviser to my family and assist me in the guardianship of the King. If you agree.'

'Gladly, John. I never expected this, but it would be an honour to serve you again.'

'It will be good to have you close. You look weary, Michael, so I will bid you goodnight. Margaret has given you your old room. Tomorrow I thought we would visit your family. They will no doubt be anxious to see you again. I visited them often during your absence and they are both well. After that we can go to Inchmahome.'

'I thought I might enjoy the night air from the roof before I sleep.'

John Erskine nodded. The time away had obviously not lessened Michael's grief over Kate. The roof had been their special place and he hoped being there again would bring him comfort.

Michael was excited to see his parents again. The years had wearied them, or was it grief still clinging to their hearts? His cousin had remarried, to a lawyer known to his father, and the family was happy to accept his parents' invitation to make their home with them. With a promise to return, Michael and John headed to Inchmahome.

Moira and Niall greeted him warmly when they arrived at the Port. As John and Niall tended to the horses, Michael waited by the water's edge, gazing across the loch at the priory. He smiled when he heard a whisper in his ear. 'It is good to be home.' He knew Maurice was with him.

The monks seemed genuinely happy to welcome him back, not as a man seeking sanctuary as he once had been, but as one of their own.

Father Joseph showed where he would sleep. 'I know you will have other duties but I want you to know you will always have a home on Inchmahome.'

'Thank you, Father.'

After joining the monks for their midday meal, John bid them farewell. Michael easily slipped into the routine. He welcomed the cycle of prayer and work and spent much of the time in the scriptorium where he impressed Father Bernard with the skills he learned in Rome. He thought often of the Camino. He knew he had learned much about himself and his relationship with God but even with his new found peace he wondered if he would ever know for sure if God had truly forgiven him for what he did at Flodden.

The first winter of Michael's return was so cold the water surrounding the island froze. There was total silence as Michael stood by the edge of the loch on the mainland. The brightness of the cold blue sky hurt his eyes. He did not mind. All around him the snowy hills sparkled like jewels. In the distance smoke rose from the houses in the village.

Michael pulled his cloak tightly around his body and stepped onto the ice. It was a strange sensation, walking on the loch that normally lapped gently, and sometimes not so gently, against the shoreline. He forced his eyes from the beauty that surrounded him to pay attention to his cautious footsteps.

Snow covered the ice beneath his feet and he was glad of his sturdy leather boots. In parts he could see air bubbles frozen beneath the surface. He caught sight of an eagle flying high against the blue sky. It would be a hungry time for it as prey would be hard to come by. If it was lucky it might spot a small rabbit darting across the white expanse of the mainland. A few swans were gliding on the patch of water at the outlet to Goodie Water which had avoided the spread of ice. They would have sensed the eagle and know that this was the only spot where it might catch a fish. The eagle flew low but then took off again into the sky. The swans were safe for now.

The purity of white covered everything, purging darkness and despair. Michael felt a lightness of spirit he had not known for a very long time as if both he and the earth were being cleansed. Here, on the frozen loch, he was between worlds. The mainland held the ghosts who searched for eyes that could see them. The island held the life of constant prayer to a God who had never spoken to him. But here in this stillness, a strange feeling overwhelmed him. It pierced his heart and flooded him with peace. It was a deluge that drowned his senses and took his breath away. For the first time in his life, Michael felt the presence of his God. He knew in a single moment of clarity that there was no right or wrong on the path to Heaven. As it was with the Camino, it was the journey that mattered. No matter what he did or how harshly he judged himself, his feet were firmly planted on that path.

An intense cold began to penetrate his body. He tried to ignore it for he wanted to stay in this place. If he died standing here with his God he would willingly give up his life. But it was not to be. He knew his journey was not complete. Regretfully he moved his legs and arms. He turned in a circle, taking in the beauty for a moment longer, and headed towards the island.

The bell tower was etched against the sky, its top covered in white. He sighed with pleasure when he eventually stepped onto his beloved Inchmahome. A bullfinch, its black cap and red chest highlighted against the canvas of white, was sitting peacefully on the branch of a tree, watching him.

Being here always made his spirit soar. Here his demons could not slyly creep from the edge of his awareness. They would bide their time until he again ventured forth into the world.

Chapter 10

Michael was working in the scriptorium one cold March morning when a messenger came from John Erskine asking him to come to Alloa Tower. From there they rode to Rosslyn Castle.

Michael had been to the Castle on a few occasions with John. On his first visit there, while John met with Sir William St Clair, Michael had been joined in the chapel by Sir William's wife, Allisone. She had told him of the great history of the St Clair family. A previous Sir William St Clair was among those who accompanied Sir James Douglas on a journey to take the heart of Robert the Bruce to the Holy Land. They never reached their destination and died in battle in Spain. Sir William's remains were now buried in the chapel.

The family also had a connection to the Knights Templar who it is said fought at the Battle of Bannockburn with the Bruce, having sought refuge in Scotland after the great atrocities inflicted on them by the Pope and French king. The chapel contained effigies of past Templars and the most magnificent carvings. Michael remembered with fondness the spirit of Jacques, the Templar he had met at Ponferrada. On his visits to the chapel he would often catch glimpses of the spirits who were still tied to the place. He did not feel any anger or sadness from them as he did with most ghosts. It surprised him that they emanated a sense of purpose.

After greeting the St Clair family on their arrival, Michael headed to the chapel to pray, leaving John to discuss business. As he was leaving he heard the sound of horses and saw twelve riders, their faces hidden by the hoods of their white cloaks, heading for the castle. The stable lads were leading the horses away by the time Michael reached there.

Michael dined with the family but there was no sign of John or Sir William. The servants were clearing away when John appeared.

'Michael, will you say Mass for us in the chapel?'

'Of course, John. Now?'

'Aye. There will be a few guests.'

Michael followed John up the pathway. The moon was full and helped light the way for them. John opened the door and motioned for Michael to precede him. As his eyes quickly adjusted to the light of many candles, Michael stared at the sight before him. The men were wearing chain mail under a white cloak emblazoned with the red cross of the Knights Templar. Sir William walked over to him and smiled.

'I would like you to meet my friends, Father.'

One by one he introduced Michael to the Templars. They were of various statures and ages. They gripped Michael's arm firmly.

'We have a reason for asking you to say Mass for us tonight, Father,' Sir William said. 'As you know, the Templars were betrayed in 1307 and many were killed. The last Grand Master, Jacques de Molay, was imprisoned for many years. He suffered greatly and was finally burned in Paris on this day in 1314. We are gathered here to honour him and the many Templars who died in the service of the Order.'

In that instant Michael felt himself once again sitting by the fire at Ponferrada. Now he knew who Jacques was—not just a Templar whose demons kept him tied to this earth, but the Grand Master himself. It was not a coincidence that he had met Jacques, or that he had been invited here tonight.

John Erskine laid his hand on his shoulder. 'Michael, you have gone quite pale. Are you ill?'

'No. Just a little overwhelmed. I am honoured to do this.'

The chapel became silent and everyone stood with their heads bowed as Michael gave his blessing and said the opening prayer. Suddenly the candles began to flicker. Michael felt a tingling begin in his body and when he lifted his eyes, the sight before him took his breath away. Many spirits, dressed in the robes of the Templars, were walking down the main aisle and along the side aisles, mingling with the men. And then he watched as something truly magical happened. One of the spirits laid his hand on a Templar's shoulder. The man jerked his head around in surprise. He had felt the touch. The others too began to smile. Some laughed at the shock of it. Michael allowed them time to absorb what was happening and just as he was about to turn back to the altar, he saw one last figure approach down the centre aisle. It was Jacques. He walked right up to stand in front of Michael and smiled.

'I took heed of your words, Father. I have finally found peace. I have come to say goodbye.'

Michael knew that for all the days of his life he would remember this night. As he made the final blessing at the end of the Mass he saw that many of the Templars were openly crying, so affected were they by the experience. No-one stirred for a long time. Eventually they all stood up and faced each other. 'Non nobis, domine, non nobis, sed nomini tuo da gloriam,' they said. The ghosts gradually faded and each man there sensed their leaving. Jacques de Molay smiled at Michael and followed them.

One of the Templars walked up to Michael. He was a giant of a man whose face reflected years of battle and pain. His face was wet with tears and glowing with emotion. He grasped Michael roughly and hugged him to this body. No words were said. None were needed. As he stepped back the others did the same. By the end of the line Michael felt bruised but humbled. If he had ever doubted the value of his gift, those doubts were forever gone.

'I have something to tell you before we leave this place,' Michael said. He told them of his journey on the Camino, of Ponferrada and his meeting with Jacques. 'He was here with the others,' he told them quietly. For a long time they stared at him in silence and then elation set in. Not a one doubted Michael was telling the truth.

In silence they all walked down the path to the castle. Servants greeted them with wine when they entered. The Templars were anxious to hear every detail of Michael's encounter with Jacques and he delighted in being able to talk openly of the things he mostly kept hidden. The release for him was profound. The rest of the evening passed with laughter and talk. The Templars spoke of battles and adventures and much wine was drunk.

The Templars were no-where to be seen as John and Michael bid farewell to the St Clair family in the morning. Sir William led them outside. He opened the door and indicated for Michael to exit first. For a moment Michael shielded his eyes against the bright sunlight.

The Templars stood facing each other, six on either side. They grasped the hilt of their swords with both hands in front of them, the tips resting on the soil. Michael smiled at each of them as he made his way past them to the waiting horses and the Templars only broke their line to watch as he rode off with John.

They journeyed in silence for a while then John moved to his side. 'They paid you a great honour, Michael.'

'I know.'

'You are under their protection now. They consider you a friend. They know you will not break their trust.'

'It is been an eventful trip, John. I will never forget it.'

'I felt the presence of the others. They were not lost souls, were they?'

'No. It was if they were honoured to accept an invitation to be there. Truly an occasion to remember.'

Chapter 11

Michael walked softly on the sea of green grass. He listened. Birdsong and the gentle lapping of water. Two white butterflies fluttered nearby and in this stillness he imagined he could hear the movement of air beneath their wings. After the harsh winter it felt good to be warm again. The sensation of the sun's rays penetrating his habit and seeping through his skin to his bones, made him sigh with delight.

It was moments like this on a perfect summer's day on Inchmahome that he felt perfect peace—a treasure beyond price.

Michael walked over to the oak tree, its branches reaching to the sky and its canopy of leaves shading the earth below. He loved this tree. He knew it had been there for a long time, perhaps even before the monks came. It had likely even witnessed the comings and goings of those who practiced the old Celtic religion.

'Well, old soldier,' for that was how he saw the tree, a living thing that had seen beauty and destruction, life and death, and still stood tall and strong, 'how are you on this beautiful day? Do you mind if I seek the shade of your branches for a time?'

Michael watched the patterns the dappled sunlight made on the ground. Suddenly a sensation of dizziness overtook him. He reached out to the tree to steady himself. Dark clouds rolled across the sky, blocking out the sun. He shivered in the sudden cold and pulled his cowl over his head. He closed his eyes until he felt himself again.

Tufts of thick grass and nettles fought the wind that whipped the land. Michael realized he was no longer under the tree but in a place he did not recognize. He fought to calm his panic.

He saw a lone figure sitting against the stone wall of the long forgotten ruins of a building. The man was motionless, his eyes fixed on the horizon and his sword beside him. Michael approached but the man either did not see him or chose to ignore him. Michael sat on the ground beside him, resting his back against the wall. The wind became a faint whisper. The man's cloak was ragged and stained. His shirt would once have been white but was now drained of brightness. He was sturdily built and his long thick hair hung on his shoulders, only a little shorter than his beard.

'Have you come for me?' he asked, still not looking at Michael.

'No. Are you waiting for someone?'

'A long time now.'

'Who is coming?'

The man laughed. 'An angel I am wishing but perhaps it will be a minion of the devil.

'You are a soldier?'

'That I am. These bones are weary and my spirit depleted. I will fight again though, when I am needed, but I am tired. I want to close my eyes and slip into a peaceful slumber beside my wife instead of my sword. But my wife is dead and I will not rest until Scotland's freedom is won.'

'Where did you last fight, friend.'

'Falkirk. We were defeated. It was not like Stirling Bridge when we sent those bastard English fleeing for their lives. We still need to keep fighting though. Scotland should not be ruled by anyone but Scots. We are a nation, not an acquisition to be had by the English. We fight among ourselves, I know this, but we are Scots, and Scots we will always be.'

Michael sensed the passion of this man. 'What is your name, friend.'

'Wallace, William Wallace.'

A chill passed through Michael. This man had died over two hundred years ago. Michael had somehow travelled back in time. How could this be? Wallace had fought valiantly for Scotland's freedom and was one of the country's greatest heroes. Every Scottish child knew of him. Wallace was obviously in hiding and did not know of the fate that awaited him. He would be betrayed and taken to King Edward I in London in August of 1305 and tried for treason. Wallace would suffer the agony of being hung, drawn and quartered.

Just before nightfall, Wallace's men came for him. He asked Michael to join them but he declined. Long after they rode away, Michael stayed with his back against the cold wall. His shallow breathing exasperated his growing anxiety. His spirit had actually moved in time. He closed his eyes and could hear only the pounding of his heart as panic overcame him. His body began to shake. He opened his eyes and knew he was back in his body under the old tree on Inchmahome. He had been in another place, another time. Michael was shocked by the possibility of it. Could he do it at will? Did he want to?

In the years that followed, Michael could not resist the temptation to try and repeat his experience. Many times he sat under the same tree and nothing happened but when it did he was amazed by the places he visited. It was not as in a dream for he became part of the history and people of the time. His yearning to understand why peace was so hard to attain found him amidst old battles. He was able to connect to spirits who died there and was humbled by the fact that he could still help them to move on. The thought that they could wander for centuries seeking the light of release was not acceptable to him. Eventually he learned to control his journeys but always he travelled to times where his gift was of use. When he found himself again on Inchmahome, no time seemed to have passed even if he felt he had been gone for days. Sometimes he lingered too long in those places and the sadness remained with him. He had to fight to release it. Each time he thought he would not do it again but in his heart he felt in some way he was making up for the lives he took at Flodden. He told no-one of his experiences knowing they were unexplainable.

Inchmahome was a haven of peace and contentment for Michael in turbulent times. John Erskine was in need of his counsel and much of his time was spend either at Alloa Tower or Stirling Castle.

In 1526 Margaret Tudor was again regent and, along with her husband, the Earl of Angus, took custody of the young King James. John was distraught but could do nothing. He saw the King rarely as Angus was virtually keeping James a prisoner. He gave many positions in court and the church to his relatives and supporters, strengthening his position even further.

In 1528, with the assistance of loyal subjects, the 15 year old king eventually escaped and one of his first acts was to seize his stepfather's lands and banish him from the kingdom. The events of his childhood and the neglect by his mother had made James distrustful. Who could blame him? He did however appear to have a fondness for both John and Michael and the men did what they could to support him. Michael sensed in James a nature of contradictions.

The King managed to increase the royal coffers but spent large amounts of money renovating and extending his palaces. Although not a devout Catholic, James would not tolerate heresy of any kind. Episodes of aggression and growing fits of depression also hampered the King. John Erskine and his wife worried greatly when their daughter Margaret became one of the King's mistresses. Michael remembered the time in the nursery at Alloa Tower after Flodden when baby James lay with his little arm resting on a sleeping Margaret in the crib.

The events in England added tension to affairs in Scotland. King Henry VIII sought an annulment from his marriage to Katherine of Aragon in order to marry Anne Boleyn. Anne was a Protestant and her influence over Henry resulted in him breaking with Rome, declaring himself Supreme Head of the Church of England and marrying Anne. In 1533 she was crowned Queen of England. Henry's suppression of the monasteries led to much death and destruction as the Protestant religion took a firm hold on England. In 1536 Katherine of Aragon died and it was also the year that Henry had his new queen beheaded for adultery and treason.

There were, however, happier events to celebrate. Michael and John accompanied King James to France for his marriage to Madeleine of Valois, daughter of the French king, in Notre Dame Cathedral. Michael again met Marie de Guise, now a beautiful young woman. She was married to the Duke of Longeuville and had a year old son, Francis. Marie gave an outward face of being happy with her life but Michael sensed a hidden sadness. He was reminded of the vision he had when he held her as an infant. They were standing by a bell tower on an island which he now knew was Inchmahome, but he was still unable to understand what it meant.

Chapter 12

Summer started early in the year 1537. By late August it was not hard to believe it might never end. Michael sat with John Erskine on the bench by the edge of the loch in the shade on an old elm tree. Wild flowers were everywhere and high on the hill they could see the clear outline of a stag.

'This place always brings me peace, Michael. I can see why it is hard for you to leave. Perhaps you would be content not to be at my bidding.'

'You know I will always be there to help you when I can.'

'That I do, my friend.'

'It is not been a good year so far for Scotland.'

John sighed. 'No. It started well though. The King married at last and to the daughter of the French King. Poor Madeline. She should not have come to Scotland in winter. Such a fragile child. Her death was not unexpected.'

'When I met her at court I sensed she would not be long for this world but I did not think it would be so soon. She is at peace now.'

'And the Guise family. Dear Marie. Too young to be a widow. She is coping well I hear from her brother, but she has a child to care for and a new one due any time now. I will see her again soon. The King has asked me to go to France. Because of my friendship with her family he wants me to help negotiate Marie's hand.'

Michael stared at John. 'Surely not so soon. The Queen is barely cold in her grave and so is Marie's husband.'

'Kings need sons, Michael. James thinks only of himself as you know.'

'The darkness around him is growing. I know he grieves for Madeline but it is more than that.'

John shook his head. 'He is again sullen and depressed. Not even the fortune he forfeited from the Countess of Glamis has lightened his spirits.'

'Poor woman,' Michael said. 'To be burned alive is a dreadful death. Do you think she tried to poison him?''

'I do not know, but I find it hard to believe. I think her misfortune was being the sister of Angus. James blames the whole family for what was done to him. I wish I could have stopped the execution but he would not be told. There is a madness in him sometimes. One day he might not be able to come back from it.'

'You may be right. At least you got the potion to the Countess in time.'

'Thank you for that, Michael. She still seemed in great pain though.'

'By the time the flames licked her body she would have felt nothing more than fear. The potion would have stopped her mind from recognizing the pain but it would not have stopped the fear of it coming.'

'A blessing indeed,' John said. 'I would rather feel fear than the pain of my flesh roasting.'

'So when do you leave for France?'

'Soon. Will you come with me?

'Aye.'

Cardinal David Beaton, one of James V's trusted advisers, was to lead the contingent of Scottish nobles to France. The Cardinal had played a key role in arranging James's marriage to Madeleine.

Michael and John stood at the bough of the ship looking out into the darkness. The moon was obscured by the clouds although no rain had come. The Captain had predicted fair weather and Michael hoped he was correct. He knew he would never like sea travel. Give him a horse or let him walk on this own two feet any day.

'Well Michael, not far now. How are you feeling?'

'Not too bad, so far.'

'Good. I wonder what Marie is thinking. I am not sure she will welcome our visit.'

'Do you think she will accept the King's proposal?' Michael asked.

'I doubt she will have a choice. The Guise family will be delighted of course. And King Francis will have no objection.'

'It will be good to see her again, John.'

'Indeed. I did not get to speak to her for long at the King's wedding but you spent some time with her.'

'She was a delight. I told her I had held her as a baby and she was gracious enough to say she felt she knew me.'

'She is a beautiful woman, Michael. And has great strength. She will be good for him I am hoping.'

'Why did you want me to accompany you on this occasion? Cardinal Beaton does not seem pleased I am here.'

'I am sure he is not. What I did not tell him was that Marie asked if you would come.'

'She did?'

'She would like your counsel. She obviously has trust in you. She will need friends when she comes to Scotland.'

Marie de Guise's son had been born by the time Michael and John Erskine reached France. Her other son Francis was thriving but the new baby Louis was weak. A widow at 21, she was not happy at again being considered a pawn in the marriage stakes, but she welcomed them with a smile. She formally greeted Cardinal Beaton but offered her cheek to John.

'It is good to see you again, John. Margaret and your family, are they well?'

'They are, Marie. Margaret sends her love.'

'Father Michael, I am happy to see you. I remember fondly our conversation at dear Madeleine's wedding. I hope we will have time to talk again on this occasion.'

'I am at your disposal,' Michael said.

'Well, I know my brothers are anxious to speak with you, Cardinal Beaton, so perhaps once you have refreshed yourselves you can meet with them. That will give me a chance to show you my home, Father.'

So while Cardinal Beaton negotiated the future of Marie de Guise, Michael walked with her in the gardens.

'You know King James, Father. Will I be happy with such a man?'

'That is something I cannot answer.'

'I remember he showed Madeleine great respect and kindness at the wedding. I think of you as a friend, Father. I am not being presumptuous I hope.'

'I am honoured, Madam.'

'Good. Now as friends all we say will be secret between us. In private I would like you to call me Marie. Will you do that, Father?'

'Yes, Marie, in private we will talk as friends.' Michael returned her smile.

'Tell me, Father, about King James.'

'He is not the easiest of men. He likes to get his own way and can be quite ruthless. There is a kinder side to him though. He can become emotional at times and depressed, but I am sure you will become his friend and when he learns to trust you, your life will be easier.'

'Thank you. I will try to earn his friendship and trust and hopefully we may have many sons together.'

'The deal has been done?' Michael asked John as the coach took them back to the docks.

'Indeed it has.'

'You do not sound too happy.'

'It went well enough but I was thinking of Marie. It was decided that her children stay in France with her family. I did not know this was the plan until Beaton told her brothers. James will not allow them to come for the selfish streak in his nature would regard Marie's attention to her own sons as a threat to the love and care she should be giving to his future children. Also, there are many who do not want this French alliance and it could put the children in harm's way. She will be distraught but it may be best they stay with the family here.'

Michael left Alloa Tower as the light tinged the black sky, and headed home. He was weary to the bone and had been ill on the return voyage. He reached the Port as Moira and Niall were having breakfast. They were a loving, caring couple, helping those in need when they could. He considered them both friends and enjoyed their company.

'Here Father, sit down and have something to eat,' Moira said. 'You look tired.'

'And hungry. Are you going to the island today, Niall?'

'Aye, Father. I will row you over when we are done here.'

'Have you been with Lord Erskine?' Moira asked.

'We went to France.'

'You will be glad to be home?'

'That I am, Moira.'

As Moira spooned the porridge into the bowl, Michael sensed sadness in her smile. She caught him looking at her and took a moment to turn her eyes away. They ate the food in silence for a while and then Moira brought him up to date on the happenings around the village. Michael had come to realize early on that in a place as small as the Port of Menteith, nothing was considered gossip. The villagers looked on it more as a sharing of information.

'Auld Lockie hurt his arm last week, Father. Molly said he must have had a wee bit too much of the whisky for it could not have been him doing any hard work for a change. She gave him a right tongue lashing instead of the sympathy he was expecting.'

Michael laughed. 'Poor Lockie. You would think he had have learned after all these years not to try and get one over on Molly. How are their daughter and her family doing in Glasgow?'

'Fine. Archie got regular work and Mag just had another bairn.'

'How many does that make now?'

'Seven. And her only a lass. Still, Molly says they are happy.'

Niall abruptly got up from the table. 'I will get the boat ready, Father. You take your time.' Niall kissed Moira gently on the cheek, gave her shoulder a squeeze and was off.

'Is everything well with you, Moira?'

'I am fine, Father. Thought I was with child again but...'

'I am sorry.'

'I do not think God wants me to have a bairn. I am getting too old now.'

There had been many false hopes over the years. Their good solid marriage and the fact that they adored each other saw them through their disappointment. Michael had tried to pick up any disruption in Moira's energy but found none. Perhaps it was indeed God's will.

'I will pray for you, Moira.'

'Thank you, Father.'

Chapter 13

The King was well pleased with the settlement on the marriage. It took him out of his depression and he started to work feverishly on plans for changes to Linlithgow Palace.

The sad news arrived that Marie de Guise's son, Louis, died and in May of the following year it was with a heavy heart that she greeted Lord Robert Maxwell who had been sent by King James to be his proxy at their marriage in France.

Marie de Guise landed at Fife in June accompanied by some of her family and household. Their formal wedding at St Andrews Cathedral in June of 1938 was a fine occasion, followed shortly thereafter by a journey around Scotland as the King showed off the kingdom to his new wife. James was delighted with his people's reaction to the gracious way she conducted herself.

Michael accompanied John on several occasions to the various Royal palaces and while John attended the King, Michael spent time with Marie. She talked often of her family in France and how much she missed her son, Francis. He look forward to his visits and he felt Marie enjoyed being able to freely discuss anything with him.

In February of 1540 a pregnant Marie de Guise was crowned Queen of Scotland at Edinburgh Castle. Michael accompanied the Erskines to St Andrew's Castle later that year for the christening of James, the new heir to the throne.

The King greeted them warmly at the feast afterwards. 'John, Margaret, it is good to see you both here. Looks like you will have a Stewart child to watch over again, John. And many more to come I hope. A king cannot have too many children. And your family Margaret, I hope they are well.'

'They are, your Grace.'

'I remember many happy times at the Tower when your mother was alive, bless her soul.'

'We still miss her,' John said.

'I must visit you soon and bring my son and the Queen.'

'It will be an honour,' John said.

'We will arrange it.'

'And Father Michael, you are welcome. The Queen speaks highly of you and I appreciate you being a friend to her, as you have been to me. It would please me greatly if you could attend her when she desires. There are a few too many of her kinsfolk around and I am happy to know she seeks counsel from a Scot.'

'The Queen is very kind, your Grace.'

With that the King was off to mingle with his other guests.

'He is in fine form,' Margaret said.

'Let us hope he stays that way,' John whispered.

King James was known for his moments of darkness. No-one knew what brought on the episodes but everyone around the King feared when it happened. Only one person seemed able to temper the King's moods—John's daughter, Margaret, who remained his mistress despite her marriage to Sir Robert Douglas of Lochleven. Margaret bore the King a son, James, given the title Earl of Moray. Michael had met young James, who was now nearly 10 years old, on a few occasions when he visited his grandparents at Alloa Tower. John and Margaret were fond of the young lad, despite his sometimes selfish ways, and Michael knew they both hoped James took after the Erskine side of the family rather than that of the King.

Later in the evening Michael was handed a message by Lady Cassillis asking him if he would meet with the Queen in private. He was escorted to the Queen's rooms and welcomed warmly by a glowing Marie.

'Oh Father, it is good to see you again. Please sit with me. Have some wine.'

Michael took the chance to look around the room as one of her ladies poured wine into two beautiful red goblets embossed with gold leaf. The fire blazed pleasantly in the large hearth. The walls were covered in exquisite tapestries and paintings and the light from the many candles was reflected on the highly polished imposing furniture. It was indeed a room fit for a queen.

Marie dismissed everyone and asked not to be disturbed. 'What do you think of my son, Father?'

'He is a bonnie child, Marie, and seems very robust.'

'Indeed he is.'

'And you are well?' Michael sensed an agitation in Marie.

'Yes, Father. I still grieve for my little Louis but I know God is looking after him. I miss Francis but we correspond often. There is one matter that concerns me. I do not know if I should speak of it. You are, after all, a friend of my husband's and...'

'I am also your friend, Marie. You know that anything that passes between us will stay that way. I am a priest. I would never betray you. Never!' Michael surprised himself with the passion of his response. As he looked at Marie, he felt a strange longing. He wanted to be close to this woman. He was just about to drag his eyes away when she looked straight at him. Surprise registered in her eyes but they held each other's gaze.

'Thank you,' she said.

'What is it that worries you?'

'James has mistresses and I am aware that one of them is John's daughter, Margaret. There have been children too. I am not naïve and know this is the way with kings. I accept this. But I am disturbed by another matter—a most delicate matter. I find it painful to speak of it, but I must.'

Michael waited.

'You know of my husband's friend, Oliver Sinclair?'

So the gossip had reached the Queen. 'I do,' he said. Many at court disliked the fond relationship between the King and Oliver Sinclair. At first Michael thought it was based on jealousy but when he first saw the two together he sensed their relationship was something deeper than friendship. The two were inseparable and King was always eager to take Sinclair's counsel.

The Queen took a deep breath. 'Some weeks ago Oliver was to be a guest at dinner along with many others. Although I hear James speak of him often it was only the second time I was to be in his company. James seemed a little anxious as Oliver was late. He drank more than normal. Oliver arrived some hours later, limping badly. He apologized and said he had fallen from his horse. I...I was...' She hesitated, took another deep breath and turned her gaze to the fire. 'James made such a fuss of him. He ran to his aid and assisted him to the table. He insisted Oliver take the seat next to him and in fact quite abruptly asked Lord Maxwell to move. He had the servants bring a stool for him to rest his leg. The other guests had gone quiet and I could feel their gaze on me. James noticed and quickly ordered the musicians to play and more wine to be brought. Everyone seemed embarrassed and although James conversed with the others, I noticed he kept looking at Oliver. Father, it did not seem...natural. Do you think James and Oliver are...? I cannot even bear to say it or think it? If it is true then James...' Marie stood up and began to pace around the room.

'Please calm yourself, Marie. Take a sip of wine.'

She did as he asked and then looked at him, waiting for his response.

'I tell you this as a friend, not a priest. My personal belief is that love comes in many forms. There is the love of a child, the love of a husband, a friend, an animal, God. To me it comes from the same place inside each of us but it manifests itself differently depending on who it is being directed to. If you were asked to love only one person in your life you could not do it. How could you choose a mother over a dear sister, one child above another? We are capable of endless love, Marie. It should pour from us and engulf the world. I believe we have no control over who we love, but we are responsible for the actions we take because of it.'

'You are saying James loves him?'

'I do not know, but what if he does? What if he has no control over it? He does not always make the best decisions for himself and those close to him, and he can be very self-indulgent, but to understand him you have to consider how he lived his life until now.

'As you know, John was one of his guardians when he was a child. John did his best to protect his Grace after his father died at Flodden. He never knew him, and his mother cared only for herself. He was surrounded by people who wanted something from him. He did not understand the way love should be or how to give it freely. I watched him at John's home at Alloa Tower when he was with the Erskine children. They were surrounded by love and laughter and they knew they were protected. The King was able to let himself be a child. He laughed and joined in with the games and I know he loved his times there. I have watched him with Sinclair. To me the King is that child again and realizes that he can give love and have it returned freely. Sinclair is a silly young man who enjoys fun and adventure, but in my opinion he cares deeply for the King. I do not think you can stop that, Marie. The question is how you will deal with it.'

The Queen had been watching him intently. Now she turned to stare into the fire again. And thus they sat for a long time. Michael waited. Perhaps he had said too much but he owed this woman the truth of his thoughts. At last she turned to him, a smile on her lips.

'You are a kind man, Father. Your compassion makes me ashamed.'

'I did not intend...'

'I know, but your words have given me much to think about. I also see the child in him on occasions. I cannot deny him a chance to be like that. He cares for me, I know. He is overjoyed with our son. I will be content. Thank you for your honesty. I know I can depend on you.'

He stood up to leave. 'Take care, Marie.'

'You too, Father.'

Chapter 14

It was an unusually mild day in September when John Erskine brought Queen Marie to Inchmahome. Michael was working in the scriptorium when Father Bernard came rushing in with the news.

'We had no word of the visit, Father. The Queen asked if you would join her.'

Michael tidied away his work and made his way to the Chapter House where he found a rather nervous looking Father Joseph in conversation with the John and the Queen.

'Father Michael,' the Queen said, 'it is good to see you again. You spoke so highly of your island sanctuary that I knew I must visit. I was apologizing to Father Joseph for not giving warning but it was on impulse. I was visiting with John and his family and he said he had business here.'

'You are most welcome, Madam.'

'While John speaks with Father Joseph perhaps you would be so kind as to escort me around your home.'

Their first stop was the church. The Queen knelt and prayed for a while and then followed Michael outside. He showed her the scriptorium, the infirmary, the refectory and other buildings. She was very gracious to the monks who were surprised to see the royal visitor.

They walked to the loch's edge and stood on the soft grass. The water lapped gently on the shore and sparkled in the sun. It was nature at its best.

'It is indeed beautiful, Father. I can see why you like to return.'

'I am at peace here.'

'There is much praying in priories is there not?'

'There is.'

'You do not find it too much?'

Michael smiled. 'Sometimes, but do not tell the others.'

'I promise.'

'You are well, Marie?'

'I am, Father. Although I find myself weary. I think I may be with child again.'

'That is good news indeed. The King will be happy.'

'I have not told him yet. I am foolish I know, but I wanted to keep it my secret for a while. Something that is just mine. It is not easy for a Queen to find time to herself. I think the only time I am alone is when at prayer and even then I am sharing the time with God.'

Michael laughed.

'I should not be telling a priest that, should I?'

'Perhaps not to anyone but me.'

'I agree.' A sadness passed over her face.

'You are missing your Francis?' he said.

'How did you know that? I think you can sometimes read my mind. Yes, I miss him. He is growing up without me. I do not see young James as much as I would wish. He has so many people looking after him that I feel he does not need me.'

'You are his mother. You should be more insistent.'

'Are you always this honest, Father?'

'I am more honest with my friends than perhaps I should be.'

'Oh no. Do not change. I rely on that. I need you to be my friend.'

'Always, Marie, always.'

They stood in silence looking over the loch to the Menteith hills and beyond. Michael again felt a stirring inside him. He did not turn to look at her lest she see what was in his heart. He knew he would never love anyone as he did Kate but the feelings Marie aroused shocked him. He felt a closeness to her. He wanted to reach out his hand and make contact with her. He wanted… Quickly he reigned in his thoughts. What was he thinking? He was a priest and she the Queen. It was a moment of madness. He tried to still his mind with a skill learned long ago. Gradually the panic subsided. He was himself again.

The Queen had remained silent during his inner turmoil. He turned to her and for an instant saw an unguarded look of intimacy in her eyes before she blinked and looked away.

When Marie finally left the island with John, Michael went to the church with the other monks. While they prayed, he fought a new demon into submission. This one he could never allow to manifest itself again. Why did he find it so hard to be a priest?

Despite the beautiful spring day, Michael's heart was heavy as he rode to Falkland Palace. He had been deep in prayer when the messenger arrived from the Queen with a request that he attend her immediately. Both the Queen's infant sons, born almost a year apart, had died from an unknown cause within hours of each other.

Michael was admitted immediately to the Queen's apartments upon his arrival. Her ladies in waiting were gathered in the outer room, some crying gently, others praying. Lady Cassillis rushed up to him.

'Father, I am so pleased you are here. The Queen is distraught. She will take no sustenance. I feel she will make herself ill.'

'And the King?'

'He is still at St Andrews with little Prince James. We hope he will return soon with the child for they are to be buried together.'

Michael was shown into the Queen's private chamber and the door closed quietly behind him. Marie sat on a winged chair, staring into the fire, the blackness of her dress emphasizing the paleness of her skin. She did not appear to see him.

'Marie,' he whispered.

She slowly turned and looked up at him. Tears began flooding down her face as she reached out her hand to him. He knelt on the floor in front of her and enclosed the icy hand in both of his.

'Thank you for coming, Father. How could this happen? Both my babies gone. My heart is breaking and in my pain I truly hate God. I do, Father, I do hate Him so. First He took Louis and now James and Robert. I can find no comfort in my God or life itself. Why did I come to this country? I should have refused to marry James and stayed at home with Francis. I have not seen him for so long. Father, help me. I am losing myself.

'Hush, Marie. I cannot heal your pain for grieve you must. I will try to give you strength. Close your eyes. Michael knelt before his queen, his friend, holding both her hands in his. He felt the warmth begin in his body and let it flow through him to her. He stayed there, praying and healing and he did not stop until he felt the warmth subside. When he opened his eyes she was looking at him. She seemed calmer.

'What would I do without you, Father? Thank you. My pain is unbearable but I feel an easing of my despair.'

Michael looked into her eyes and felt a jolt, not of compassion but an overwhelming need to take her in his arms and protect her from the world. She seemed to be holding her breath as she held his gaze. He reluctantly let go of her hands and sat on the other chair by the fire, his heart pounding in his chest. He felt ashamed for his weakness in allowing his feelings to be so transparent.

Michael was greeted by an anxious Lady Cassillis when he eventually left the room. 'Take the Queen something to eat and drink.'

'Oh thank you, Father, thank you.'

The death of his sons and the events of the next year heralded the King's spiral into depression. His only consolation was that Marie was again with child.

King Henry's demands for Scotland to abandon the Church of Rome, and King James's refusal to oblige, led to increased fighting between the two nations. In November 1542 Michael rode with John Erskine and his men to Solway Moss, just over the Scottish border, to join the King's army. Indecisiveness and quarrelling among the nobles led to the superior force of Scots being defeated by the English. King James himself was not present and when he heard that

Oliver Sinclair had been captured along with many of the nobles, he went to Falkland Palace, humiliated and ill.

The devastation of Solway Moss left Michael drained. As he rode back to Alloa Tower with John and his men, he thought about the cycle of death and destruction that had been going on for so many years and wondered if Scotland would ever know peace. If the nobles and clans were not fighting amongst themselves, they were fighting the English. He often wondered why a land which held so much beauty and mystery could not find contentment.

After only a short time to rest Michael and John were off again—this time to Linlithgow Palace. The Queen had sent a messenger asking Michael to be there at the birth of her child to ward off any evil spirits that such an event might attract. He spent the days leading up to the birth talking to the Queen and trying to ease her anxiety. When the time came he waited in the outer room, listening to the Queen's painful cries, but he knew before the child was born that it was a girl. Marie de Guise named her Mary.

Hearing he had a daughter, not a son, contributed to the King's delicate state of mind and all feared for his sanity. When the news reached John and Michael that the King was gravely ill and unlikely to survive, they left for Falkland Palace. They arrived weary and cold on the 12th day of December 1542. The Lords of Scotland were gathered there, waiting. The death of a King was a serious and unsettling time for all. The Queen remained at Linlithgow Palace guarding her daughter, for their fate would depend on the outcome of the struggle between the Lords as to who would rule Scotland. While the Lords squabbled, Michael sat with the King who was in a world remote from reality. Michael knew that the time of the King's death was near and he struggled to keep his demons away. But they remained, even as the Lords gathered at his bedside to await his final hour. When it happened there was a short time for sorrow, and then it was on to the business of deciding what needed to be done. Michael stayed close by John Erskine's side as the manoeuvring for power continued. Eventually it was decided that James Hamilton, Earl of Arran, who was next in line to the throne after the infant Mary, be proclaimed Regent. The little princess, now the uncrowned Queen of Scotland, was put in the care of John Erskine and Lord Livingstone. Weary and in need of solitude, Michael returned to Inchmahome.

A month later, yet another death–this time it was Moira's husband, Niall. It began with him not being able to eat and his strength depleted rapidly. He continued to work on their farm and also on the island as long as he could but eventually had to take to his bed. The folk around the Port were a great support to Moira but Michael saw the light in her eyes fade as each day Niall's condition worsened. He exhausted all his healing abilities but to no avail. It only took two months from the onset of Niall's illness to Michael saying Mass for the repose of his soul. He spent as much time as he could with Moira but despite the cheerful face she put on to others, he knew her heart was broken. He remembered Kate's death and knew the pain his friend was going through.

Chapter 15

The first time Michael set eyes on her he knew she was special. She was but a child, perhaps twelve years, and to him it was as if she walked with a guard of angels. Was she aware of them? No, he did not think so. He hesitated for a moment and then turned back to the altar.

Michael loved saying Mass in this old priory. It was not just the beautiful wall hangings and polished wood, or the sunlight that shone through the stained glass windows, but the sense of peace, of history, of belonging. It was his spiritual home. His longing to return here always began the moment he stepped from its shore.

When the service was over he made his way to the church door as quickly as he could to farewell those who had rowed over to the island for the service.

'Good-day, Moira. I hope I did not disturb you last night when I stabled Rusty. It was late.'

'No, Father. It is good to see you home again. You have been gone a long time.'

'Too long.'

'You have brought additions to our flock I see.' Andrew had already told him that Moira's brother and his family had arrived late one night, to Moira's delight, and accepted her invitation to stay with her permanently. The brother was more than eager to take on Niall's work and his wife would be a help to Moira.

'Father, this is my brother Kenneth and his family. They've come to stay with me. Kenneth, this is Father Michael.'

'Moira speaks highly of you, Father.' Kenneth grinned, showing a missing front tooth. He was a large built man, with a rough red face and big hands. His thick brown hair, sprinkled with grey, struggled to fall in any one direction.

'This is my wife, Jeannie.' The younger woman looked at Michael quickly and then down at the ground. She was small and frail. The strands of auburn hair that escaped from under her shawl were the only remnant of a beauty diminished by what Michael assumed was hard work and poverty.

'Bairns, come meet Father Michael.' The children huddled around their parents, looking up at the tall man in the white robe. The girl stood apart from them.

'This is Kenny, Father.' Kenneth proudly put his hand on his older son's shoulder. Kenny was nine or ten and the image of his father. The boy nodded politely at Michael. 'And Peter.' Although appearing to be only a couple of years younger than Kenny, Peter was more fragile, more like his mother. 'Wee Jeannie here is our youngest.' The child quickly disappeared behind her father, but not before Michael saw that she had the same beauty her mother would once have had. She then popped her head around her father's leg.

'Where is your hair,' she asked, looking intently at Michael's bald head.

'Wee Jeannie,' Kenneth said, his cheeks turning an even deeper shade of red.

Michael laughed. 'Do not worry, Kenneth, it is good for children to be curious.' He crouched down beside the child. 'My hair fell out when I was a young man. My head does get cold in the winter though, but I have my cowl to keep me warm.' He gave her a wide smile and stood up.

'And who is this?' he asked, looking directly at the girl.

'This is our eldest, Alice,' Kenneth said.

Alice was a little taller than her mother but in contrast had long straight brown hair which hung down her back. Her green eyes, the colour of wet moss on the hills, gave nothing away. She had obviously learned early to close down. Michael knew what that was like, for had he not spent most of his life doing the same.

'You must be kept busy helping your mother look after the young ones,' he said. From where he stood he could feel her power. She looked directly at him and he realized that at some level she had felt his. What he was not sure of was if she realized she had done it.

'Aye, Father.'

'Our Alice can read and write well and helps the wee ones with their learning,' Kenneth said.

'You will be going to the school at the Port, I presume. Father Andrew is a very good teacher.' Andrew kept a small cart and horse at Moira's stable and picked up children along the way. 'He tells me you will be doing some work for us, Kenneth.'

'I am ready any time.'

'We will be delighted to have the help again.' Michael turned to Moira and laid a hand on her shoulder. 'We sorely miss your Niall.'

'I do too.'

'He is watching over you, Moira.'

'I know that, Father, I know.'

'Well, I hope you and your family will be happy here, Kenneth.'

'I will be doing my best to make sure they are, Father,' Moira said, slipping her arm around Jeannie.

He watched them walk to their boat. Alice quickly looked back at him before drawing her shawl further over her head.

Spring was filled with the flurry of light breezes and a renewal of the earth. The daffodils began their journey to display their faces to the sun. The snow on the higher hills was gradually melting, and colours again adorned the hillside.

Michael could hear the laughter of children as he stood outside the school. There was nothing nicer than that sound. Andrew had taught the children of the area for a long time and he loved that part of his work. He nurtured them, was a friend to them and never reprimanded them. Because of his giving nature the children responded to him in kind. Andrew was totally content with being a monk and a teacher, happy with his life in every way. Michael sometimes craved that sense of contentment for his own restless spirit but he knew he would always be a seeker, searching for what lay beyond the reality of this earthly existence.

He and Andrew were great friends, based on an acceptance of each other's values and choices. When Andrew told him Alice had a beautiful writing hand and a yearning to learn, Michael hoped this was his chance to offer her guidance. He opened the door quietly and was greeted by ten pairs of eyes. He immediately saw Alice at the back of the room. She looked straight at him and returned to her task.

'Father Michael, welcome. I told the children you might be visiting us today. They are anxious to show you what they have been up to.'

'Good morning, children.' Michael's smile encompassed them all. 'I am sorry it has been so long since I last visited. Ah, Alexander,' he said, bending down in front of one of the younger children 'what are you drawing?' The child's eyes lit up at being acknowledged first.

'I have drawn Angel Michael,' he said. The monks kept their discarded or poor quality parchment for use at the school. 'He has the same name as you, Father.'

'Aye, he does. My, that is a fine angel, Alexander, a fine angel indeed. In fact, Michael is one of God's special angels—so special he is called an archangel. He protects souls from evil and is a special favourite of mine.'

The child's smile widened. 'Alice told me he was special. She helped me start it. Alice said I should always ask Angel Michael to look after my Ma in heaven. Will he Father? Will he take care of my Ma?'

Alexander's mother had died giving birth to her fifth child the previous year and Alexander and his siblings were cared for by their father and grandmother. Life was hard for them but they were a loving family.

'He certainly will, Alexander. You should never worry about your mother as Archangel Michael will always be by her side.'

Alexander looked around to Alice. 'You are right, Alice. Father Michael says you are right.'

Alice smiled at the child, a smile so tender, so caring, that it took Michael's breath away.

He spent time with each child, talking to them, praising their work and at the same time laying his hand gently on them for a few moments, asking God to bless them. Eventually he reached Alice.

'Can I see what you are writing, Alice?'

'I copied Psalm 23 from Father Andrew's bible to give Auntie Moira for her birthday tomorrow,' she said. She slowly raised her eyes to look at him and handed him the paper. 'I am just making it bonny.'

Andrew was right—Alice did indeed write beautifully. The words flowed perfectly on the paper. The drawings of flowers around the words were delicate and precise.

'This is good work, Alice. You have a special gift I see.' He was amazed that a child of her age could produce such delicate work on poor quality parchment, resting on just a wooden bench.

'You like to read and write, Alice?' he asked.

Her face lit up. 'Oh aye.'

When it was time to leave, Michael blessed the children and thanked them for letting him see their work.

'Children, take some milk while I talk to Father Michael.'

'They are such a joy, Michael, such a joy,' Andrew said once they were outside.

'Indeed they are, Andrew.

'What did you think of Alice's writing?'

'She is truly gifted. Some of our brethren cannot write as well.'

'Including me, Michael. It would be a shame to let such a gift go unheeded. She also has the ability to remember everything. I have never known anything like it. I only have to say something once and she remembers it precisely. God must have a plan for her.'

'I think you are right. I will have to give it some thought.'

'I trust you to do what is best for the child.'

'I will, Andrew, I promise. We will talk to the others and see what can be done.'

The next morning after Prime, Michael walked along the cloisters with the other monks to the Chapter House, praying that a way could be found to allow him to help Alice. He had already spoken to Father Joseph and Andrew and they would now discuss it with the others. He joined them on the stone benches around the walls. It was practice in Chapter for misdemeanours to be brought up and suitable disciplines allocated but here at Inchmahome there were very few, so after prayers were said for deceased benefactors, general business was dealt with.

Michael had no apprehension about bringing up the subject of Alice with his fellow monks, whom he liked immensely. He told them about Alice's writing. Concern was voiced at the appropriateness of Michael's plan but it was accepted that as their numbers had depleted over the years, it would greatly assist the work of the scriptorium.

Chapter 16

Michael found Kenneth in the orchards. He was wiping the sweat from his neck and brow.

'And how is the fruit faring, Kenneth?'

'Fine, Father. It is all healthy but there is much work to be done. That last storm damaged some of the trees.'

'You do not mind the hard work?'

'I am used to it.'

'I visited the children at the school recently and I wanted to speak to you about Alice.'

'She has not been up to mischief has she, Father? She is a good lass, but sometimes she gets a wee bit restless.'

'No, Kenneth, she is not in any trouble. She is a bright child, is she not?'

'We think so. She is a great help to Jeannie and the other bairns love her.'

'You and your wife should be very proud of her. She is a kind-hearted girl and writes well.'

'The local priest where we lived saw that in her. His eyes were bad but he taught her how to read well and copy passages from the

Bible for him in large writing for his sermons. He gave her parchment to practice on. She would spend her time writing when she finished helping Jeannie. Is that what you want to talk about?'

'It is. We have many books in the priory, some very precious, and copying of these requires much care and attention to detail. Our world is changing, Kenneth, and with that change these books will become even more important to us. There may come a time when our way of worshipping God the way we have always done will be difficult and we must be ready for what the future holds.'

'What has this to do with Alice?'

'We would like Alice to help us with the copying of our books.'

'On the island?'

'Aye. As you know we are small in number and the work on the books is slow. We will pay her a small remuneration and ensure she receives a good education. I will take care of it personally when I am there, otherwise Father Joseph or Father Andrew will see to it. We were thinking perhaps three days a week. Either you could row her over or one of us will come for her, depending on whether you have work on the island.'

'She is only a bairn. She would be afraid on the island, away from her family. I know you are offering much, Father, but she is shy and the children would miss her. Jeannie's health is not good and she relies on Alice.'

'I know this is a big decision for you. If the family need her then that would always come first. She would be the one helping us, so we would be grateful for any time she can give us. I will give you time to think about it? Discuss it with your family and Alice. I could come to your home after Mass on Sunday and we can discuss any concerns you or your wife might have. More importantly it would always be Alice's choice. We would not want her to come if she has any doubts.'

Kenneth seemed relieved he did not need to give an answer immediately. 'Aye, Father, come on Sunday.'

'Good. I will see you then.'

As Andrew set up for Mass on Sunday, Michael knelt in front of the crucifix. He banished the demons who whispered words of doubt in his ear and prayed to God for guidance and strength. He knew that if given the chance to help Alice it would be a sacred trust, but if he assisted her to open to all the gifts he sensed she possessed, he would also open the way for any demons to gain entry to her soul. Would she have the strength to overcome them? He knew what that fight entailed.

Michael saw the family arrive in the church. Alice looked over at him but gave nothing away of her thoughts. Andrew's sermon that day was about the importance of trusting in God and being guided by Him. He hoped that Alice in particular was listening.

After completing his other duties, Michael rowed over to the mainland. Moira was playing in the garden with the children.

'Go in, Father, they are waiting for you.'

'Thanks, Moira.' He hoped her smile was a good omen.

Inside the house he found Kenneth, Jeannie and Alice sitting around the table. It was neatly laid out with bannocks and a pitcher of milk. The house was of stone, with two levels. The room they were currently in was where the family had their meals and sat around the fire. There was also another small dwelling annexed to the side of the building to accommodate any travellers who were prevented from crossing the loch in bad weather. Niall's family had owned the farm for generations and he and Moira had extended the place with money Niall inherited from an uncle. They had made it a comfortable and welcoming home.

Kenneth stood up and pointed to a spare stool. 'Sit down and have some food, Father.'

'Thank you, Kenneth.' Both Jeannie and Alice followed him with their eyes, although Jeannie quickly lowered her gaze when Michael smiled at her.

'Very good bannocks, Jeannie, did you make them?'

'Aye, she did,' Kenneth answered for her. She is a good cook, my Jeannie. Moira is glad of her help around the place.'

Michael took one more sip of the milk and wiped his mouth with the back of his hand. 'Very nice indeed. Thank you for your kindness.'

Kenneth patted his wife's arm and smiled over at Alice. 'We have talked about what you said, Father, about Alice working on the books. It was up to her to decide and she wants to do it.'

'And you are both in agreement?' he asked.

'We think she is too young but she is eager to learn. She is always asking questions and wanting to know everything.'

'I am pleased, Kenneth. You know she will be safe with us and we will take good care of her. If at any time you want to change your mind, just tell me. We will be glad to have the extra help and I am sure Alice will brighten our lives. Thank you, Alice,' he said, looking directly at her. He was unable to read her thoughts.

'When will you want her to start, Father?'

'You could bring her tomorrow if that will be convenient. We can acquaint her with the place. Would that be in order?'

'Well, lass, what do you say?' Kenneth said. Alice looked from her father and mother to Father Michael.

'Aye, that would be in order.' Michael tried not to laugh at her mimicking. This girl would be a challenge to teach.

'Good, good. Well, I will get off and let you enjoy the rest of your Sunday.'

As he rowed back to the island Michael was filled with a sense of being part of a destiny greater than his own.

Chapter 17

Michael stood in the stillness of a morning filled with promise. Droplets of dew hung like lanterns from the bushes and trees, sparking for but a moment before surrendering to the grass below. The birds had long finished their dawn chorus but some continued their joyous singing as they flew from tree to tree. Michael loved all creatures but for him birds were God's special gift to mankind, to remind us of our freedom of spirit and to give gratitude for a life blessed. He was glad Alice was to begin her time on Inchmahome on a day such as this, when the beauty of the island was displayed to perfection.

He was being given a chance to guide a child who stood where he once had, on the edge of a world that did not seem possible. He wanted to do right by her. For the first time since meeting her, he experienced doubt about his resolve to help her accept and then develop the strange gifts they shared. What right had he to do this? She was still young. It would change her life forever. But what else could he do? He could have been like she was now, confused and alone with her fears. No, he must not waiver. He must help her as Maurice had, and still did, for him.

Had it been almost 30 years ago when he stood in terror on the battlefield at Flodden? His mind drifted back to that time and the years since. He had known both great sorrow and moments of joy but still he wondered if there had been another road he should have taken.

Michael's journey through his memories ended when he spotted Kenneth's small boat making its short journey across the loch. He shrugged off the sorrow of past times and smiled in anticipation of the beginning of this new journey with Alice. It would not be easy. He would have to work hard to gain the child's trust, and then keep it. She would no doubt struggle to share her secrets and accept guidance. She would have perhaps spent all her young life being haunted by visions of a world she did not understand. He would take it slowly and with care, for his fervent wish was to take away her fear which he knew she carried like a stone around her neck. He could not let Alice live her life like that. He would find a way to protect her from a world that few knew. He must somehow ease the way for her.

Father Andrew joined him at the jetty just as the boat approached. Alice looked such a tiny thing, her cloak wrapped tightly around her. She took the hand Michael held out to her but avoided looking at him. He felt her uncertainty, her fear of the unknown. She smiled when she saw Father Andrew.

'Alice my dear, welcome to Inchmahome. We are very grateful you agreed to help us with our work.'

'Thank you, Father. I will try my best.'

Kenneth bent down in front of his daughter. 'You are sure you want to do this, lass?' he asked.

She kissed his cheek. 'I will be fine Pa, really I will.'

Kenneth patted her head and went over to Michael. 'Remember your promise, Father,' he said.

'We will take very good care of her, Kenneth,' he said.

Alice walked between the two monks up the gentle slope to the priory.

'Our order has been here since 1238,' Father Andrew said, 'although it is believed an earlier church was once on this site. It was built by Walter Comyn, the Earl of Menteith, one of the most important men in Scotland at the time.'

'It may take you a while to get your bearings as you have only seen the church but I will show you where everything is,' Michael said, with what he hoped was a reassuring smile.

Father Andrew left them in the cloisters with a promise to see her later.

Michael opened one of the doors and indicated for her to enter. 'This is our kitchen and warming room.' The heat hit them as they crossed the threshold. Two monks looked up from the table as they entered.

'Alice, this is Father Callum and Father Donald. This is Alice, who will be helping us in the scriptorium.'

Both monks stood up and bowed to her. 'Welcome, Alice,' Father Callum said.

'Yes indeed,' Father Donald said. His broad smile showed several missing front teeth. 'Come by the fire have some milk.'

Michael watched Alice as she sipped the drink, wrapping her hands around the cup. She looked so young, so vulnerable.

'Father Callum is our cellarer. He makes sure we have food on the table. Father Donald helps with just about everything. He is quite a wonder. Oats are one of the few things we have brought from mainland to be ground into meal for porridge. We also fish for trout and pike in the loch.'

Alice handed her empty cup to Father Donald and whispered her thanks to the two monks.

'Well, let me show you our home, Alice.'

'You come here any time you wish, my dear,' Father Callum said. 'You will be most welcome. Even if we are at prayer, just make yourself comfortable and help yourself to food or drink.'

'Thank you.' She smiled at them before following Michael to the door.

'The cloisters are completely surrounded by buildings,' Michael said. 'This helps protect us from the cold winter winds as we are greatly exposed here on the island. The garden in the centre is where Father Callum grows herbs both for cooking, and medicinal purposes for Father Malcolm who takes care of any of our sick brothers. I also have a way with plants and herbs. I will teach you.'

'You will?'

'If you wish it, of course.'

'My granny taught me a wee bit but I would like to learn more.'

'Those are the stairs we use during the day. At night there are other stairs that lead us to the choir of the church. A blessing on winter nights.'

They stopped at the entrance to another room. 'This is our Chapter House. We come here after morning mass. A chapter from the Bible is read and the business of the priory is taken care of including what work is to be done for the day. We are bound by a set of rules and certain times each day is allocated for prayer and work. We pray many times together, starting not long after midnight and ending when we go to bed.'

'You pray all day and night?'

'It seems that way, but we also study and work. We call it Opus Dei—the work of God. And we have time to eat and sleep.' Michael was not sure Alice believed him.

'And as you know, this is our church,' Michael said as he opened the large wooden door. Although she had attended Mass here, Michael could see she was still in awe of it. The highly decorated stained glass on the five lancet windows behind the high altar depicted Christ and the saints. Rays of colourful light streamed through onto the floor. There were eight smaller windows on the side walls so there was always light in the church during the day. Parishioners sat in the nave at the other end from the high altar but they could still see the painted walls and the many colourful tapestries that adorned the walls. To the left was the belfry. Between the nave and high altar were the seats for the monks. These were made of dark heavy wood, richly carved and polished.

They returned through the door to the cloisters and walked to the right. Michael pointed out the refectory where the monks ate their meals, the stairs leading to the Prior's room and where accommodation was provided for visitors.

'And here is our scriptorium,' Michael said. Alice walked a few paces into the room and stopped. Her eyes were wide as she looked along the rows of books on the shelves. There were four wooden tables, each with a slanted frame secured on top. Attached to each table was a solid tray with ink pots slotted into holes. There was a wooden seat at each table.

She slowly walked over to one of the tables where a large volume lay open. She went to touch it but drew back her hand.

'It is beautiful. Will I be working on books like this?'

'That you will, Alice.'

'Perhaps I will not be able to do this.'

'Father Bernard will show you. He is a good teacher. Do not worry. You will do well. You have a steady hand.'

Just then the door opened and a monk came into the room. 'Father Bernard, we were just talking about you. This is Alice.'

Father Bernard limped towards her. Michael saw that he did not instinctively put his hand to the birthmark on his face as he usually did when meeting strangers. 'Father Michael says you have a beautiful hand. It will be a pleasure to have you working here. Welcome my dear, welcome. Do you like our scriptorium?'

'I do, Father.'

'Let me show the Book of Hours I am working on. We lay the books we are copying open on the top part and the parchment on the frame. It makes it easier to write. The ink pots are by the side so there is no danger of spills. We have to be very careful. And over here,' he led her to a smaller table, higher than the rest, with doors below, 'is where we keep the inks and pigments.'

They eventually left Father Bernard to his work and went outside to the gardens. In the vegetable patch two monks were kneeling on the ground, working in the soil. They seemed absorbed in their task but got up and dusted off the dirt as they approached.

'Alice, this is Father Joseph. He takes care of the priory business for us and keeps us all in line. And Father David. He looks after the gardens and animals.'

'Good morning, Alice,' Father Joseph said. 'We are grateful for your help with our work. It is very important, especially in times like these.'

'And over there,' Michael said pointing to a figure sitting on a bench under a chestnut tree a short distance away, 'is Father Colin. He does not keep good health and sleeps a lot but he is a joy to us. He has many stories to tell.'

Father Joseph laughed. 'He does indeed. Father Daniel is another of our older monks. He cannot hear but still enjoys being part of our community. He is sleeping, I think, but we will introduce you to him another time. Now, let us show you our garden. We take great pride in it. We all help out here. Father Callum does wonders with what we grow.'

Alice followed the monks as Father David pointed out the different vegetables laid out neatly in rows. 'We grow what we can and are able to store much of the food for the winter months. Now let me introduce you to some of our other companions.' Father David led the way to the hen house near one of the trees. 'These little angels provide us with our eggs and a fine job they do too.'

Alice laughed and went over to them. 'They are bonny hens.'

'Now where is Maisie?' Father David said. 'Maisie, Maisie, where are you? Ah, here she is.' A large black cow appeared from around the side of the building.

She came right up to Alice and stared at her with her large dark eyes. Alice stroked her gently and the cow lifted her head high in appreciation.

'Father Callum has prepared some food for you and your father, Alice,' Michael said. 'We thought you might like to join him in the orchard.'

'Aye, I would.'

'I hope we will be friends, Alice,' Father Joseph said. 'I will be helping with your lessons when Father Michael is away from the island. It will take you a while to get used to things no doubt but please look to us for help. We will do everything we can to make you feel at home during your stay. Well, I will let you get on.'

Instead of returning through the cloisters, Michael led Alice around the outside of the building. Spring flowers were everywhere and the sun felt warm on their faces. 'Look up there, Alice,' Michael said, pointing to the sky. 'An osprey. There are many around the island. You have seen the swans no doubt?'

'I take them stale bread when I walk by the water. I saw one yesterday with her babies. They swam right up to me.'

For a moment Alice's eyes were unguarded as they had been when she smiled at Alexander the day Michael visited the school. He was now more determined than ever to help her overcome her fears and be the happy child she should be.

They walked in the cool shade of the trees. The only sounds were the birds and the humming bees. The island was carpeted with bluebells and lush green grass. Michael told her the names of the different species of trees and plants and the various places on the mainland that could be seen from the island. He stopped and pointed to land that stuck out from the mainland towards the island.

'That land is known as Arnmach. There is a story about it. That hill over there is Bogle Knowe and that is where the fairy folk live.' Alice turned and stared at him. 'The story goes that a long time ago the Earl of Menteith released the fairies into the world by accident. They were bored and pestered him for work so he asked them to build a rope of sand from the south shore to the island. Of course they did not finish it but it is said they still live on Bogle Knowe.'

'Do they visit the island?'

Michael was pleased at her question. The experiences of his life had taught him that nothing was impossible. 'I believe they do. I have never told anyone this but one evening, just as the light was fading and I was standing on the shore, I am sure I saw them fly from one of the trees and make their way across the water to their home.'

'You did? What did they look like?'

'Very pretty creatures, small, and they had such delicate wings. I am sure I heard them laughing. I think they visit the island during the day and fly among the flowers. Perhaps some of them live on the island. I believe they keep an eye on us all.'

'Why did you not tell anyone?'

'There are times when it is acceptable to keep a secret. It makes it special. It somehow does not seem so special when you tell someone else.'

'You told me.'

'I think we will be friends and friends share secrets and keep them safe. I trust you, Alice. You will keep my secrets.'

Alice stared at him in silence. He could not read her thoughts.

'Let's go and get the food then find your father.'

Father Callum had wrapped up some bread and cheese and put them in a basket with some ale for Kenneth. 'We make the best cheese in the district, Alice, so I hope you enjoy it.'

'Thank you, Father.' Alice smiled at him and went to take the basket.

'Here, let me carry it,' Michael said.

Alice's eyes took in everything as they made their way through the trees to the orchards. On the way they passed some sheep munching quietly on the lush grass.

'We have four sheep. They keep the grass down for us and also provide the wool that Father Malcolm spins. We just let them go where they want on the island. They are very docile.'

Kenneth was on a ladder which rested against one of the apple trees. When he saw them approach he came down, a big smile on his face.

'Alice! I was not expecting to see you till later.'

'Father Callum thought you and Alice might like to share your midday meal together. He has packed some things for you.' Michael handed Kenneth the basket.

'Very kind of him. I was thinking about you and wondering how you were doing.'

'Fine, Pa. Father Michael showed me round and I have met the other monks.'

'So you think you will like it here?' he asked.

'I like it, Pa.' Alice turned to Michael and for the first time smiled at him.

'Well, I will leave you two to enjoy your meal,' Michael said.

'You will not join us, Father?'

'I have to be in church and then I will be in the scriptorium.' Take as long as you like, Alice. Do you think you will be able to find your way back by yourself?'

'Aye.'

'Good. I will see you there.'

Michael turned when he heard the door open.

'Look who I found wandering around outside,' Father Joseph said. He stepped aside to reveal Alice, clutching the empty basket. 'I think she was a little lost. Come in, Alice. It will probably take you a while to find your way around. I will leave you in the capable hands of Father Michael. I will take the basket back to the kitchen.'

Michael went over to her and noticed she took a small step backwards. He did not sense fear but thought rather she had felt his energy field. He drew it back.

'Let me show you where you will be working. The tables and benches are made so that there is no movement to disturb us while we work. In the winter it is hard to stop shivering so heated stones are put under the tables to keep our feet warm. As you can see the room is well lit by candles but they are kept well away from the manuscripts. We have to be very careful as months, even years, of work would be ruined if an ember landed on one of the books. And this is your table. Father Joseph made this for you.' Michael pointed to the black cushion on the seat. 'He filled it with wool from our own sheep. We old monks are used to the hard benches but he wanted you to be comfortable.'

He heard her sigh and saw a tear start to form in the corner of her eye. 'What is wrong, Alice?'

'I am not clever enough to do this. I will make mistakes, I know I will.'

'Oh Alice, do you really think we would ask you to help us if we did not think you could do it? Your writing is beautiful and very precise. God has given you a gift but above all this I watched you when I came to the school. You love to write. There is a passion inside you for words.'

For a moment Michael closed his eyes and the smiling face of another lover of books flashed before him. As always, the memory tugged at his heart. He opened his eyes to find Alice staring at him.

'We will take it slowly. You can practice until you think you are ready. You can do this, but only if you want to.'

'I want to.'

'Good. Now let me show you some our most precious books.' Michael took a book from the shelves and carefully placed it on the table.

'It is beautiful,' she said as he opened an elaborately decorated Bible.

'This is very old and precious. Let me show you the book I am working on.' He moved to one of the open books on the table.

'You do this too?'

'I find it a peaceful and rewarding occupation. When I am not occupied with Lord Erskine I treasure the times I spend here. There is comfort in the silence and rest for my mind. I feel I am with God.'

'I thought priests were always with God.'

'Not always Alice. We are also men and like everyone else we have our demons.

'Do you see your demons?'

'I see lots of things that others cannot, but I do not tell anyone. Another of my secrets I hope you will keep.'

She looked at him without expression. 'I will keep your secret.'

'Would you like to watch me for a while?'

For the next hour Alice sat silently on her cushion at his side watching every stroke he made. The only sound was the scratching of the quill on the parchment.

'Well, Alice, it will be time for you to leave with your father soon and I have prayers.'

She looked at him as if coming out of a trance and smiled. The magic of that smile would stay with him always. It was not with words of encouragement or understanding but in the silence that the bond between them had been tied. He took a package from one of the shelves.

'I have a welcoming gift for you.'

She stared at it. No-one other than her family had ever given her a gift and she always knew what it would be as she watched them make it. Wee Kenny had a gift of whittling wood and spent many hours shaping pieces into birds or animals. Her mother would spin wool and make her some clothing. This was the first time she had ever been given a surprise. The gift was wrapped in cloth. She slowly unfolded it to reveal a book bound in red leather. Her eyes widened.

'It is a journal, Alice. The pages are blank and if you look underneath there is a clasp and a tiny lock. This is the only key so whatever you write in the journal will be private.'

Alice reached out and took it. She carefully inserted the key and the clasp sprang open. She stroked the first blank page then closed the book and locked it. 'I thank you, but why are you giving me this?'

'Remember we talked about secrets, things we do not want to share with anyone. Sometimes it helps to put our thoughts and fears in writing. I find it helps to clear my mind.'

'You think I have secrets?'

He smiled, not wanting to frighten her with questions she was not ready to answer, fears she did not want to confront. 'The power is strong in you, child,' Michael said.

'What power? I have no power.'

'You do not recognize it yet but it is there. One day you will trust it, believe in it.'

'You are a strange man. You do not speak to me as a child.'

'You are an old soul, Alice. You have still to learn what that means.' He smiled at her again, hoping she would sense the truth in his words. 'Will you help me put out the candles?'

The routine was set that first week. When Alice arrived with her father they went to the kitchen where either Father Callum or Father Donald had a warm drink ready for them. Father David would discuss with Kenneth what he wanted him to do that day and Alice would go to the scriptorium. Both Michael and Father Bernard were impressed with the practice lettering she did and the care she took with her task.

The following week they gave Alice a real manuscript to work on. She smiled at them, her eyes sparkling. She took a deep breath and let it out slowly before sitting down in front of the parchment.

Everyone was delighted with her efforts and recognized the great gift she possessed.

While the monks were at prayers, Alice took the basket of food prepared for her and her father to whatever part of the island he was working. They sat together to eat and talk. If he was not on the island she ate by the edge of the water, always keeping back some bread to feed to the swans. Michael watched over her and was happy to see her become more relaxed.

Chapter 18

The morning had begun in a blaze of sunshine but by the time Alice and her father reached the landing place on Inchmahome the clouds had rolled over the bright blue sky. By noon the monks working outside scurried to Mass, trying to avoid the onslaught of sudden rain, their robes billowing in the wind.

Alice waited in the warming room where the huge fire blazed and crackled. She and her father would not be sharing their meal outside today. When Kenneth appeared he was soaked to the skin and hurried to stand by the flames. He tried to dry himself while sipping a warm drink.

'The day has certainly taken a turn for the worse,' Father Callum said.

'And I think it will only get worse,' Kenneth said. 'Alice, I think we should head home now.'

Michael came through the door and struggled to shut it behind him. 'What a day. I think you should leave now, Kenneth. Looks like this will keep up.'

'I was just saying so to Alice, Father. We will go now.'

Michael and Father Callum went with them to the boat shed. Lightning flashed and the sky became even darker. Greyness descended on the lake and swirled around, almost obscuring the mainland.

'It will not be a pleasant trip in this. I have never seen it so rough.'

'It is only a short distance and Jeannie was sick this morning. I need to get back. I do not think I should risk it with Alice.'

'I agree, Kenneth. She can stay here.'

'I will go and see to it,' Father Callum said and hurried off back to the priory.

'Pa, I want to go with you.'

'It will not be safe, child. Father Michael will look after you. I will see you tomorrow.'

'But Pa...'

'I cannot take you in this.'

Alice knew any more delay would make the crossing worse and she too was worried about her mother.

'We will take care of her.' Michael shouted over the increasing wind. 'Kenneth, wave the lantern when you get back so Alice knows you are safe.'

Kenneth hugged his daughter. 'You will be fine, lass.'

Michael helped Kenneth drag the boat to the water. He and Alice remained in the shelter of the shed until eventually through the rain they saw the light on the mainland.

'He is home.' Alice sighed with relief.

They ran through the storm to the warming room. Inside Father Callum fussed over Alice, taking her cloak and hanging it on a hook.

He made her sit down on a stool by the fire and gave her a cup of hot milk and honey. He took off her boots and laid them on the hearth.

'We cannot have you catching a fever, my dear. More milk?'

'No thank you, Father.'

'Well, I suppose I had better help myself then.' Michael said.

'Oh Father, I...'

Michael laughed. 'I am jesting. I will get my own. You continue your fussing.' This old monk had lived most of his life in a cloistered existence, many years here at Inchmahome, with only men for company. It was heart-warming to see the pleasure he got from taking care of Alice.

'We have readied a room for you, Alice,' Father Callum said.

The room was used for storing blankets and Father Callum had set up a pallet. 'I would have given you one of the other rooms but I thought it would be cosier here. The kitchen is on the other side of the wall so the room will stay warm. Come back to the fire now. You can help me make the bread for tomorrow if you want.'

After the final prayers of the day, Michael did not go to bed, but instead made his way to the warming room. He was surprised to find Alice sitting alone by the fire.

'You could not sleep?'

'No, Father.'

'Can I sit with you a moment?'

She nodded. Michael sat on one of the other stools. He saw a shadow around her.

'Do you not feel safe here?'

She turned to him. 'Why do you ask me that?'

'I can sense it. I feel your fear. What is it that you are afraid of?'

'I cannot tell you.'

'I told you I have secrets, and I know you have them too. That first time I saw you at the church I knew you were different. I knew you were like me.'

He saw the fear return to her eyes and he wondered if it was too soon. Perhaps she was not ready. He did not want to rush her.

'What do you mean?' she said.

'I see what you see, Alice. I see the dead and I can talk to them. I have dreams, visions. There are times when I wish it was not that way but I cannot deny it. We have a gift you and me. You might not see it like that now. I too was afraid when it started. I can teach you how to control your fear, how to put it behind you and live in peace with your gift.' Michael knew what she was feeling. He had once been where she was now.

'Live at peace. How can I live in peace when the dead will not leave me alone? What do they want from me?'

'They live in darkness, Alice, wandering a lifeless landscape and are drawn to the light of your spirit. Some of them are angry at the manner of their death. When they see your light and realize you can see them, they vent their frustration on you. Some are just lost. They have not accepted their death. They do not realize they have left their bodies. Then there are the others—the ones who have been assigned to help you, to protect you.'

'Protect me,' she whispered. 'They do not protect me in the night.

'You have much to learn, Alice. I can teach you how to protect yourself from the spirits who torment you. I can show you how to help them as well as the ones who are simply lost and need to find a way home. I can help you recognize and call on the ones who wish to walk your path with you.'

Alice watched him as he spoke. He knew she wanted to trust him. 'I cannot talk about it, Father. Ma and Pa made me promise.'

He put his hand on her shoulder and looked into her eyes. 'Will you trust me, Alice? I give you my oath that I will never discuss with others what passes between us. I would never betray you. I am a priest, your priest. I offer you my friendship and my protection. Will you trust me?'

She stared at him for a long time. 'Aye. I will trust you.'

He smiled. It had begun. He saw the relief in her face. This was probably the first time in her life she had confronted her dark secret.

'My granny knew what plants and flowers to use to help people, and when it was going to rain or snow. She had the sight and would know when a woman was with child even before she knew it herself, and she would know whether it was a lad or a lass. She would warn people not to do things if she sensed danger. She taught me the healing way. I dream a lot, about places and people I do not know. Sometimes even when I am awake I see things. Granny treated Father Luke when he was sick. He was the one who taught me how to read and write. Then he died and we got a new priest. He was not like Father Luke. He was very strict. Did not think women needed learning.

'When he found out from the villagers that Granny helped them when they got sick and about her knowing way, he was very angry. He ordered her to stop helping and said only those under the influence of the devil could know the future. He said it was in the Bible. Granny got really scared when she heard him tell the neighbours she might be a witch. She quickly made plans. One night we all just left. She went north to find her sister and Pa brought us here. Granny said she could not leave on her own because if the priest came for her and she was gone he would go after me because everyone knew she taught me her ways. Poor Ma. She cried and cried all the way here. If Auntie Moira had not been so kind I think Ma would have died from all the fuss. Ma made me promise I would forget all Granny taught me and never tell a soul about it.'

'That must have been hard for you.'

'I could always see shadows from when I was wee, but as soon as we came here they became more real. Now I see them everywhere. I try so hard but they will not go away.' Alice looked around then shivered.

'Do you believe I am your friend?'

'Aye.'

'Good. Then tomorrow we can begin. But you must guard our secret well. No-one must know of the world we see.'

'You said there is much for me to learn, that you will teach me.' Alice said.

'As best I can.'

'Can you teach me first not to be afraid?' she whispered.

'I promise. And no matter what happens in your life I will protect you. That is my pledge to you.'

She smiled at him and he knew could never let her down.

'You said you were like me. You see spirits and have visions?'

'I do.'

'How did it begin for your, Father? Were you young like me?'

'Not as young as you. It took a nightmare, a time of great madness, for it to begin for me.'

'Tell me?'

'I cannot.'

'Do you not trust me, Father,' Alice asked. He saw a hint of a smile at the edge of her mouth.

Michael laughed. 'I will tell you.'

'Will you spare nothing?'

He was reminded that the age of her body was nothing compared to the journey her soul had travelled. 'Nothing.'

She sat on the floor beside the fire, wrapped her hands around her drawn up knees, and gave him her full attention.

'I was 16.' he said, as his mind again journeyed to the past.

Chapter 19

Michael could see that Alice was agitated when she arrived on the island with her father. He sought her out in the scriptorium when he knew she would be alone.

'Is all well with you, Alice?'

She immediately jumped up from her bench. 'Father, I have seen one in the woods.'

'A ghost?' His revelation of his past led to a deeper trust between them and she gradually opened up about her visions. He did his best to help her let go of the fear she still had of the ghosts who were drawn to her.

'Aye. Sometimes he comes near the house. He wears a short skirt and his legs are bare. His sandals are tied up to his knees. His helmet has red feathers.

'It is said that the Romans passed this way. Perhaps this one died nearby. Has he spoken to you?'

'No. I think he wants to but he always turns away.'

'Next time you see him, Alice, speak to him. Encourage him to leave this world behind and move on. Are you afraid of him?'

She smiled. 'Oh no, he seems gentle.'

'Then he can do you no harm.'

'This is what you do? You want me to do the same, to help him move on?'

'We can both help the lost souls who linger in this world.'

When Alice arrived on the Wednesday, Michael noticed her excitement. It was not until mid-morning that he got the opportunity to be alone with her.

'I saw the soldier again yesterday. He did not disappear this time. I did what you said. I told him my name and asked him his. He is called Marcus. I asked him what happened to him and he said he caught a fever. His legion was camped nearby but he could not get off the ground when it was time to leave. Two of his friends stayed with him until darkness came. He had not long joined the legion and wanted adventure and glory. He did not want to die. At first he thought his friends had abandoned him in the night but after a while he realized he was dead. He was angry because he did not get the chance to make his family proud. He said he could not find his way home. I told him he could find glory in heaven if he moved on—that God was waiting for him. He asked me which God. I just told him his God. Did I do right, Father?'

'Aye, Alice, you did.'

'We talked for a long time. He said he would try. That is when I saw the light, Father. It was beautiful. He saw it too and I told him he should go to it. He did. He did. The light wrapped itself around him and he was gone.'

'You did well, child. How did you feel?'

'Oh Father, I feel happy. I did that. I helped him. I did not know it could be like this. I have always been afraid of the ghosts, but now I can help them.'

'Remember, they may not always be so willing to move on.'

'But some will.'

'I told you it was a gift. Has it taken away some of your fear?'

Her eyes were sparkling and she smiled. 'It has.'

'Good. Good. Now I had better go. Father Joseph is waiting for me. We will talk again soon.' He headed to the door. She called his name and he turned.

'Thank you, Father.'

The morning mist still lay gently on the lake. Michael stood silently by the water watching Alice scattering the grain for the hens. He pushed back his cowl and waved to her.

'Good morning, Father. I saw you earlier but you seemed far away,' she said.

'I was. Far, far away.'

'When do you leave, Father?'

'Noon.'

'You look sad for a man going to the crowning of a queen. It will be a grand affair, will it not?'

'Indeed. A light in dark times. The King wanted a son badly but his daughter on the throne will suffice. It will keep the Lords in check for a while, although King Henry will be thinking to the future. A bride for his son. He will be a hard man to deny.'

'Will the Queen's mother be strong enough to resist?'

'Despite being French she knows what is best for Scotland and will not give away her daughter's heritage easily. She is clever and well used to the diplomacy needed in these matters.'

'Then why are you sad?'

'As I watch little Mary being crowned Queen of Scotland tomorrow, it will be 30 years since Flodden, the day I lost my brother. So long ago. It was the end of many things, but also a beginning.'

'Does Robbie come to you?'

'No. I see so many spirits and at the beginning I resented he was not one of them. He was the only one I wanted to see. Only when I understood fully what was happening to me did I realize that the spirits I see have not moved on. They are still clinging to this life. With Robbie, he must have gone quickly. He left nothing unresolved. I like to think he chose his time to leave but that he still keeps a watch over me.'

'How long will you be gone?'

Michael shrugged. John wants me to sense the way of things. There are still those who want an alliance with the English, some who do not want the French involved, and some who play both sides.' He looked back over the lake. 'I am weary of all this intrigue. There are times when I feel I will never leave this island. Perhaps one day I will get my way.'

'I miss you when you are gone a long time.'

Michael smiled. The blush on her cheeks told him that her words had come unbidden.

Chapter 20

Alice stood by the stone wall looking across the lake at the island, bathed in moonlight. The air was cool and the stars flickered brightly in the night sky. Had it really been a year? In that time she had learned much. Father Michael had kept his promise about her education. She especially enjoyed when he talked of Scotland and its place in the world and was always sorry when the lessons ended. He had a deep, gentle voice that brought alive the people and the places he described to her. Her little world had expanded and she felt pride at being a Scot. He talked of battles won and lost, of mistakes and brilliance, but above all she felt the spirit of the Scots. She was part of an ancient and noble people.

And France and Spain and Rome. Her mind formed the pictures as Father Michael spoke the words. It fired in her a passion to learn everything. He had laughed when she told him that but she could see he was pleased. She was surprised how easily her trust of him happened. It was his gentle way and the fact that he always looked her straight in the eye when he spoke. He did not treat her as a child and was eager to share his knowledge.

Sometimes he came and stood behind her in the scriptorium as Father Bernard instructed her on technique and she was comforted by his presence. She sensed in him honour and honesty but also a loneliness. He had shared his secrets and his fears and listened to hers. He was her friend.

She could hear the voices of her siblings coming from the house and the sound of Moira's laughter. Life had changed much since her family left their little home and the runrigs behind. Pa always spoke kindly of his sister and he knew his family would be made welcome. The journey with their meagre belongings had been difficult and confusing but the loving welcome they did indeed receive from Moira completely wiped out all memories of the hardship. She opened her arms and her heart to them all.

Alice heard footsteps behind her.

'What a beautiful starry night,' Moira said. 'It can get fair noisy in there sometimes. I love it but I know a young woman needs time to herself. Do you miss the family when you are on the island, Alice? Are you lonely there?'

'Oh no. There is so much for me to do.'

'They do not work you too hard?'

'They are very kind to me. I love the books; the way they smell and how they feel. And I have my lessons. I am learning so much from Father Michael.'

Moira turned to Alice. 'You know your mother is ill?'

'Aye.'

'I have seen you touch her. You put your hand on her shoulder and close your eyes. I also see she seems better afterwards. I asked myself if you have the healing way with you.'

Alice sucked in her breath. She had been so careful. Father Michael's words echoed in her head; his warning of the danger if her gifts were to become known.'

'Do not worry,' Moira said. 'Your secret is safe with me.'

'Father Michael said I should not talk about it, just do it without raising suspicion.'

'He advised you well. The times are such that fear often takes over in the hearts of good people. Alice, with your mother, the healing you give her, it does not mean...it might not...'

Alice put her hand on Moira's arm. 'Father Michael explained my healing will not cure her unless it is the will of Ma, and God.'

'He is a wise man and you are a brave girl. Know I will always be here for you. I would never betray you and anything you ever say to me will be between us. I hope you will come to me if you need to talk about anything.'

Alice kissed Moira's cheek. 'Thank you.'

Chapter 21

It had been a long harsh winter and the snow was long on the ground. Michael felt the cold in his bones as he sat alone in the chapel at Stirling Castle while John Erskine was meeting with some of the Lords of Scotland. His mind drifted back to his time in Spain when he walked the Camino. He often thought of that journey on a cold Scottish day.

He felt uneasy but did not know why. He became aware of someone else in the chapel. He turned to find Jeannie walking towards him. He knew now what had been disturbing him. Alice's mother was dead.

Michael could hardly believe it was the same woman. All the pain and weariness had gone and she looked as he imagined she once was. Her red hair was shining and hung long down her back. Her skin was clear and she walked towards him straight and strong. Her smile when she reached him held no regrets, no sorrow.

'Jeannie, I am happy you came.'

'I could not do it any more, Father. I had no strength left but I hung on for the sake of Kenneth and the bairns. I tried hard but I had to let go. I need them to understand that.'

'They will, Jeannie.'

'They will be sad, and I do not want them to think they could have done more for me. Moira will care for them I know. She loves them and they will be safe with her.'

'She is a good woman. She will care for them as her own.'

'It is Alice I am most worried about. I do not want her thinking she should have stayed home more. She loves the learning and working on the books. I do not want her to think she should not have spent all that time on the island, or needs to give it up to help look after the young ones. You will make her understand that she needs to keep at the learning. She is special. I knew it the day she was born.'

'Do not you worry yourself, Jeannie. I will talk to her. I will make the family understand you are at peace now. You are happy?'

'Oh aye. I did not know it could be like this. I was afraid you know. It was dark and then suddenly everything was light. I feel a peace I never had. Father, does Moira know you can see us?'

'She might suspect, but I do not think she knows for sure.'

'If you can, will you tell her that when I got to the light, her Niall was there to meet me. I never met him but it was him. He talked to me and helped me with the new place. He says there is so much to see, and lots of people wanting to meet me. Imagine that, Father, folks wanting to meet me. I saw my Ma too. Niall took me to her. I had a fine time. Will you tell Moira, please? Niall was handsome and smiling all the time. He told me you were with him when he passed and to tell you everything you said was right. He just wants Moira to know that he loves her and not having children did not matter to him as long he had her beside him.'

'I will find a way to tell her. I promise.'

'And you will look out for Alice? I know she has the gift like Ma and I tried to get her to stop it because I was afraid. She needs to be careful. There are many folk who are afraid like me. You promise me you will look out for her?'

'I will protect her with my life.'

'Thank you, Father. I had better be leaving you now. Niall is waiting for me. God bless you, Father. God bless you.'

Michael immediately headed to the Port.

Kenneth was leaning against one of the trees when Michael arrived at the cottage. He looked cold, sad and weary. Michael embraced him.

'You go in and see the others, Father. They need you.'

Michael put his hands on Kenneth's shoulders. 'Will you believe me when I tell you that all her sickness has gone and she is at peace now? She loves you and the family but she had to go. She needs you to understand that.'

Kenneth looked at him for a long time. Michael sensed his conflict. 'You saw her?'

'I did.'

Kenneth smiled and wiped a stray tear from his cheek. 'Thank you, Father. You go in now.'

Alice was sitting on the rocking chair with Wee Jeannie on her lap. Peter and Kenny where sitting on the floor by the fire next to Moira's chair, their heads leaning against her. He sat down on the empty chair.

'I am glad you got back in time for the burial, Father,' Moira said. 'Will you say the Mass for her?'

'I will, Moira. May I see her?' He turned to the others. 'I am going to say some prayers for your mother.'

They all followed him, silent in their sorrow. Jeannie was dressed in her Sunday best. Her long hair had been combed and framed around her face. Her hands had been placed across her chest. The children began to cry and clung tightly to Moira.

'Dear Lord, we know that Jeannie is with you now and that you will take care of her. She is much loved by her family and they are grieving for her and I ask you to give them comfort. Wrap your love around them and help them understand that one day they will be reunited with her in Heaven. I know she will watch over them. They only have to think of her and she will be beside them. They cannot see her but they can know her arms will hold them and that she will be with them always. When their turn comes to be with you, she will meet them at the gate to paradise and look after them. Until then Lord, give them strength to endure their grief.'

Michael pressed his finger to his lips and placed them on Jeannie's forehead. 'I will keep my promise, Jeannie,' he whispered.

Alice walked with him to the landing place. Kenneth had left a boat ready in the water.

'You saw Ma?' Alice said.

'She came to me in the church at Stirling. She was beautiful, Alice. Her face was glowing and her eyes bright. She is truly at peace.'

'What did you promise her?' Tears streamed down Alice's cheeks.

'That I would help you all. She especially made me promise to look out for you. She did not want to you to have any regrets about being away so much.'

'She forgives me?'

'There is nothing to forgive. She is proud of you and what you are doing. She said you are special.'

'Will I see her, Father?'

'I do not know.'

'But she is happy?'

'She is. It will be hard for you but try to think of her healthy, and looking forward to her future.'

'I will, Father. Not today, but I will.'

Early the next day Michael made the journey to the cottage. Moira was alone, feeding the hens.

'Those were fine words you said for Jeannie yesterday, Father.'

'Moira, I need to talk to you. I have a message for you.'

'From Jeannie?'

Michael smiled. 'Aye, from Jeannie?'

'I always knew you had the gift, Father. Since that first time we met when you came to the island I knew there was something about you. And what you did for Niall when he was dying. I know Alice is special too. It is just something we do not talk about in case the younger ones repeat it. It would not be good for her. You know how superstitious folks are. What did Jeannie say? I hope she will trust me to look after her bairns.'

'She wanted me to tell you that when she passed the first person she saw was Niall.'

'Niall! But they never met.'

'I know, but she said he looked after her and took her to see her mother. She said he is happy and that he wants you to know he loves you. Not having children was not important to him. Only having you mattered and he is keeping a wee eye on you.'

Moira put her hands to her face and let the tears flow freely. 'Oh Father, thank you for telling me. I miss him so. I never wanted him to think he was not enough for me. You do not know how much it means to me to know he is happy.'

Michael said Mass for Jeannie and in the weeks following spent as much time as he could with the family. Moira enfolded them all in love and gradually the darkness lifted a little. Jeannie did not appear to Alice but she understood that she had to let go. She returned to work at the priory. Kenneth too seemed lighter. Both he and Alice were content to leave the children with Moira.

Chapter 22

The following years were turbulent. A treaty was signed agreeing peace between Scotland and England and to the young Mary, Queen of Scots, marrying King Henry's son, Edward, This did not sit well with the Scottish people and when Henry insisted that the Scots break their alliance with the French, the Scottish Parliament used this as an excuse to break the agreement. Henry's response was swift. He sent the Earl of Hereford to invade Scotland in an attempt to force the Scots to accept the betrothal. Many Scottish towns were burned and the people terrorized as Hereford made his way through Scotland.

On the island it was easy to think that the world was at peace. Michael watched Alice from a distance, as she waited for him by the fallen log at the edge of the loch. Over the years their friendship had deepened. There were no barriers between them. When she talked of strange happenings, dreams that seemed so real, voices that no-one else could hear, he listened. He helped her nurture her gift and in taking away her fear it allowed the gift to grow. She had such a hunger for knowledge and was a delight to teach. She remembered everything and it was not that she just repeated dates learned in the history lessons. She would remember the events in detail, the circumstances of the battles, the linkages in history. She was eager for the seeds of knowledge to be planted in her fertile mind. Although she loved working on the books he knew she loved her lessons more and in the warm weather they would go outside.

Michael went over and sat beside her.

'History today, Father?'

'Not today, Alice. I am going to Rosslyn with Lord Erskine.' He saw the disappointment on her face.

'What is it you do there?' she asked.

He smiled. She asked him that each time he went and always seemed dissatisfied when he said it was business with Lord Erskine.

'I hope one day to go there,' she said. 'It sounds so beautiful the way you describe it.' Alice looked intently at him. He knew that look. 'Do you see ghosts there, Father? There are bound to be ghosts in such an ancient place?'

'There are. Some of them are not ready to leave yet but I am working on them.'

'If you took me with you I could help you. Some ghosts do not like me seeing them and disappear.'

Michael laughed. 'You know you are not supposed to frighten them, Alice. You should help them move to the light, not just to a corner where you cannot see them.'

'I do not do it deliberately, you know that. They sometimes disappear before I get a chance to speak to them.'

'I know, I know.'

'Can I go with you to Rosslyn?'

'I cannot take you.'

'I know,' she interrupted, 'Lord Erskine's business. When you come back from there you always look strange.'

'Strange?' he said.

'You have secrets you have not told me about Father? Big secrets.'

Michael laughed. 'Oh Alice, what an imagination you have.'

'I feel the power is strong in you when you come back. Can you tell me what you do there?'

'No, Alice, I cannot tell you.'

She laughed. 'One day you will, Father.'

'You might be right, Alice. I promise you that one day you will go to Rosslyn and you can see it for yourself. Now go and get something to eat. Father Joseph said he would take your lessons today and because you are doing so well with the book you are working on we thought you might like to stay home for the rest of the week and spend some time with your family. It is your birthday tomorrow, is it not?

'Aye.'

Michael took a package from the sleeve of his robe and handed it to her.

Her eyes widened. 'Oh thank you, Father, thank you,' Alice carefully unfolded the cloth. It was a Book of Hours. The cover was decorated in shades of blue and grey and gold. He watched her as she gently opened it.

'It belonged to my grandmother. My mother gave it to me when I returned from Rome. She will not mind me giving it to you.'

'It is so beautiful. I cannot take such a precious thing.'

'I have no-one else to pass it on to. You are my friend and I know you will care for it. I want you to have it.'

A tear ran down her cheek and she quickly wiped it away lest it fall on the book. 'I will treasure it.' She carefully folded the linen around it. 'Will you be gone long?'

'The English have wreaked havoc. They have destroyed more villages and monasteries. We are bringing some things back here for safe-keeping in case the castle or chapel are attacked.'

'The English are close?' she said.

'They are.'

'Will you say a prayer for me at Rosslyn, Father?'

'I always do, Alice.'

Three days later, as Alice was leaving the kitchen to feed the hens, she saw Father Michael and three men land on the island. As they unloaded four wooden boxes, Alice saw that under their black cloaks the strangers wore white robes adorned with a red cross, and swords hung from their belts. She watched them carry the boxes to the scriptorium.

When she had finished her duties she made her way there. Father Michael was kneeling by an open box, reading a manuscript.

'That looks very old, Father.'

'Indeed it is, Alice. Very old indeed, and very precious.' He gently rolled it up, put it back in the box and replaced the lid.

'Your friends did not stay long,' Alice said. She knew she had failed to mask her curiosity.

'Can you keep a secret?'

'Father! You ask me such a thing? You know you can trust me.'

Michael laughed. 'I am only teasing. I told you of the history of the Knights Templars. Well, my friends are Templars. That is all I can tell you.'

Alice shrugged her shoulders and sat down to continue the illustrations she was working on. Michael wandered over to the table and looked over her shoulder.

'Your work is beautiful, just beautiful,' he said.

'I have good teachers.'

'No, Alice, the gift is yours. We merely passed on some guidance.

When Alice returned the next day, the boxes were gone.

Chapter 23

1546

Alice did not let her wish to finish the book detract from her usual careful attention to detail. She applied the last stroke to her work and stretched her body as she walked away from her bench. She loved this places—the smell of the leather and ink, the gentle sounds of scratching on the parchment. She had learned so much over the years from the gentle monks. They seemed to sense her thirst for knowledge and she was never short of a volunteer for her lessons when Father Michael was absent from the priory. She headed to the kitchen as her stomach was making rumbling noises and arrived there at the same time as her father. They found Father Callum agitated and flushed.

'Father Joseph rowed over to the mainland at noon. We are expecting a new arrival. The news is not good. The English King is destroying more monasteries around the borders. Brothers have been killed. Sad, very sad. Here, the milk is still warm. Please help yourself. Everyone is so upset. Not good news at all.'

'Are we in danger?' Kenneth asked.

'I think we are safe for now.'

'Terrible times, Father.'

'That they are, Kenneth. All we can do is pray that it will end soon.'

'We had better be off,' Kenneth said.

Father Michael joined them as they walked to the landing place. He smiled at them briefly but Alice sensed his unease. Father Joseph was tying up the boat. His passenger had his cowl pulled over his head so Alice could not at once see his face. He was carrying a small bundle. He uncovered his head as Father Michael approached him.

'Welcome to your new home. I am Father Michael.

'Thank you. I am Father Feandan. It has been a hazardous journey.'

'Come, we have food ready for you.'

Father Feandan went to follow Michael but stopped abruptly when he saw Alice and her father standing on the grass.

'This is Kenneth, Father Feandan,' Michael said. 'His sister owns the farm you passed on the mainland where we left the horses. Kenneth works on the island and Alice does great work on our books.'

'A girl lives in the priory?' Father Feandan asked.

'Kenneth here is Alice's father. She comes every day but sometimes stays when the weather is bad or when we cannot pry her away from her work.'

'This is allowed?' Father Feandan said, as he continued to stare at Alice.

'The arrangement is acceptable to all, Father. We are very fond of Alice and the work in the scriptorium could not be done without her.'

'I have never heard of such a thing.'

'Well, let us get into the warmth,' Father Joseph said. 'Kenneth, you and Alice better be on your way. It looks like rain.'

Without another word, Father Feandan pulled his cowl back over his head and walked away.

'I do not like the new one,' Kenneth said, as they were rowing back across the loch.

'I do not think I have ever heard you say anything bad about anyone, Pa.'

'I do not trust him. You be careful of him. He does not like the idea of a woman being on the island.'

Alice said nothing to her father of the darkness she too had sensed around the new monk.

The rain did come late on the Friday night. The family gathered around the fire after their meal. The younger ones were sprawled on some blankets on the floor talking about the new hen Moira had bought.

'I want to call her Dougal,' Kenny said.

'That is a boy's name. Anyway, you gave Mary her name,' Wee Jeannie said. 'It is my turn.'

'You can name the next one.'

'Not fair.' Her small lips quivered. 'It is my turn. Tell him, Alice. Tell him.'

Kenneth just smiled, knowing that Alice would sort it out. She sat down on the floor beside the children and put her arms around Kenny.

'Let us see now. How many hens came to live here this past year?'

'Three,' said Peter.

'Mary and Lizzie and Maggie. Who named Mary?'

'Kenny did,' Wee Jeannie piped up.

'And Lizzie?'

'I did,' Kenny whispered.

'And Maggie?'

'Aunty Moira said she already had a name when she bought her.'

'So, Maggie already had a name and you gave Mary and Lizzie their names. Who do you think should name the new one?'

Kenny signed. Left by himself with his siblings he could usually get his way but Alice always made him do the right thing. 'Wee Jeannie.'

The little girl clapped her hands and bounced up and down on the floor.

'What are you going to call her then?' Kenny asked.

'Jenny,' she said with authority.

'Jenny is a stup...' Kenny started to say but caught Alice's glance.

'Well, that is settled then,' Moira said. 'You children get off to bed.'

'But...'

'No buts, Kenny. Time for bed. I have put warm stones in your beds so you should be nice and cosy. Now off you go.' The children gave them all a kiss. Alice got a special hug from Wee Jeannie and they headed off to their room.

Moira and Alice lingered by the fire after Kenneth went to bed. Moira watched Alice as she stared at the flames. From a shy, awkward child, she had grown into a confident, beautiful young woman. She was 16 now and well within the age for marrying and starting her own family, but Alice showed no interest in the various young men who tried to catch her eye. Moira knew that next to her family, Alice loved her work on the island. Father Michael and the other monks had provided her with the best education she could have received anywhere, and certainly not one usually available to the lassies.

Some nights Alice would sit by the fire and share what she had learned with the children. Of course she and Kenneth would be just as fascinated by the things Alice talked about. She knew so much about the history of Scotland and they were treated to stories of kings and lords and family intrigues. Alice told them about the local history and that even King Robert had visited Inchmahome. When the locals spread their fear about the English coming to kill everyone, Alice was able to explain where the battles were and that they were all relatively safe in Menteith.

Although she knew that Alice loved her family dearly, Moira recognized that the relationship between Alice and Father Michael was very special. They were often seen together wandering the forests or standing on the hilltops. Alice said Father Michael taught her all about plants and herbs that could be used in healing and how to be still and observe the animals and insects. Moira remembered seeing them atop one of the hills. Father Michael was pointing to something in the distance and Alice was shading her eyes with her hand as she followed his direction. She remembered thinking how the light seemed to form a circle around them and at one point they seemed to shimmer against the backdrop of the sky.

Now and again Moira heard the whisperings in the village about their relationship. They would ask her if Alice had found a young man yet and say that a girl of her age should be married and having bairns. Moira was quick to reprimand them but every now and then the gossip resurfaced.

Moira knew there was something different about Father Michael. He seemed more than a priest. She knew he had fought at Flodden and Lord Erskine held him in special regard. She remembered the first time he came to the island so long ago. He had a power inside him that was obvious to those who dealt with him. When Moira spoke to him she felt he could see into her soul. He was also a healer, that Moira did know. When Niall was dying Father Michael came to see him. Moira left the room thinking Niall might want to make his confession. They spent almost an hour together and after Father Michael left, Moira went in to see her dying husband. Instead of the weary, sad man she had watched him become as the disease took hold of his body, he had a smile on his lips. They talked for hours that night, of their life together, the good times and the bad. There was laughter as well as a few tears and when his spirit left his body at dawn, Moira thanked God and Father Michael for making Niall's last hours so peaceful.

Moira knew that Alice had been in awe of Father Michael at first but as the years passed this transformed into friendship. Moira wondered if Alice had heard the gossip and what would happen if one day she did find a young man. Would he be able to accept Alice's friendship with a priest? Moira knew the value Alice placed on it and did not think she would be prepared to give it up.

The villagers still came to Alice with their ailments and she freely dispensed her herbal remedies to them. She never told them the herbs would cure them, only help them feel a wee bit better. Moira knew that Alice's healing gift came through her hands and somehow she always managed to touch others without them knowing of this gift. After all, she had experienced it for herself. When Alice had seen her limping from a pain in her ankle, she laid her hands on the area. Moira felt the heat penetrate her skin and go deep into the bone. The next day the pain had eased and the following day it was gone completely. It was the same with the bairns. With any bumps or scrapes they would rush to Alice, knowing that she would take away their pain.

'I am off to bed, Auntie Moira.'

'Are you still having those dreams?'

Alice nodded. 'The images I see are strange. I spoke to Father Michael but he does not know what it means.'

'Hopefully they will go away soon.'

But it was not to be. One moment Alice was asleep and the next awake, her body rigid. She listened, but heard only the beating of her heart. There were no spirits there and the house was at peace. What had roused her? She closed her eyes and focused inwards. Nothing. She knew something had pulled her from her dream state. There was no fear, no panic, no indication whatsoever of what had disturbed her. She thought perhaps Father Michael was trying to communicate with her but she did not sense his energy.

Finally Alice gave up trying to relax and quietly got out of bed. She opened the door and slipped out into the night, wrapping her shawl tightly around her. The moon was full and lit up the world. She walked across the grass to the edge of the garden and looked over to the loch. The moonlight laid a path of white from the island to where she stood. She could see the shadow of the trees and the bell tower rising into the night sky. She sensed no danger, only a strange calmness surrounding her and felt if she wanted, the path of light would carry her to the island. She tried to make sense of the feeling but could not. Why was this happening to her? Suddenly the moonlight seemed to wrap her in a cocoon of warmth. She felt a pull towards something yet to come. At that moment she connected to a source that made all things possible. If she wanted to fly she knew that she could. If she wanted to rise above the earth and stand on the surface of the moon, she could. Her mind flashed with pictures, of places she did not recognize. A figure, covered with a while cloth, floated in front of her. She knew well enough to allow the images to run their course. She felt no fear, only an overwhelming sense of loneliness. Gradually the images faded. Alice opened her eyes and felt again the earth beneath her feet. She stilled her mind and body, took a deep breath and returned to the house. Once in bed, sleep came quickly and easily.

The next night Alice was not so fortunate. No sooner had she fallen into a deep sleep than she was wide awake again. This time she stayed in her bed and when she closed her eyes the pictures came. Again the figure in white floated in front of her and the feeling of loneliness overcame her. She saw the figure float to the edge of the loch, and then a wind blew up, carrying it slowly above the water.

Half way across it was as if the body was sucked by some unseen force and was gone.

The sadness of the dream remained with her in the daytime.

Chapter 24

Alice was working alone in the scriptorium. Father Bernard was not feeling well and had gone to see Father Malcolm. She did not look up when the door opened as she was at a crucial point with a design. Eventually she lay down the quill and turned around to find Father Feandan staring at her. As he moved closer the hairs on the back of her neck stood up.

'Father,' she said, holding his gaze. His dark eyes darted quickly around the room and then back to her. Alice admonished herself for thinking what a horrible little man he was. His bushy eyebrows overhung the dark beady eyes sunk deep into their sockets. His skin was the colour of dough and speckled with red eruptions. He was an odd shape with large shoulders and a short slim body, and the top of his head came to her nose. There was a sour smell about him that permeated through his robes and made her want to step away from him whenever he was near. His meanness of spirit projected itself towards everyone. Even the other monks avoided him when they could. At every opportunity Father Feandan mentioned his uncle, Archibald Douglas, the Earl of Angus, the late King's stepfather, who had kept him a prisoner when he was a young man. He had returned from exile following the death of his stepson. Angus was known for his treachery and habit of switching sides when it suited him, but had now joined his countrymen in defending Scotland against attacks by the English.

From the day he arrived, Father Feandan made no effort to be part of the tight community of monks on Inchmahome and sullenly went about his duties with barely a civil word to anyone. He was, however, particularly outspoken when it came to his objection to Alice's presence on the island. Alice tried to keep out of his way but there were times she was sure he sought her out just to glare at her.

A month earlier, Alice had been working on a delicately decorated Bible when Father Feandan leaned over her table.

'The colours are the wrong mix and your decoration is careless. I will never understand why a girl is allowed to do the work of monks. This is of low standard indeed.'

Father Feandan had not heard Father Michael enter the room and nervously jumped when he realized he was standing behind him.

'Alice is here at our request, Father, and her work is deemed excellent. Her presence is fully authorized by Lord Erskine.'

Father Feandan's face became so red Alice thought it might explode. He said not a word but headed to the door. Alice saw the look of pure hatred in his eyes as he turned and stared at Father Michael's back before exiting.

'That man makes me so ...'

'Perhaps we should say a prayer for his improved disposition, Father,' Alice said. Michael saw her smile and started to laugh.

'We will do that, Alice. Not right at this moment but I will take heed of your suggestion.'

And now again, Father Feandan was seeking out her when he knew she would be alone in the scriptorium and Father Michael was not on the island. Alice finished what she was doing and tidied up the quills and inks. Without a word she pulled her shawl over her shoulders and made for the door.

'What is your hurry, Alice?'

She left without a word. Outside she stood for a moment and stretched her arms above her head. Although she loved her work on the books it was tiring to be bent over them for so long. She noticed the boat approaching the landing place and smiled when she realized it was Father Michael. She stood under a tree watching him. His cowl was drawn over his head and she could not see his face. His strokes were even and strong and she sensed his eagerness to be home. He saw her as he tied up the boat but did not smile.

'Finished for the day, Alice?'

'Aye, Father. You look tired.'

'That I am, Alice. Walk with me to the kitchen. I need a warm drink.'

The monks were all at prayer so they had the kitchen to themselves. Alice put some honey in a cup and poured in hot water from the caldron.

'Here, Father. This should warm you. Something has happened?'

Michael looked at Alice and slowly lowered his eyes to stare at the cup.

'It has, Alice.' He sipped his drink. She waited.

'I often wonder if I made the right choices in my life. A monk, a priest of God, is expected to believe that those who lead our Church are good, caring people who follow the teachings of Our Lord. I still struggle with many of their decisions. In fact I feel it in my heart that some of their actions are against the Lord's intentions. Their justification does not sit well with me. Cardinal Beaton had a man called George Wishart sent to the fire. I cannot get it out my head. How he must have suffered. I ask myself, was that the only choice, and I know it was not.'

'What did he do?'

'He was accused of heresy but he spoke the truth in his heart. I too could be accused of the same thing.'

'You, Father? I do not believe that.'

'Aye, Alice, me. I have many secrets that would see me sent to the same fate. The Church has many a good soul looking out for the children of God, but they cannot see any good in the new way of worship that is spreading. People want to know God directly. They want to be able to pray to Him and have those prayers answered without having to put a coin in the coffers of the Church. The Cardinal is one of those turning the people against the Church with his ways. He has the power of a man of God but lives the life of the devil, with his mistresses and his children. As long as we try to suppress people with rules and punishment, they will never find their own way to God. If only we accepted each other's beliefs we would all be better off to meet our Maker when the time comes. I remember when King James was a young man, he ordered the burning of the Countess Glamis. I was able to get a potion to her in time to block her pain before she was put to the torch but I could do nothing for Wishart.'

'You could not have stopped it, Father. It would be dangerous to go against the Cardinal.'

'I know, but I feel no less anger and disgust and shame that such a thing happened.'

'Could the Queen Mother not have stopped it?'

'The Cardinal is a law unto himself and she would not interfere with the work of the Church. I hope she did not know.'

'You said she is a good woman.'

'She is, but she is also Catholic, and will not entertain heresy. She has to play the game of politics to ensure her daughter's rule. It is not always easy being the Queen Mother.'

'It is not always easy being a priest.'

He smiled. 'No, it is not.'

'What made you want to be a monk? Is it because you lost your Kate?'

No-one had ever asked him that question. It seemed so long ago that the reason of his decision to become an Augustinian Canon was blurred. 'I felt it was the path to take at the time. I lost Kate and knew I would never love that way again. I also thought God could protect me from my demons. How foolish was that? We must be responsible for the demons we create. I think I did seek peace in ritual and silence but it was not to be. I could not hide from the lost spirits. They always found me. The reasons seemed right at the time and I would not have it any other way. But still I struggle. I feel with my heart what is right and what is wrong. No-one can tell me that. The burning of a child of God is wrong. Are we not all God's children, no matter how we live our lives? If the Cardinal gave me the torch and asked me to light the fire, I would refuse. It astounds me that so far I have not been caught out. I have never had to openly refuse a request from the powers above me. Perhaps God has been looking after me all this time. Sometimes I feel a coward and a liar. I live under the protection of a Church which would burn me if they knew what I was capable of.'

'No-one could condemn you, Father. You help both the living and the dead.'

'I wish it was that simple, Alice.'

'Could you leave if you wanted?'

Again, no-one had ever asked him that question. 'I could, but I would be breaking a vow I hold dear.'

'You have changed the world, Father.'

'What do you mean?'

'You changed my world. You change the world of the lost souls and the sick. What you do for Lord Erskine changes the world.'

Michael stared at Alice for a long time. He laughed. 'How did you get so wise?'

'I have a good teacher.'

Chapter 25

Michael struggled to control his mood of sadness. Since his conversation with Alice the question of whether he had made the right choices in his life seemed to overtake him and fill his every thought. He often dreamt of Kate, seeing her smile and holding her close. Other times he was again standing on Inchmahome with Marie de Guise and the longing he felt for her stayed with him when he was awake. In his questioning he could not remember why he had chosen this way of life. Even if at the time he had been running away from his loss, there had been other choices. In the autumn of his life he wondered if his life had been wasted.

Michael tried to work in the scriptorium but he felt a need to be near the oak tree. He was weary and should not be attempting the journey to another time, but perhaps the tree was calling him because there was somewhere he needed to be. His mood eased as soon as he stood by the tree. He sat down and rested his back against its cool bark. 'Well, old soldier, I trust you. Take me where you will if that is why I am here.'

Michael expected the dizziness to overcome him as it usually did when he travelled to another place, but it did not come. He sat with his eyes closed and stilled his thoughts but nothing happened. He opened his eyes, intending to return to his work, but he realized something was very wrong.

He was still under the oak tree but the grass was tall, intermingled with wild flowers and brambles. He made his way to standing. He could now see the loch, shimmering in the sunlight. The hills were less wooded than he knew them to be. A sense of panic arose from his belly. He took his bearings and headed through the trees towards the priory. He stood there in shock. It was not there. In its stead was a circle of stones. He looked over at the mainland. He was definitely on Inchmahome. On reaching the stones he touched one of them and felt the heat it had absorbed from the sun. He walked past it and entered the circle. There was power here, similar to what he had experienced when he first entered St Paul's in Rome. It was the result of centuries of prayer.

Out of the corner of his eye Michael watched a tall figure walking towards him. He was wearing a white robe under a dark green cloak with his hood pushed back. He was smiling and did not seem surprised to see Michael there.

'Welcome to Innis-mo-Thamh,' he said. 'My name is Goraidh.' The man's voice was deep yet soft.

'I am Michael. Do you live here, Goraidh?'

'I do. I am a priest. We worship here and perform our rituals. It is a sacred place.' Goraidh stared at Michael. 'You are not of our time, are you Michael?'

'No. But I am of this island.'

'You are an Ovate?'

'What is that?'

'You are a seer, a healer. You understand death and rebirth.'

'How do you know that?'

'I too can see what others cannot and I know the ways of healing. I see the future and the past and my spirit, like yours, can travel through time.'

'But why did I come to this time? I was sitting under the oak tree and then I was here.'

'You have a connection to the oak tree,' Goraidh said. 'It is sacred to Druids. You are a Druid?'

'No. I am a Christian priest.'

'But you believe in the spiritual path, in the sacredness of nature?'

'I do.'

Goraidh smiled. 'Then you are a Druid. Shall we find out why you are here? Let us sit in silence and journey to the Otherworld. We will find the answer there perhaps.'

'What is the Otherworld?'

'You know, Michael. You know that world.'

Michael followed Goraidh to the centre of the circle and sat down facing him. He did consider for a moment that he was dreaming but Goraidh was familiar to him. When he looked into his eyes there was recognition, of what he was unsure, but it was there.

Almost immediately Michael was hovering above Inchmahome. He saw the priory and landing place, the village and Moira's farm. He saw the monks walking in a line to the church. There was stillness and then he could hear their chanting. He saw himself standing by the water's edge. A mist gathered around the island. It began to whirl slowly and spread outwards until all he could see was the island itself. The whirling increased and as it did, the island changed. He was the only thing that remained the same. The bell tower disappeared, and then the roof and the walls until there was nothing left of the priory. The vegetation became thicker. Stones appeared where the priory had been. Still he was standing there, silent and unmoving.

Michael felt a rush of wind through his body. He gasped for breath. He opened his eyes to find Goraidh watching him.

'Take a moment, Michael. Settle your body and your mind.'

Michael did as Goraidh said and gradually he became himself again. 'Did you see what I saw?'

'I did. Do you now understand why you came here?'

'Everything changed but me. The island changed to as it is now. I do not know what it means.'

Goraidh stood up. 'Look at me, Michael. What do you see?'

Michael got to his feet and moved closer to Goraidh who put his hands gently on Michael's shoulders. Michael looked deep into Goraidh's eyes and again he sensed he knew this man. The more he looked at him the more the feeling of recognition increased. In an instant he knew.

'I am you,' Michael said.

Goraidh smiled. 'We are one. It is you, standing where I am now, on this island. You learned the old ways. You saw the earth as sacred and understood we are no greater than all other creatures. You knew the cycles of the seasons and what they meant. You were able to heal and reach other realms through silent contemplation. You saw your life as many yesterdays, each holding a promise of endless tomorrows. To me, you are one of my tomorrows. You were a Druid.

You still are. You may now be bound by rules set by man, but in your heart you are a Druid. The old ways are still part of you. You wonder why you struggle but it is because you have forgotten who you are. You carry regret and pain but it does not have to be. You once lived in peace and joy. You will again. You only have to remember that your life it part of an eternal cycle. You were, you are and you will be. Use your knowledge and gifts wisely, Michael, and remember that God will never let go of you. He will not allow your spirit to expire.'

When Michael found himself again under the oak tree he was breathless and his heart was racing. He tried to understand what had just happened. How could it have been possible for him to go back in time and meet himself? And he had been a priest then too–a Druid Priest.

Chapter 26

September 1547

Michael felt the power of the stallion beneath him as his hooves pounded the hard ground. The cold wind stung his face and the cloth of his robe chaffed his legs. He sensed the horse's fear as if he knew what was to come.

The greyness of the early September day was reflected in the faces of the men who rode alongside him. Most of them had known him since the day he first appeared at Alloa Tower, a mere boy, just after Flodden. They had shared his sorrow when Kate died before their wedding and could not hide their surprise when he returned wearing the robes of a monk.

They were on their way to where the English were gathering at Pinkie Cleugh outside Musselburgh. King Henry VIII was dead but Edward Seymour, Duke of Somerset, had come to Scotland to continue the dead King's plan to force the Scots to agree to the betrothal of the young Queen of Scots to the new King of England, eight year old Edward VI.

The English were very well equipped and supported by a fleet of ships. The large Scottish army included pikemen, archers, and canon. John Erskine expressed his concern at the battle being under the direction of James Hamilton, Earl of Arran. It mattered not, for they were committed. Arran set himself up on the slopes of the west bank of the River Esk with the Firth of Forth on his left flank and the bog protecting his right. Canon was mounted with some of the guns aimed at the English warships.

Michael prayed with John Erskine's men and gave them his blessing. He then left as he always did. After Flodden, he vowed never to lift his hand in anger against another creature. Instead he knelt beside an outcrop of rocks and prayed. He tried to drown out the dreadful sounds of men trying to destroy each other, but could not. He only returned to the battlefield when the sounds of fighting ceased.

Michael did not need to ask how the battle went. The ground was covered with bodies. The English troops had slaughtered the Scottish forces and many of the retreating Scots drowned as they tried to escape across the Forth. John's son, Robert, was among the dead. Those who survived were weary and appeared as if in a trance. He sat with his friend in silence, knowing that there would be no words to comfort him. He then tended to the other men as best he could. He did not pray with them either for nothing could erase the horror they had endured. He merely placed a hand on a shoulder when he sensed it was needed and prayed over those they buried. While John and the men rested and attended to the injured, Michael returned to the battlefield where many of the dead still wandered. The painful memories of Flodden flooded his mind. He struggled to let go of his sadness and concentrate on helping those who needed it. When he had done all he could, he found a stream and tried to wash off the blood and the grief.

He returned to John's camp and they began the journey home. As they neared the Tower, memories of Kate's death engulfed him. Silence reigned throughout the Tower, broken only by the cries of grieving families. He spent time with Margaret but she was inconsolable. A rider came with a request from Marie de Guise for John and Michael to attend her at Stirling Castle.

Despite Michael's plea to him to stay with his family, John could not refuse the request of the Queen Mother. The English were not far from Stirling and the danger to the young Queen was great. After much discussion it was agreed that she be taken to Inchmahome for safety. Michael went ahead to make the arrangements.

Michael stood at the water's edge. The mist lay low on the water and the stillness surrounded him. He loved this island. It was a place that held its history in the walls of the priory and the trees that had adorned the island for centuries. This place had a sense of knowing its importance in the lives of those who crossed the Loch of Menteith and stepped onto its shores. It would remain this way, even in the centuries to come. For those whose hearts were open, it would always be a place of beauty, a sanctuary to heal wounds of the body and soul, a haven where seekers of truth could connect to their God. It had been all of these things to him, and more.

Alice came to stand beside him. 'When will she come?'

'Soon,' he said. 'The others will be her governess, the Lady Fleming, whose husband died at the battle, and her four young companions. One of them is Lady Fleming's own daughter. They are all in mourning. John and Lord Livingstone will also accompany the Queen and she will have her guards. Is everything in readiness?'

'Aye. It is not been easy to find room for them all. You have met Queen Mary. What is she like?'

'She is a bright and happy child, considering the tragedies in her life. She struggles between being herself and who others want her to be. I think she will carry that struggle with her always. The Queen Mother asked that I take charge of her spiritual education while she is here.'

'She will learn much from you, just as I have.'

'She does not have your gifts, Alice, but despite her age I do think she has the capacity to understand many things. It will be an interesting time.'

'Father Feandan seems excited by it all. He told me I should not be on the island when the Queen comes. Why does he distrust me? I have done him no harm.'

'I think he is a man who embraces his demons rather than fights them. He fears me and he senses you and I are the same.'

'We have come a long way together,' Alice said after a long silence. 'Without you I would have spent my life afraid.'

'It was the first thing you asked me to teach you, not to be afraid.'

She smiled. 'I remember. And you kept your word.'

'We need to be careful, Alice, especially with strangers. There is a shift taking place over which we have no control. Father Feandan is dangerous, especially with his connections. Be very careful, Alice. He will be watching, so guard yourself well.'

'There are so many seekers of the truth who fear what they will find,' Alice said. 'Then there are those who want only their own little world, somewhere to be safe with no thoughts of what their lives are about.'

'You think we are better off than any of them, because we venture into the unknown?' he asked.

'It is a gift to see that this world is not all it seems,' she said. 'I would change nothing. And you?'

Michael shook his head. 'It is indeed a gift to see a world of endless possibilities, to lift the veil and see what lies beyond.'

They again stood in silence and looked over the loch.

'I must go now,' Alice said. 'I have duties in the kitchen.'

'I will stay a while,' he said. Both wanted to reach out and touch the other, to extend the hand of comfort to a friend, but they knew that eyes were watching, eyes that were windows to a hostile heart.

Alice heard the excited calls of the monks at the approach of the royal visitors. She watched from a distance as they all headed to the landing place to greet their Queen. The loch was still shrouded in mist but she could see her father as he rowed the first of the boats towards the landing place. There would be many trips this day, carrying those who were to stay on the island with the Queen, and their belongings. Father Michael told her that some of the Queen's soldiers would camp on the mainland, ensuring the safety and privacy of the royal family. Alice did not wait for the arrival of the guests but returned to the kitchen where she went about her duties.

Some time later, Father Feandan walked in and stood by her. 'Girl, you are needed to take milk to the Queen.'

Alice picked up the large jug from the table and headed to the door.

'You will be introduced to the Queen and her mother, he said. 'Curtsey respectfully. You know how to curtsey? Do not speak unless you are spoken to, which will be unlikely. It has been explained that you will be their servant and attend to anything they need. Hurry girl. Do not keep them waiting, and be careful not to spill the milk,' he shouted.

Alice looked straight into his eyes, her face expressionless. 'I am always careful, Father.'

As she approached the door to the Queen's quarters, Alice found herself looking into a pair of smiling grey eyes, framed with long dark lashes. Her focus took in the rest of the face. A beautiful face, she thought. His dark hair rested on his shoulders and his face had no beard. He was young yet held himself with authority. He made no move to open the door. How long they stood like that she did not know, but then she felt the weight of the jug pull on her arm.

'Can I carry that for you?' His voice seemed to float gently towards her like the sound of music in the distance.

'Thank you, but I will manage if you open the door.'

He did so and stood aside to let her pass.

'Thank you, sir.' Her arm gently brushed his as she walked through. She paused and quickly took in the scene before her. She assumed the woman in quiet conversation with Father Michael, Lord Erskine and two other gentlemen was the Queen Mother, Marie de Guise. She was indeed a beautiful woman despite the seriousness of her expression. She was wearing a black gown to her neck and a black cap framed her face. Another woman, dressed also in black, was removing clothes from a box but her sad eyes seemed far away. This was surely the lately widowed Lady Janet Fleming. Five little girls were looking out the window and whispering to each other. Alice could not tell which one was the Queen as they too were dressed in black. As Alice moved to put the jug on the table, one of the girls noticed her presence and walked over to her. She was a beautiful child. Her dark eyes sparkled against a flawless skin. Her red hair was perfectly dressed and dotted with pearl clasps. Alice did not know if the girl was the Queen or one of her friends.

'Who are you?' the child asked.

Michael joined them. 'Your Grace, this is Alice. She will help attend to your needs while you are here.' Alice curtseyed to the little Queen.

'That is a very pretty name,' the Queen said. 'Alice,' she repeated slowly. 'Yes, I like that name. I would like some milk please, Alice.'

Alice poured it and handed a goblet to the Queen.

'Thank you, Alice,' the Queen said.

Marie de Guise joined them. 'Father Michael has told me that you are a gifted young woman, Alice, well read and of great assistance to the work of the priory.'

'I have good teachers, Madam.'

'Thank you for leaving your family to stay with us during this time of trouble. The rest of our belongings will be coming soon. Perhaps you can help us to unpack them.'

'I hope the accommodation is not too much of an inconvenience to your party,' Michael said.

'It is sufficient under the circumstances. I often think of my brief visit here with Lord Erskine some years ago. It is still as beautiful as I remember. I believe that your island has been visited by Kings in the past, Father?'

'King Robert the Bruce graced the island with his presence in the early 1300s.'

'Was he seeking refuge as we do?'

'One of his supporters was the Earl of Menteith and the King came here after his coronation at Scone in 1306 and also before Bannockburn. I believe he found this to be a place for quiet meditation. I hope it will be the same for you.'

Marie de Guise smiled. 'I hope so too, Father. We will need to build our spiritual strength for the days ahead.'

'Perhaps when you have had some food to sustain your bodies we can pray together to ask God for sustenance for our souls.'

'Everything is ready,' Alice said. 'We will bring the food now.' When she turned to curtsey to the little Queen, the child was staring at her.

'I think we will be friends, Alice,' the Queen said.

The young man was standing by the door when she exited the room. He turned to her immediately and smiled.

'My name is William.' He came to stand in front of her, barring her way. 'I am one of Lord Erskine's men. Do you live on the island?'

'No. I stay sometimes as my work is here but my home is on the mainland. My father takes care of the boats.'

'He has had a hard job today.'

'Aye.'

'May I ask your name?'

'Alice.'

'Alice.' He repeated softly. 'I am honoured to meet you, Alice.'

Again she seemed unable to pull her gaze from his.

'I hope we get the chance to meet again,' he said.

Alice felt his eyes follow her as she made her way along the corridor and down the steps. It was a pleasant feeling. She made her way outside and stood with her back against the stone wall. She felt different, somewhat lightheaded. Laughter bubbled up from inside her. She closed her eyes and saw his face. She opened them and could still picture his eyes and his smile. She whispered his name. What had just happened to her? She had always been so sensible and now here she was, repeating a stranger's name and feeling excited by the thought of him. She let out a deep sigh and made her way back to the kitchen.

The next two days were busy. Alice was in and out of the Queen's quarters and despite the comings and goings, William always smiled in her direction. Lord Erskine and Lord Livingstone came and went but there was always one of them on the island at all times.

Chapter 27

Alice wearily wiped her brow with the back of her hand. She put down the brush she was using to scrub the refectory table and sat on the bench. It was not that she was unused to hard work but she missed those moments of quiet meditation. Since the arrival of the Queen's party she had been unable to seek solitude. She thought how much harder it must be for the Queen who was never allowed a moment by herself, except perhaps when she was asleep. Alice hoped that her dreams were peaceful and happy. She liked the Queen very much. She seemed to grasp the importance of her position and the part she played in her world.

It took Alice a moment to register the screaming. She rushed to the door and saw William, Lord Erskine and some of the monks rushing towards the bell tower. Alice followed them and was shocked by the scene that greeted her. The four Marys were huddled together crying, being comforted by Lady Fleming, and Marie de Guise was kneeling over the still body of her daughter.

'What happened?' Michael asked, his hand on the Queen's forehead.

'I do not know, I do not know. Is she dead? There is no heartbeat. I cannot find her heartbeat. I thought she was resting so Janet and I went for a walk by the loch.' Marie de Guise turned sharply to the crying children. 'What caused this?' she demanded.

The four Marys were instantly silent.

'Tell me.'

Mary Seaton took a step forward. She looked down at the Queen and began to cry again. 'The Queen was bored,' she whimpered. 'She did not want to rest. She said she was going to explore the bell tower. She asked William to fetch her some milk and then left the room. We could not let her go by herself so we came with her. She tried to get us to follow her up the stairs but we would not. We begged her to come down but she just laughed at us and kept climbing. She was halfway up when she turned but her foot became caught in her gown and she fell.'

'Did you touch the child?' Michael asked.

'No, Father, we did not know what to do but we did not touch her.'

'We should take her to her bed,' Marie de Guise said.

'No. We cannot move her yet.' Michael turned around. 'Alice, come help me examine her. Quickly, Alice. Everyone stand back. Give us room.'

Marie de Guise stood up and moved away a little. Alice took her place, kneeling down beside Michael.

'I will start at the bottom, Alice, and you at the head. Be sure to miss nothing. We cannot move her until we are sure what is happening internally.'

Alice placed her hands gently on the Queen's head. She stilled her mind, as she knew Father Michael was doing, and very slowly moved her hands over the Queen's face, then her arms and the upper body. Meanwhile Michael was doing the same to the Queen's legs.

Alice stopped moving when she reached the Queen's stomach. 'Father,' she whispered, 'there is bleeding.'

Marie de Guide gasped and the four Marys started to cry again.

'Do what you have to, Alice.' He turned to Marie de Guise and then looked around at the audience to the drama.

'Yes, yes.' Marie de Guise waved her hands at the others. 'Everyone wait outside. Give them space to work. Quickly.' John Erskine and William guided everyone away.

'Father, I do not know...'

'You can do this, Alice' he said, 'you can do this.'

Alice moved to the Queen's side and Michael took her place, cupping the child's head in his hands.

Alice laid her hands gently on the Queen's stomach. She again stilled her mind and focused all her energy, her thoughts, on channelling God's healing power through her body. She felt it surge and did not stand in its way. Time stood still for her. Eventually she felt the energy slow then finally stop. She brought herself back and opened her eyes. Both Father Michael and Marie de Guise were watching her. Alice sighed. 'The bleeding has stopped. We can move her now.'

Marie de Guise stared at Alice. Michael gently picked up the Queen. 'Madam, we must keep her warm.'

'Yes, yes.' Marie de Guise followed Michael outside but Alice remained where she was. She stood still, closed her eyes, and allowed the natural flow of her body to completely return. When she opened them she saw Father Feandan in the doorway, a look of glee on his face. He turned and walked away.

When Alice returned to the kitchen, Father Callum asked her to take a pitcher of milk and honey to the Queen's room. William smiled at her as he opened the door. 'Thank you,' he said as she walked past him.

Father Michael was standing by the window, deep in conversation with Marie de Guise and John Erskine. They looked at Alice and smiled. The little Queen was sitting up in bed playing a card game with her friends.

'Alice, come talk with me,' the Queen said, shooing the Marys away.'

'Sit here,' the Queen said. She patted the space beside her. 'I have been naughty, have I not?' Alice smiled. 'Mama said I caused great distress sneaking away like that. I told her it was not William's fault but he is upset.'

'We were very worried about you.'

'They do not understand. I have such energy, such a hunger for adventure. I dislike embroidery and being indoors all the time. Mama says I am too like my father. I never met him, Alice, did you know that? He died soon after I was born.'

'I did know, your Grace. I am sorry you did not get to know him.'

The Queen looked around the room and indicated for Alice to move closer. 'Can you keep a secret?'

'Of course, your Grace.'

The Queen checked that no-one was listening. 'When I fell down the stairs, I heard the others screaming but gradually the sounds disappeared until I could hear not a single sound. Alice, I saw my father. He was exactly as he is in the portrait in my room at Stirling Castle.'

Alice looked into the little girl's eyes and knew she spoke the truth. 'Did he speak to you?'

The Queen's eyes widened. 'You believe me? You believe I saw my father?'

'Of course.'

'He was very handsome. I loved him instantly. He knelt down and put his hand on my head. He said I was beautiful and that he had been watching over me. Then I felt as if I was being pulled away from him. I told him I wanted to stay, that I did not want to leave him. He said I had to return, that it was not time for us to be together. He said I had a destiny to fulfil but I told him I cared not for destiny or being queen but that I wanted to be with him. He looked sad, and gave me a cuddle. He said there would be great happiness in my life but also great sadness and that when I felt lonely or afraid, just to think of him and he would come to me. I might not see him but would feel him. He said when it was time for me to die he would walk with me to heaven. I so wanted to stay with him in that peaceful place but then I saw you. You were standing at a distance and waiting for me. My father kissed me and told me to go with you. Then suddenly I was lying here in my bed with Mama and Father Michael and Lord Erskine around me. What happened to me? Why did I have to leave? I do not understand, truly I do not.'

Alice took the Queen's shaking hand. How was she to explain this to her? 'There is so much more to this life than what most people think, your Grace. When you started to climb the stairs of the bell tower, what could you see?'

'The stairs. I was trying to be careful as I climbed them.'

'But if you had reached the top and were able to look out you would have seen across the loch to the village. You would have seen the hills and the sun and the grass.

'Yes, but I did not reach the top.'

'But the loch is still there, the hills and the people in the village. They still exist even though you did not get to the top and see them.'

The Queen was frowning in concentration. 'Yes,' she answered. 'They are all there but I did not see them.'

'That is how it is with your father. His body has passed from this life but his spirit, the part of him that loves you, that is still there but you cannot see it. It is as if he lives in a place far away from here and no matter how many towers you climb you are unable to see him but you know he is there. You will be able to hold the thought of him in your mind, allow him to be with you in your heart. One day when you are very old he will come for you and walk with you to heaven as he promised.'

'And cuddle me again?'

'He told you so.'

'He did.' The Queen reached forward and kissed Alice on the cheek. 'Thank you, Alice. I believe what you say. I will try to be content. I want to ask you one more thing. Why were you there when I saw my father? You are not dead.'

'I truly do not know, your Grace.'

'Was it you who pulled me back?'

'That was God. It was not your time. Your father said you had a destiny to fulfil.'

'I wonder where my destiny will lead,' the Queen said, her eyes closing softly.

Alice got up from the bed when the Queen was fully asleep. Marie de Guise came to her, put her hands on her shoulders and kissed both her cheeks. 'Thank you, Alice. I will never forget what you did for my daughter.'

Father Michael found Alice at the water's edge looking towards Arnmach. He had not been able to speak to her alone since the Queen's accident. There was much to talk about and he was concerned for her.

'Are you looking for the fairies?' he asked.

'Aye, but they do not seem to want to show themselves tonight.'

'It has been an eventful day.'

'The Queen has an adventurous spirit,' Alice said. 'I think she will struggle with her destiny. She saw her father.'

'How did he appear to her?'

'Kindly, loving.'

'Good. He obviously passed to the light and is just keeping a watchful eye on her. Was she afraid?'

'No. I think she has good instincts.'

'May they serve her well in her darkest hours.'

'Will she tell her mother?'

'I do not know but I think Marie will understand. And you gave the child sufficient explanation?'

Alice nodded and turned to look back over the loch. 'I was not sure I could do it, Father, use my energy to heal her, but I felt the power. It surged through my body and I knew I was connecting to hers. I have never felt it so strong before.'

'It grows daily in you, but you must be careful.'

'I think Father Feandan saw what happened. I do not think he left with the others. He holds much resentment for me.'

'And me, Alice. It starts with me. He senses the powers I have. He cannot see that he too possesses gifts. He only sees what he does not have. I do not think he will let this rest. He will not do anything while the royal family is here but will wait until they leave. There will be those who will delight in hearing that the Queen Mother is associating with ungodly people. She will do all she can to assist us.'

They both stood in silence, deep in their own thoughts. Their love for each other surpassed that of teacher and pupil, father and child, man and woman. Their spirits had connected at a level attained by few. Sometimes it almost seemed they were one. Often there were moments when each felt the need to reach out and touch, to give some physical connection to what they shared. They knew it was impossible, because a touch could be misconstrued by others. A single doubt about their relationship as teacher and pupil would debase their connection forever. Michael often thought about his love for Alice. It was not like the overwhelming love he had, still had, for Kate. Or the feelings he had for Marie de Guise. What he felt for Alice went beyond understanding or explanation. It was indeed a love born of heaven—a touching and binding of two spirits.

Chapter 28

'The message has safely been dispatched to France, Marie,' John Erskine said. 'The King is eager to send the ship for the Queen when you're ready.'

'It saddens me greatly to let her go without me,' Marie de Guise said. 'But there is no other way. The English will feast on their victory but when they realize my daughter is gone, their revenge may be swift. Many more may die before this is over.'

John Erskine sucked in air and held it.

'Oh John, forgive me. I cannot believe Robert has gone. He was a loyal friend and a brave man.' Marie de Guise rested her hand on his arm.

'Indeed he was,' John said. 'He made our family proud even though it has broken our hearts.'

'You should go home, John,' Michael said. 'Margaret and the family need you, and you need to be with them.'

'I will go soon, once I know all is in place for the Queen's safety.'

'I want you both to know that you have my eternal gratitude for your friendship and your loyalty,' Marie said. 'You have my complete trust and I know that whatever happens, I can count on you.'

Alice finished her duties for the night and went for a walk in the cool evening air. She needed time by herself to think about William and why she was unable to put him from her mind. She smiled. She did not want to stop thinking about him. It gave her such pleasure. Every morning her first thought was of him and his face was the last thing she saw before she fell asleep.

She eventually sat down on the fallen tree by the side of the loch. A rustling from behind startled her. She turned to find John Erskine walking towards her.

'May I join you or do you wish to be alone?' he asked.

She moved along the log and smiled at him. Together they sat watching the moonlight play games on the rippling water.

'You could not sleep either, Alice?'

'No. And I do love the peace at this time of night.'

'You must be tired. There is much to do for the royal family.'

'I do not mind. Although I miss my time with the books and my lessons.'

'I find it hard to sleep since the battle. Since...' He let the words drift into the night.

'You miss him?'

'He was too young to die. I was remembering when he was a bairn. It does not seem so long ago. Where does the time go? The King is dead, my father and dear mother, and now Robert. I never expected to outlive any of my children. It has torn my heart apart and yet I must go on. Margaret and the children need me and I have my duty to the Queen. I will do my best to protect her, as my family has always done for the monarchs of Scotland.'

'You will go with her to France?'

'Aye, she is not safe here. Not from the English or some of her own people. I will stay until I know she is safe. Alice, I asked Michael if he sensed Robert but he did not. Do you?'

'I am sorry but...'

'Michael said not all linger after their death and that it is a good sign he has passed easily to the next world. I just wanted to feel him near me again. Do you know how Michael and I first met?

'He said he took a message to you from your father after the battle at Flodden.'

'I learned not to wait until I died to let my children know how much I love them. I make sure they know in word and deed. Robert knew, knows, I love him.'

They sat there for a long time watching the path of moonlight on the loch.'

'Father.' The faint sound startled John and he quickly turned to Alice. Her eyes were closed and she appeared to be asleep.

'Father.' The word came from Alice's mouth but the voice belonged to his son.

'Robert.'

'Aye, Father.'

In the stillness of the night, side by side on a fallen tree, John Erskine had a final conversation with his son. When Alice was again aware of where she was, the tears that streamed down his face told her she had succeeded in linking to Robert's spirit. John took her hand in his and their gaze returned the shimmering loch.

Chapter 29

It would be a glorious autumn day. Alice wondered if there was anyone who doubted the existence of God on such a day as this. The dew on the grass sparkled in the morning sunlight and the leaves on the trees displayed their most magnificent colours just before they dropped to the ground to form a carpet of reds, yellow and orange. On the hillside across the loch the heather was a burst of purples, and blues. Alice thought there could not possibly be any other part of the world that could match this breathtaking sight.

She had been busy since well before dawn and now felt the need for a few moments peace before the royal family awoke. She thought the monks set in their ways, but she smiled when she realized how she had become like them, appreciating the need for routine and quiet. The arrival of the Queen's party had put an end to the usual pattern of life on the island. Some of the monks were excited by their royal visitors while others pondered on why the priory had been chosen to keep their Queen safe. The fearful ones worried about the heavily armed soldiers camped on the mainland and that Lord Erskine and the other men who accompanied the Queen always wore their swords. It was not hard to feel their constant state of alertness.

Alice was concerned about the safety of her own family. She had managed to get a little time to talk to her father when he brought Lord Livingston to the island the previous day. Kenny and Peter were excited by the comings and goings but Wee Jeannie was afraid and would not settle. It had taken lots of cuddles and soothing words from Moira to calm her down.

'You seem deep in thought,' the voice said.

Alice turned around to find William a short distance away.

'I am sorry if I startled you but the Queen Mother asked if you would bring some warm milk. The Queen had a bad night it seems you have a calming influence on her.'

Alice smiled at the handsome young man who caused such unexpected flutters in the pit of her stomach. He walked to her side and she forced herself to take a deep breath lest he heard her heart pounding.

'This is indeed a beautiful place,' he said. 'A sight that makes everything in the world seem at peace. Come, I will walk back with you'.

As Alice started to move away her foot caught on something hidden under the canopy of leaves. A pain burned her ankle and she let out a cry. William reached out instantly to steady her. With one arm around her waist and the other on her arm, their eyes met and held. Alice's cheeks burned but she could not look away. She felt the loss when he let her go.

'Did you hurt yourself?'

'Just a little. It is easing already.

'May I assist you,' he said, holding out his arm.

'Thank you.' She again felt his warmth.

William walked with her to the kitchen. He smiled and was gone. She was kept busy for the rest of the morning. The little Queen's nightmare was soon forgotten. She settled down for a sleep with her companions after their midday meal so Alice wrapped herself in her cloak and went for a walk in the cloisters.

She saw Michael in conversation with Lord Erskine and both turned and smiled.

'Well, I will see you shortly, Michael,' Lord Erskine said. 'Is your ankle better, Alice?' he asked.

'It is.'

He winked at Michael as he walked away.

'Why would William tell him about that?'

'I think perhaps the young man just likes to say your name.'

'He does?'

'By the colour of your cheeks I would say it does not upset you too much, child.'

'I...'

'Do not worry, your secret is safe with me. You like the young man I can tell. He obviously likes you too. John thinks highly of William. He is well educated and is highly thought of by the Queen Mother. She knows he would give his life for her daughter.'

'I see that in him too.' Suddenly Alice felt sad. 'He will marry well I think. It would be expected.'

'You think you are not good enough for him?'

Alice remained silent.

'None of us knows what the future will be, Alice. William is of noble birth and is not without means. John will not forget how he guarded Robert's body during the battle until John could reach him.

William is part of the Erskine family now. He will no doubt be free to marry anyone he chooses.'

'He will have to go away soon. To France with Lord Erskine and the Queen.'

'Aye, he will. I think you do like him, Alice, very much. In the time I have known you, you have been content to live in the present. Now you think of the future. That is not a bad thing, child, but do not let it overcome you.'

'No, Father.'

'And thank you for what you did for John. I could not sense Robert at all. You did well.'

Michael watched her as she walked away. He had known that one day Alice would fall in love and marry. How could it be otherwise? She was a beautiful, caring young woman who had much to offer. Had he not benefited from her friendship, her gentle spirit? His life had been enriched by her and part of him felt sorrow that he would no longer be her sole confidante, the one with whom she shared her thoughts, her hopes, her fears. Someone else would be this to her now. He felt a sense of loss, and perhaps a glimpse of jealousy. William was a good man. He had feelings for Alice, that was obvious, but he was leaving and did not know when he would return.

Later that morning as she climbed the stairs to the Queen's quarters, Alice wondered if William would be there. She was not disappointed.

'Good morning, Alice,' he said.

'Good morning, William.' He opened the door for her and she was surprised to see the young Queen standing there, wearing her outdoor cloak.

'Alice, I have been waiting for you to come. Mama said I can walk around the island with you. Can we go now?'

The Queen Mother was smiling. 'I have agreed, Alice. William will go with you.'

'Why can we not accompany the Queen,' Mary Seton said.

'Because I wish to go alone and that is the end of it,' the Queen said. 'No buts, Seton. I am the Queen and it is my wish.'

Little Mary Seton looked as if she would cry. The Queen glared at her for a few moments then abandoned her queenly persona and again became the friend. 'Do not be a cry baby, Seton. You can all come next time, I promise.'

The Queen led the way, followed closely by William and Alice. When they reached the stairs, William went first. The tender way he held out his hand to the Queen and gently guided her down the stairs, tugged at Alice's heart. They walked slowly on the path through the trees. The Queen glided over the ground, her small feet hidden under the long gown and cloak.

'Shall we walk to the south of the island?' Alice asked. 'From there you can see Arnmach. There is a story about the place.'

'I love stories,' the Queen said. 'Tell me. Please tell me.'

The Queen gave Alice her complete attention as she related the story as Father Michael had told her. 'Sometimes the fairies still come down the hill and fly across the loch to the island. They love Inchmahome and it is said they go the church and listen to the monks singing. Sometimes when an apple is found with a small hole in it, it is thought that a fairy has taken a bite.'

'Do you think we will see the fairies? 'Will we?'

'I hope so, your Grace.'

'Have you ever seen one, Alice?'

'I cannot be sure but I think so. Some days I take a walk and stand by the water. I have seen tiny creatures flying in the air, most often when it is a clear day. I look really closely and although they move very fast, I am sure they are fairies.'

'Oh Alice, that would be so wonderful. I do hope they will come today. Let us not tarry as I am anxious to see this place.' The Queen darted ahead.

William's hand was covering his mouth. He was unsuccessfully trying to hide a smile. 'That was a good tale,' he said.

'What makes you think it is a tale?'

'It is true?' The smile broke into laughter.

'Perhaps,' Alice said. 'Can you tell me it is not? Just because you have not seen something for yourself does not mean it cannot exist. I like to think that fairies do exist and they are part of God's universe.'

William's smile disappeared and was replaced with a look of tenderness. 'You may be right, Alice. I will believe in fairies from this day until I have absolute proof they do not exist.'

They both turned as the Queen called to them. She had stopped beside a growth of purple wild flowers. 'They are so pretty,' she said. 'I will pick some for Mama.'

They watched the little girl gently pick one of the delicate flowers and place in the grass before choosing another. As she moved further away, William went to follow her but then decided to stay by Alice's side.

'The Queen is enjoying herself,' he said.

'It must be hard for her being so closely guarded all the time. Not much time to be a child.' Alice looked at him but his eyes were fixed firmly on the little Queen. 'Will you continue to guard the Queen when you leave the island?' she asked.

'Not all the time. Lord Erskine is only one of the Queen's guardians so there will be others looking out for her. She seems to have taken a liking to me and his Lordship and the Queen Mother think it best to have someone familiar close by during this time.'

'What will you do then, when you leave here?'

'Whatever his Lordship commands of me. I think I will be going to France with him and the Queen's party.'

'Have you been to France before?'

'No. Lord Erskine told me about his visits. The Queen's father sent him to France many times. He is a friend of the Queen Mother's family. I thought I would like to go. Now I am not so sure.'

'Why is that?' Alice was surprised that given the chance a person would not go to France. She looked at him and found him staring at her. Her heart was beating so loudly she thought he must hear it.

'Alice, come quickly.' The Queen's voice startled her. Alice went over and knelt down beside her.

'Look, Alice.' Perched on top of one of the wild flowers was an insect, its red spots shining against the black. 'I have never seen one of these before. What is it?'

'A ladybird.'

'Why is it called a ladybird?'

'It is named in honour of the Virgin Mary. See the shell on its back. It protects it and its wings fold against its body. They are considered a good omen and the monks love them very much. They eat parasites.'

'How do you know all these things?' the Queen asked.

'Father Michael told me. When I was younger I thought he must know everything but he said you just have to watch the creatures in nature. They have much to teach us.'

'Can I touch it?'

'Only if you are careful. Put your hand next to the leaf.'

The Queen held out her delicate little hand. Alice gently touched the leaf, raising it a little. The ladybird crawled on to the Queen's open palm.'

'Oh, I have it,' she said. 'It is beautiful. I wish I could take it back to my room.'

'That would not be fair on the wee thing, your Grace. Its life is out here, going from plant to plant. They do not live long so we should leave them to do what they enjoy.'

'You are right, Alice.' Suddenly the ladybird stuck out its little wings and flew out of the Queen's hand.

'Oh, I have lost it,' she said.

'No, it is free and off to do what ladybirds do.'

Alice helped the Queen gather up the flowers she had picked and they continued along the path. Alice pointed over the water to Arnmach. 'There is the land the fairies built. See how close it is to the island? They almost finished it.'

They all stood in silence as the Queen stared over the water, her little face alert with concentration. Alice smiled for it looked like William too was actually looking for the fairies.

'I do not think they are here today, Alice.' The Queen's bottom lip quivered.

'We will come another day. Perhaps they are resting on the hill.'

'Yes, we will come another day. I so want to see them.'

William escorted them to the Queen's quarters and left them at the door. The Queen's little companions rushed to greet her.

'You were gone a long time, your Grace,' Mary Livingstone said, 'we were bored without you.'

'If you are going to pout then I will not tell you about my adventure.'

'Oh you must, please,' Seton said.

'Well, sit by the fire and I will join you shortly.'

'You obviously enjoyed your walk, Mary,' the Queen Mother said.

'I did, Mama, and look what I picked for you.' The Queen handed her the flowers she had been holding behind her back

'Oh Mary, I love them.' She took them from her daughter and kissed her on both cheeks. 'Thank you, my darling.'

'Alice told me a wonderful story about fairies. I wish to come back here one day. Can I, Mama? I do not have to stay in France forever. I can bring the Dauphin here to visit.'

'When Scotland is safe you will be able to do anything you wish, my child.'

'Will I have to wait long, Mama?'

The Queen Mother half smiled at her daughter. 'I do not know.'

A sadness came over the little girl's face and she turned to Alice. 'Thank you, Alice. I hope we can go for another walk together before I leave.'

'I would like that, your Grace.'

The Queen joined her friends. At least she could re-live her adventure in the telling of it.

Chapter 30

Michael was on his way to prayer when he saw Alice approaching from the kitchen.

'You look tired, Alice. Are we working you too hard?'

'No, Father. The dreams keep me awake.'

'Still the same one?'

'Always the lady in white.'

'There must be a reason you are having the same dream so often. I have meditated on it but nothing is clear. I worry about you.'

'Oh Father, I have strength. You taught me well.'

'It will not be too much longer I hope, and we can get back to the way life was.

'I would like that.' She laughed. 'I am beginning to think like a monk. I crave routine in my life.'

'Ah. Except for young William. You would not forsake the adventure of knowing him, would you, Alice?'

'Perhaps not.'

'Take care, child. You are very precious to me.'

As he walked away, William came towards them. The two men exchanged a greeting. William's face was set in a serious frown as he came to her side.

'Good day, Alice. Have you time to walk with me a little?'

Her tiredness evaporated at the thought of spending time alone with him. They strolled by the water and sat on the fallen tree. William was silent for a long time.

'You are well, William?'

'I am. All the better for seeing you.' He smiled briefly and then turned his gaze away. 'Father Michael is a good man. I like him.'

Alice knew this time would come. 'Aye, he is.'

'You and he are great friends I think.'

'We are. I owe him much.'

The silence dragged. Perhaps William had heard the gossip. 'William, Father Michael is my dear friend. We are bound together in friendship and loyalty. He is my teacher and I care deeply for him. There are those who are suspicious of our friendship but I cannot care or respect him less because of that. He once told me that we should honour love in no matter what form it appears.'

'You love him, then?'

'I love him as I do my family but it is different. I can never explain it. He would give his life for me. I know this. I would give mine for him. I would no sooner betray him than I would my family.'

'You would not leave him then?'

'Distance would not alter our feelings for each other. He is often away and if for any reason he never returned I would still feel the same for him as I would if I had to leave. There are things about me only he understands. The tie that binds us can never be broken.'

'You think a husband will accept your relationship with him?'

'I hope so, because I am who I am because of him. Without him I would have been a frightened woman, afraid of my own shadow. I would have trusted no-one and sought refuge in solitude. Anyone who would love me would need to know this. I know there is gossip but that is because people do not understand.'

The silence lingered. Eventually William stirred. He turned to Alice and took her hand in his. 'Any friend of yours, Alice, will be a friend of mine. I know you to be an honourable person and I would be grateful if one day you held me in the same regards as you do Father Michael.'

Alice was tidying away the dishes in the kitchen when she saw Father Michael in the doorway. The others did not appear to notice him as he nodded and walked away. She calmly finished her chores and headed to the scriptorium where she knew he would be waiting. He was facing the wall of books but appeared to be looking at none of them. He turned when he heard her approach.

'We are safe for the moment.'

'Is something wrong, Father?'

'I under-estimated Father Feandan. He did not wait until the royal family left. He spoke to the Queen Mother this morning and expressed his concern about the influence you have on the Queen. He said he has been worried for some time about your behaviour, that you are too familiar with the monks. He did not mention me specifically. He said he thinks you used unnatural healing on her daughter and he is afraid you have put a spell on her.'

'Surely he cannot believe that.'

'I think his desire to destroy us has overtaken his logic. The Queen Mother told him it was nonsense and that any gift of healing you have comes from God. She said she considered any influence you have on her daughter to be good and refused to hear any more on the subject. But she does not think he will leave it there.'

'What can he do?'

'If he manages to get a message to his uncle or the Bishop and mentions the word 'unnatural' they will investigate. There are those who will insist on it. If he uses the word 'witch' there will be great trouble.'

'Dear God, not that. What can I do? Must I go away?'

'There would be no-where you could hide, Alice. We will have to think of another way.'

'If I cannot stay and cannot hide, what can I do? I do not want to put my family in danger.'

'Do not let fear fill your heart. I promised you I would protect you and I will. I will think of something but be careful in your words and actions. We must give Father Feandan no excuse to take the matter further. We have talked many times of the voices you hear and the people you see in your dreams,' he said. 'Tell me again about the woman.'

'I feel there is a connection between us but no matter how hard I try I cannot see her face. But I know it is a woman. I feel it.'

'And the voice.'

'At first she seems afraid but then she becomes sad. She asks me to help her, to bring her from where she is and take her home. When I say I do not know how to help her she answers that I do.'

'You never get a sense of where you are or any more details about her? Do you think she is a ghost?'

'No.'

'But you feel connected to her?'

'I told you this. Why are you asking me this now?'

'It is been on my mind. I wonder if there is another gift you have. You get some rest. Try not to worry.'

Alice knew he would find a way to help her. 'Thank you, Father. I will see you tomorrow.' She smiled at him before walking away.

Alice lay on her small bed, hugging her blankets. Why did Father Feandan hate her so? She had done nothing to harm him and had always been respectful towards him. She sensed his troubled soul that first time they met. She thought him a man who filled his life with resentment.

Alice came out of the kitchen to be greeted by a cooling breeze. She so loved to watch the sunset, and wandered over to the water. The darkening orange tinged sky and the sound of the monks singing gave Inchmahome a mystical aura. Alice had a sense of time reaching back through the centuries to a night such as this. Someone would have stood where she did, listening and watching. She felt the world more clearly in moments such as this. It was as if God had drawn a line that reached from the dawn of time to where she stood now, into the future and connected back to the beginning. She felt part of something so much more important than the life that bound her to this earth. She let this feeling of connectedness grow and fill her being. She sensed that all creatures must have moments such as this.

She basked in the sensations and then gradually it waned, leaving her with a sense of loss.

She turned from the water to find William standing not far from her. A strange thing happened. As she looked at him, looking at her, for a moment she again felt that connection with the universe.

He walked slowly towards her. 'You look so peaceful. I did not want to disturb you. It is a beautiful evening,' he said. 'You have finished your work?'

'Aye.'

'Will you sit with me a while?'

They sat together on the fallen tree until the monks' hymn ended.

'You can hear their singing on the mainland,' he said. 'Have you heard it?'

'Sometimes, when the air is still.'

'Perhaps when I return from France we can stand on the shore together and listen.'

'I would like that.'

He laughed. 'Then we will do it.'

Alice felt a loneliness lie heavy on her heart at the thought of him going away. 'Your family will miss you, William.'

'My parents are dead. My father died quite a few years ago and my mother shortly thereafter of a broken heart. So Alice, no-one will miss me.'

'I will miss you, William,' she whispered.

Suddenly there were in each other's arms. Their first kiss was gentle. Alice put her head on his shoulder and he held her close.

They quickly separated when they heard the sound of the monks leaving the church. 'I must go. I will see you soon.' His tender smile made her heart skip.

Alice watched him as he walked across the grass and was waiting with a smile when he turned and waved before entering the building. She made her way to the garden in the centre of the cloister to collect some fresh herbs to place in the Queen's room. She was surprised to find the Queen Mother walking there alone. She seemed to be in silent contemplation and Alice did not want to disturb her. She turned to retrace her steps when she heard the Queen Mother call her name.

'Please, do what you have come to do.'

As Alice picked sprigs of rosemary and lavender, the Queen Mother came to stand beside her.

'It is so quiet here, especially at this time of day. It has been a long time since I felt so peaceful. Ah, if only it could be like this always. Except when I pray I never feel at peace. Even then I am thinking of what the powerful men who surround me want from me. Father Michael taught me that most power is an illusion created by one person and that illusion is perceived by others to be the truth. Real power lies in self-knowledge, self-awareness, and the ability to see your place in this world. Not your place as others see it, but as you truly feel it.'

'But no-one could see you as powerless, Madam. You are the Regent, your daughter is Queen and you come from a powerful family.'

'Yes, but the leaders of this new religion that is spreading across our world are no different from the Holy Church. They refuse to see women as equals.'

'Father Michael told me about the wars since the birth of Jesus and they are all about religion,' Alice said. 'I often wonder why is it so hard to accept another's right to choose their own path to God.'

'If it was only that simple, Alice. As Regent I cannot allow that to happen. I would lose the support of my countrymen and I need France. I believe the Reformers would not be content to let us keep our way of worship. They would try to overpower us and impose their ways on us all. It has happened in England and other countries. There seems no way out of this for me. I have to protect my daughter's inheritance. She will rule this country one day.' The Queen Mother saw the sadness in Alice's eyes. 'You think I should be brave and take a stand; allow the people to choose their own way?'

'I truly do not know, Madam. If this becomes a Protestant country then places like this would probably be destroyed. I do not know the answer. I am only glad I do not have to make such decisions.'

'Come, let us talk of happier things. Have you seen much of this beautiful country, Alice?'

'No. We lived further north before we came to Menteith but perhaps one day I will get to see the world outside of here. For the moment I am content.

'You are well read. What places would you go to if you could? The Holy Land? Rome? Where Alice?'

'I would go to Rosslyn Chapel,' Alice said.

The Queen Mother stared at her. 'Rosslyn! You know about Rosslyn?'

'Only what Father Michael has described to me of its beauty and peace. Many spirits guard it he said. It is a special place, and one that holds secrets, I think.'

'It does,' the Queen Mother whispered. 'It is a place like no other.'

'You have been there?'

'Many times. Sir William is a good friend to us. Our families have been connected for many centuries.'

'And is it as beautiful as Father Michael describes?'

'Oh yes, Alice, it is indeed. Being there renews my spirit.'

'Father Michael said one day I will go there.'

'I hope you do, Alice, I hope you do.'

Chapter 31

The little Queen was gazing out of the window when Alice entered the room. She turned and smiled, indicating for Alice to sit next to her. The Marys were embroidering by the fire.

'Do you miss your family, Alice?'

'Very much.'

'Tell me about them.'

'I have two younger brothers, Kenny and Peter and then there is Wee Jeannie. She is nearly 10. She has the most beautiful red hair, like my Ma. She died and we still miss her. Kenny whittles wood. He is very good at it. Says he wants to make every animal in the world. Peter is good with his hands too. He is like my Pa. He fixes things. He just thinks and thinks about it and makes it work. Wee Jeannie is always laughing. She sees joy in everything. We live with my Auntie Moira. She has been so good to us. She helps anyone who needs it. Always giving.'

'I have my friends who are very precious to me and my half-brothers. In France I have Mama's family and she said there are many relatives for me to meet.' The Queen returned to gaze out of the window. 'This is a beautiful island, so peaceful and small. From my apartments at Stirling Castle it is as if I can see the whole world from the window. I think I prefer this view. It is a little world but it feels safe.'

'I find great comfort standing alone by the edge of the water.'

'Alone,' the Queen said. 'I am never alone. What do you think about when you are alone, Alice?'

'Usually I think of nothing at all.'

'Nothing! How can you think of nothing?'

'It takes practice. I believe that when we pray we are talking to God, but when we allow ourselves to be still, we may hear God talking to us. We can feel his presence.'

'You feel the presence of God. What does God feel like Alice?' The Queen's eyes were bright.

'He feels like peace. I feel surrounded by his love for me. I feel part of him.'

'You really feel his love?'

'I do.'

'I pray often,' the Queen said. 'I try so hard to concentrate but my mind wanders. Can you teach me to feel the love of God as you do, and to hear Him talk to me? Then I can ask Him questions and He can advise me on how to rule.'

Father Michael's words of warning echoed in Alice's mind. This was no ordinary child. She was the Queen of Scotland. She had the power of life and death over her subjects. She was Catholic and would be ruled by the Church in Rome who taught that direct communication with God was a privilege of priests. Should she tell this Catholic Queen, that when she spoke to God she could sometimes, in the stillness that followed, hear His reply with her heart, not her ears.

'Your Grace, I...'

'Oh look, look Alice,' the Queen pointed excitedly through the window. 'A swan, and she has her babies with her. 'Come Alice, I want to look at them more closely. Come.'

The others looked up to see what had caused the Queen's excitement.

'Go back to your game,' she said. 'I wish to walk with Alice.'

The Queen walked serenely across the room to the door and it was not until they were halfway down the corridor that she threw off the mantle of Queen and again became the little girl. A soldier followed a short distance behind.

'I did not want the others to come with us. They would get excited and frighten the swans away. Hurry, I must see them before they leave.'

They approached the water's edge quietly. The swans glided close to them. Alice watched the excitement in the Queen's face. If only her innocence could stay with her.

Alice watched from a distance. Father Michael's shoulders were a little stooped as if he carried a great weight. She sat down beside him on the old tree that had fallen in last winter's storm.

'Alice,' he said softly, 'I am sorry to keep you from your bed but there is much I have to say to you. The Queen is being taken to Dumbarton Castle and then she will go to France.'

'And the Queen Mother wants you to go with her?' Alice said.

'She does.'

'Do you want to go?'

'We both have an idea of what faces the young Queen. Her life will not be easy. The Queen Mother cherishes her daughter and would ease the way for her. She sees how gentle she is but fears she may have some of her father's weaknesses. The need for the right guidance is paramount to her survival. The Queen Mother cannot go with her to France but she wants me to go as her spiritual adviser.'

'It is a great honour for you, to guide the life of a queen.' Alice said.

'You see the strength of spirit she has, but she will be Queen of France one day and although the alliance is strong, I fear she may be influenced by men of power who would use her for their own ambitions. The threat from England will not go away either.'

'Then you must go.'

'Leaving will be hard. I thought of asking the Queen Mother if you could join us. After all, the child has shown a great affection for you. And it would solve the problem with Father Feandan. You would be under the Queen's protection and he could do you no harm. But it would mean you may not see your family for a long time.'

'It is kind of you to think of me but I do not want to leave my family, or Scotland. We both knew we could not be together forever. You taught me much, Father, and now perhaps it is my time to be a teacher to others.'

'You are certainly ready for that.' He looked away for a few moments. 'We have to talk about Father Feandan. I know we have never discussed it properly but his obsession with you is unhealthy. With me it is just hatred based on his jealousy and sense of inadequacy, but with you, he wants to possess you and he fights that battle every day. I do not think he will let it end.'

'I know. I have sensed it for a long time now.'

'You said nothing.'

'I knew you knew. What good would speaking of it have done. If you thought I was concerned you would not let me come here. I would not have been able to learn from you and work with the books. Anyway, I know you watch over me. You would not have let any harm come to me.'

'I will have to think of a way to protect you once I am gone.'

Alice stared into his eyes. 'There is still something for you to teach me.'

Michael smiled. 'I forget how good you are.'

'I saw you one day sitting under the old oak tree. I called to you but you were very still and did not hear me. Your body was here but it seemed somehow your spirit had wandered away for a while. Is that what happens? Your spirit is wandering?'

Michael asked himself if this was the only way he could leave her in safety. He never talked about his special gift, for he knew the danger of it. Yes, perhaps it was the only way. 'It is not that I did not want to share this with you Alice, but it is not an easy thing to control.'

'Tell me. Please.'

He saw the expectation in her eyes, the look he had seen so many times over the years.

'So far you have been able to see this world differently, clearer than others. You can sense the future, see images in your head and you have come to trust those occurrences, those visions. You know that when you heal, you are channelling energy from God. But there is much more, Alice, so much more. The wonders of God's universe are endless and our understanding is but a blade of grass in a summer field. Our spirits are bound to this body because we think that is all there is to our world. Once we realize the error in our limited thinking we can set our spirits free.'

'Your spirit can wander?'

'My spirit separates from my body and it travels to other places, other times.'

'You can travel anywhere, whenever you wish?'

'There are times when I have been able to guide my thoughts in a certain way. Mostly I am just in another place, but I know it is not our time but in the past.'

'I do not understand. How can you visit what has been?'

'It is something here on the island. Perhaps a portal to other worlds, other times. It only happens when I am in a certain place on the island.'

'Where?'

Alice followed him to the oak tree. 'This is where I come,' he said. 'I sit right here and then after a while I am somewhere else. When I return, no time has. Sit with me, Alice. Would you like to try it? I will watch over you. I think it is beyond our understanding but for now I think we merely accept the possibility.'

'Are you saying I just to have to believe it is possible and I can do it?'

'Not quite, but it is a beginning. You see it is not just visiting the past. There are other dangers out there. I have encountered many spirits in my travels whose purpose is not for good. Remember I told you about the spirits I saw on the battlefield, the ones who had not accepted their deaths and who were wandering in confusion?'

'Aye.'

'Well, some spirits continue to wander. Their confusion can turn to despair or anger, and they do not know what else to do but let those feelings grow. I have met spirits who try to drag others into their darkness. They feed off those in this world whose hearts bear the shadow of hatred, jealousy, discontent.'

'Why are you telling me this?'

'I feel it may one day help you avoid danger. I will try to teach you. Your awareness will be heightened, and your senses, so you can be alerted to the danger and take steps to avoid it.'

'Where have you gone in the past?'

Michael laughed. 'Here I am, talking about teaching you something few are able to do, and the dangers it may involve, and your curious mind thinks only of the adventure.'

She returned his smile. 'You were the one who taught me to always question, to seek the truth.'

'That I did.'

'Tell me,' she said, her smile disappearing, 'where have you gone in the past?'

'I have mostly ventured to times of war and unrest. I have sought to understand why we continue to kill our fellow creatures. Why we have this passion for destruction. The main reason I go is that my spirit is able to help the dead move on, even though it is not my time. I hope it makes up for what I did at Flodden—the people I killed. There are also other places I go that are not of my choosing.'

'How far back have you gone?'

Michael knew there was a particular searching in her question. Suddenly he understood what she wanted to know. 'No, Alice, I did not go there.'

'Could you go, Father, if you wanted?'

'I do not know. Somehow seeking to go to a time when Christ walked the earth seemed too overwhelming. I was tempted to try. To be a spectator as He fed the multitudes with only some bread and fish, or when He healed the sick. Aye, I have been tempted.'

'What stopped you trying?'

'Since the moment I first saw the spirits of the dead, and then realized that I could channel God's healing energy, I have lived my life on faith. Faith in my God and the Christ. Faith in His love for me; that one day He will forgive me and I will be in His presence. Somehow to try to go where I could touch the hand of Christ seemed to diminish that faith. I would be saying to God, I have faith but I want proof. I have faith, Alice, complete faith, and I do not need proof.'

'Forgive me, Father. You are right. My curiosity is not always a good thing.'

'Your curiosity is what allows your spirit to fly. Do not ever stop asking questions and seeking the truth.'

'What about the future, can you go there?'

'No. Like you I can only see in my mind's eye a scene, an image. I cannot be part of it.'

'When can we start?' Alice asked.

'Now. We have done this many times, Alice. Just relax and become one with your spirit. When I feel you are at peace I will tell you what to do. Listen to my voice and block out all other thoughts.'

Alice did as he instructed. She took deep breaths and focused within. Gradually her breathing slowed.

'Your body is an encumbrance to your spirit, Alice. I want you to feel your body getting lighter and lighter. There is nothing to hold you back from releasing your spirit. Give it wings. Feel yourself leave the ground. You are lifting upwards and upwards. Your spirit is flying and you can go where you wish.' He could not sense her readiness to release. Again he spoke to her softly, encouraging her to let go, but he felt her fear, the one thing that could hold her back.

Eventually she opened her eyes and sighed. 'I am sorry, Father.'

'Do not admonish yourself. It is natural to be afraid of the unknown. We will try again another time but please, do not attempt this on your own. Now go and rest.'

'Goodnight, Father. May your dreams be happy.' She smiled and turned towards the priory.

Chapter 32

The Queen and her friends were asleep when Alice brought the jug of milk into the room. The Queen Mother was sitting by the window looking out at the loch. 'Perhaps a walk would benefit me.' She smiled at Alice. 'Will you accompany me, Alice, if your duties permit?'

'I have finished for the night.'

One of Lord Livingstone's men was standing guard outside and made to follow them. 'No,' the Queen Mother said,' stay with your Queen.'

The guard returned to his position and Alice followed the Queen Mother outside. The loch glowed crimson with the setting of the sun. Insects were thick in the air and the sound of the birds bidding farewell to the day was like music.

Alice walked quietly beside the Queen Mother. She could sense a deep sadness in the woman.

'Is your family well, Alice?'

'They are.'

'You must still miss your mother.'

'Always.'

'It is good that you have your aunt. Children need a mother, especially when they are young. They need guidance tempered with unconditional love I think. I am sure you and your aunt provide that. I gave birth to five children,' the Queen Mother said, 'but they did not all live.'

Alice knew from Father Michael what the Queen Mother had suffered. 'They are with God and no doubt watch over you.'

'Father Michael said you too can communicate with the world of spirits.'

Alice held her breath. He had not told her he had spoken to the Queen Mother of these things.

'You need not fear me, Alice. Father Michael did not betray you. We have been friends for a long time. We have spoken of many things, he and I, and I hope you will trust me as he does. I lost three children and the pain never leaves my heart. My first born, Francis, was a serious child. He never cried but the night little Louis, my second child, died, Francis, he was only two, he cried so much I thought he would die from it. He was totally inconsolable. I was holding him and I remember thinking that life held only sadness. As I cuddled him he just stopped crying and began to stare at the empty space beside the window. Suddenly he started to laugh and jump up and down on my knee. He just laughed and laughed. I was so confused. I did not see anything but obviously Francis could. As I sat there I felt the dark place I was in become lighter. I had a sense of peace, of being loved. I knew in my heart that Francis was seeing his father and little brother. I could not see them but I felt them. I truly felt their presence. At that moment I believed that spirits walk among us and that the bonds of love are never severed. When I left

France to marry King James, I had to leave Francis behind in the care of my family. I miss him every day but I know that he is being watched over and that I will see him again. I also lost two other sons, James and Robert, by the Queen's father. I try to be content with the thought that their spirits still live and that they are together.' The Queen Mother laid her hands on Alice's shoulders and smiled. 'I know you believe that also, Alice. You have a great gift.'

'You are a courageous woman, Madam, to suffer as you have and to keep faith.'

'You think I am courageous? At this moment I am filled with despair. I am sending my only daughter to France for her safety. I will be without both my children. I must stay and keep the peace so that when she is old enough she can rule this beautiful land as is her destiny. I hope she will understand and forgive me for sending her away.'

'She has a strong spirit. I am sure she will know you are only thinking of her safety.'

'I do hope so. I will send John and Lord Livingstone with her on the journey. And of course Jean and her little friends. My family in France will watch over her too. I hope she will think it all an adventure. I have asked Father Michael to go with her. She will be in need of spiritual guidance and I trust him completely in that capacity. You will miss him, I know, but my daughter needs him.'

'She could have no better teacher in the world.'

'Father Michael has asked me to give you my protection when he is gone. Will you accept my friendship as well, Alice?'

'Thank you, Madam.'

Alice stayed long after the Queen Mother had left. She tried to shift the feeling of sadness. Her world was changing and she wondered if she was really ready for it. Then she thought of William and smiled.

It could not be love. Not this quickly. Not with someone she might never see again. Alice thought again of how she had felt with his arm around her waist when she stumbled, and the feel of his lips on hers.

'Alice.' She whirled around to find William standing a short distance away.

'Father Michael said I might find you here. I did not want to leave without saying goodbye. I might not get a chance again.' He moved close to her and she could feel his breath on her face.

'Can you see into my heart, Alice?'

Her cheeks were hot in the cold night air. She tried to look away but could not.

'Can you feel what I have no words to express? I will be gone soon and do not know when I will return. I have no right to say that which I cannot follow through with action.'

'Please try, William. If you were not going tomorrow what would you say?' She felt such a rush of tenderness for him.

'I would say that I feel a great fondness for you. I spend my days trying to catch a glimpse of you, hoping you will come to spend time with the Queen. And when you walk with her I pretend it is me by your side. I imagine what it would be like to hold your hand. I imagine you looking back at me with fondness and thoughts that one day that fondness will turn to love and that you could see yourself as my wife and the mother of my children.'

She held his gaze, trying to see from his eyes if he was playing with her. He took a deep breath and moved closer to her.

'And if I was not going away and I said these things, what do you think you would say in return?'

Alice had spent so long being closed to people for fear they would realize what she was. She did not want it to be like that with William. 'I would say that my heart beats faster every time I see you. Before I drift off to sleep I see your face. I can feel you near me before I see you. I would say that to be your wife and the mother of your children would be an honour.'

Instantly they were in each other's arms, and their world became only what they embraced. When he bent his head to kiss her, Alice felt she could have stayed in that moment forever.

'Alice, I will come back, I promise. Will you wait for me?'

'Aye, I will.'

'I do not know how long I will be gone.'

She put a finger to his lips.

'I will wait.'

Chapter 33

Alice sighed as she wiped her wet hands on her apron. It had been a long day, with much activity surrounding the Queen. She had managed to have a few quiet moments with her father as he waited for the Queen's men he had brought from their camp on the mainland. He told her that the children missed her and wanted to know when she was coming home. She was glad to hear news of them. They were sitting in the warmth of the kitchen when the soldiers called for him to take them back. They seemed agitated and asked him to hurry. She quickly kissed her father on the cheek before he rushed off. She would tell her family about William once she was home.

Alice hoped she would get a chance to talk to Father Michael to find out what the excitement was about but he was nowhere to be seen. She thought he was probably with the Queen Mother and hoped that the activity did not mean their departure was soon. She felt a sudden pang of loneliness.

Later, Alice was finishing in the kitchen when she heard the door open. She smiled and turned.

'Ah, you were expecting someone else I see,' Father Feandan said.

Alice ignored the comment and took off her apron. 'I have finished for the night, Father. I am going to bed.' She walked towards the door but he stayed where he was, blocking the doorway.

'Will you please let me pass?'

'Why the hurry? Stay awhile and talk to me.'

'I am very tired. I would like to go to my room.'

His eyes flashed in anger. 'You always have time for Father Michael but not for me. Why is that I wonder?'

'I would like to leave please,' she said, trying to overcome the sense of fear she felt in his presence.

'Come now, a few minutes will not matter. Answer my question and I will let you pass.'

Alice ignored him.

'I will tell you why you have no time for anyone but him. It is because you are both alike. You like secrets. You like to make the rest of us feel inferior. You think you're special. Is that the reason, Alice, or is it something else? You do spend a lot of time together?'

'Father Michael is my teacher and my friend.'

'Yes, yes, your teacher. But you are a grown woman, Alice. What is that Father Michael teaches you now?'

Alice flushed with anger and took a step closer to him.

'Nothing to say, Alice? Is that guilt written on your face? Father Michael has been teaching you some tricks, has he not? Some tricks that perhaps give him much pleasure.'

'Stop this. You have no right. Father Michael is a good man, a man of God.'

'I expect he is good, Alice.'

'Let me pass.'

Father Feandan did not move and continued to stare at her. 'Perhaps I have it wrong, Alice, and Father Michael is the victim here. Perhaps you are a witch and you have him under your spell. Are you a witch, Alice? Perhaps your skills with healing are not from God.'

'You know that is not true.'

'Perhaps, but it would make a good story, would it not? After all, I witnessed what you did for the Queen. You merely touched her and she recovered. Yes, that would be a very good story. You know how stories like that spread. And you know what they do to witches, Alice?' He took a step backwards and leaned against the closed door. 'You know he is leaving tomorrow?' Father Feandan saw the surprise on her face. 'Yes, tomorrow. He is going with the Queen. What will you do then, Alice? Who will be your teacher once he is gone?'

Alice saw the darkness surrounding him grow even denser. She instinctively stepped back but he slowly walked towards her. She remembered that Father Michael had told her that to show fear to an aggressor was to feed that aggression. She looked directly into his eyes and took a step towards him.

'You will let me pass. Now! Or I will scream.'

She saw him falter. He shook his head once and then stared at her, as if awakening from sleep. His confusion lasted an instant and then hatred again returned to his eyes.

'You will keep. Father Michael will be gone and you will have no protector.'

Suddenly the door flew open. Father Feandan spun around to find Michael striding towards him. The colour drained from his face but he quickly recovered.

'Ah, Father Michael. I was just telling Alice you would be leaving tomorrow. She will miss you I am sure.'

Michael remained silent, his eyes fixed on Father Feandan.

'Well, I must be leaving now. It is been a long day.' Without looking again at Alice or Michael, he made for the door. Michael did not move so he was forced to walk around him. When he reached the door he turned and stared at Michael's back. He seemed about to say something then hesitated and walked silently through the door, closing it behind him.

Alice sucked in air as if she had been holding her breath too long.

'Did he harm you, child?'

'No. The only thing that harmed me was my fear. I let him see I was afraid.'

'What did he say to you?'

'He said some cruel things about us. He threatened to spread a lie that I was a witch.'

'He called you a witch? Oh, Alice, I do not know what to do. He is right. I am to leave tomorrow with the Queen but I fear for your safety.'

'You cannot be here to protect me all my life. Do not worry about me.'

'I wish there was more time,' he said. 'I wanted to try again to show you how to...'

'Father, please do not worry.'

'There is so much to do before I leave. We may not get a chance to speak alone again.'

Alice felt the sadness catch in her throat. 'I will miss you very much.'

'You have to make me a promise, Alice. You will leave the island tomorrow with us and you must never return.'

'Never? But what...'

'Promise me. You will be in danger from him. I have spoken to the Queen Mother and you will accompany the Queen on your father's boat tomorrow. Gather your belongings but tell no-one you're leaving with us. I will need time to make arrangements to send you somewhere safe. I am sure John will find you a place in his household. In the meantime you must not be on the island without me.'

'I do not want to leave my family.'

'I know, but if he starts spreading rumours that you are a witch...'

'Father, I promise never to come to the island. I will live quietly. If the need arises I will go away.'

'I expect you to keep that promise.' He smiled. 'I will miss you, Alice. I want you to know that my life has been enriched by your presence in it. The times we have shared will live in my memory and I will think of you every day and pray for you.'

Alice was overwhelmed with grief. She did not bother to wipe her tears. 'I was intending to be brave and see you off with a smile.' She stepped closer to him and held out her hands. He took them without hesitation. She felt their warmth and strength.

'Father,' she said softly, 'before you leave I must tell you that I love you. I will think of you every day of my life.' She slowly reached up and gently kissed his cheek.

He could taste the salt from her tears and the love radiating from her heart. She stepped back a little, still holding his hands.

'Thank you, Alice,' he said gently. 'I love you too and I will not say goodbye to you. We will meet again, I know this. I will not have it otherwise.'

'Father, will you take care of him, watch out for him?'

'William. Of course. I will do whatever I can to keep him safe.'

'Thank you. I feel better knowing you will do this. It will be a new adventure for you.'

'It will, but I will miss my home. What is it that draws the heart to this place? There is a tie that binds us Scots to our country; a sense of belonging to the hills and the lochs and the sky. There is a part of Scotland in each of us and no matter where we travel it calls us back. I felt this in Rome and on the Camino. I had an ache in my heart that only eased when I once again set foot on Scottish soil. I stood a long time that day, allowing the power of this earth to surge through my body until I again felt like a Scot—not a traveller or a man or a priest, but a Scot. I thought I would never leave here again although I did on occasions with John, but that was only for short periods and then I was home again. This time will be different. I do not know how long I will be gone. The Queen Mother asked me to do this and I cannot deny her, but she will never know the pain it will cause me to be away from this sacred land. I do not want her to know as she is doing what is best for the Queen. She thinks with my gifts I will be able to protect her and keep her from danger. Wherever my body is, my heart will always be here, with the people I care about. You, my parents, the Erskines, the Queen Mother. Here lies the grave of my dear Kate. I will miss you all.'

They stood in silence, delaying the moment of parting. Finally Alice released his hands.

'Goodnight, Father, until we meet again.' She smiled at him and walked towards the door. He remained where he was long after she had gone.

Alice lingered in the darkness. She thought how little she really knew about life, despite the fact that she lived in three different worlds. There was the world where she was the daughter, a niece and a sister. She was surrounded by her family's love and it was something she could always depend on.

There was the world of Inchmahome and the time she spent with Father Michael and the monks. She loved the tranquil surrounds and the books. Most of all she could be close to Father Michael, her teacher and her friend. With him she could be herself. There was no need to guard her thoughts or her words. He filled a space in her very being, the space that hungered for knowledge and truth. He was the only one with whom she shared her thoughts, her fears, her hopes. When she spoke to him there were no barriers, just one spirit connecting with another. Although her aunt guessed she had healing hands, she did not know of her other gifts. Alice laughed at the fact she actually now thought of them in that way. Before she met Father Michael they were curses. They had filled her with terror and made her withdraw into herself. He taught her to embrace who she was and he took away her fear. He armed her well for when she lived in her third world. The world of spirits and visions, of dreams and nightmares. She had some control over this world now, thanks to him, but he could not enter it with her.

The spirits still sought her out, drawn to her because she could see them and talk to them. She tried to get them to see the light that waited for them, the light where loving spirits beckoned to them. It saddened her when she could not convince them to go but always she felt that the spirits of the light would try again another time.

She had never valued her three worlds more than now because one of them was being taken away. Father Michael would be leaving and she might never see him again. She would keep her promise to him not to return to the island when he was gone. Both of them knew that the darkness surrounding Father Feandan was growing and he seemed unwilling or unable to stop it.

And William. She had learned so much since he had come into her life. She now knew that there was only one kind of love but it expressed itself in many ways. There was the love for her family, for Father Michael and for William. The same but separate. They ignited in her different feelings, different reactions, but each was as important to her as the other. She knew she could not betray one for the other and to choose one above the other would be impossible. The pain of losing any of them would be the same.

Chapter 34

Alice and Father Michael had been right to say their goodbyes when they did as there was no chance to speak alone again. Alice spent most of her time packing in the Queen's room.

'Alice, will you walk with me?' She turned to find the Queen standing behind her.

She followed her outside and walked with her to the edge of the water, followed at a discreet distance by two of her guards.

'I did not get to see the fairies,' the Queen said.

'There will be fairies where you are going. You will find them.'

'I hope so. I enjoyed our stay here. It is so peaceful and I felt like a child, not a queen. It is often hard to be both.'

'Even when you are grown, you must try to keep the child within, the child that is open to her instinct, the child that follows her heart and plays when she can.'

'I will try. I will miss you, Alice.' The Queen suddenly clapped her hands. 'Alice, will you come with me? I know your family is here but if you would like I will ask Mama to take you with us.'

'Your mother has already asked me but I cannot go with you. I would miss my family and I do not feel it is the way for me. My destiny lies elsewhere. I hope I have not offended you.'

'No, you have not.' The Queen suddenly laughed. 'Each time I speak with you I learn something. You talk of your destiny. Until now I thought only kings and queens had a destiny.'

'We each have our own but sometimes we do not follow its path.'

'How do we know where our destiny lies?'

'We often do not. Each day we face choices in our lives. Sometimes we make the wrong one but we are always given another chance to return to the path. I think our hearts always know the choice to make.'

'Do you think I will make the right choices, Alice?'

Alice could not tell her of the pictures that had flashed into her head. 'You will make good choices and bad ones, as we all do, but you have to remember that God always walks your path with you. If you feel you have made a wrong choice or even if you just need comfort, reach out your hand to Him and He will take it and hold it tight and walk with you.'

'Oh Alice, you know how to make me feel better. When I told you I saw my father you took away the fear that I was seeing things. Now, at this moment, I am unafraid of the future. I will remember your words. When I am afraid I will reach out for God's hand.'

Alice followed the Queen Mother, the little Queen and her companions to the landing place where the monks had gathered to bid farewell to their guests. The Queen Mother thanked the monks for their hospitality and told them that she would never forget their kindness. The little Queen and her companions were helped onto the boat by Michael and Lord Erskine. William was already on the loch in another boat.

Michael held out his hand to Alice. Without looking at any of the monks she stepped forward and let him help her into the boat. As her father pulled away, Alice looked at Father Feandan. She saw hatred and frustration in his face and realized that leaving was the only way.

Not a passenger spoke on the short journey to the mainland. There was barely a movement in the air and a mist seemed to descend around them. The only sounds were that of the boat and the oars stroking the water. Each had turned their thoughts inwards, reflecting perhaps on what might be ahead. None knew what the future held but for a short time their lives had touched.

As they approached the mainland Alice could see Moira and her siblings, dressed in their Sunday clothes, gathered by the landing place. She felt a rush of excitement at being with them again. Michael stepped out first and helped Alice. Her feet had barely touched the ground when the children rushed to her side, overcome with excitement.

'Oh Alice, we missed you.' Kenny and Peter hugged her tightly.

'You will not go away again, will you?' Wee Jeannie asked as Alice swept her into her arms.

'No, little one, I will not go away again.'

Alice noticed that the Queen Mother and the others were out of the boat and standing silently on the shore.

'I am sorry, Madam, I...'

'Do not apologize, my dear,' the Queen Mother said,' it is heart-warming to see such a loving family. I realize how much was asked of you to stay on the island with us. Please introduce us.'

'This is my Auntie Moira.' Moira moved to Alice's side and curtsied to the Queen and her mother. 'And this is Kenny, Peter and Wee Jeannie.'

The little Queen stepped forward and smiled at each of them. 'Alice has told me all about you. I am sorry we kept her away from you for so long. I hope you will accept these small gifts in appreciation.

The Queen handed Kenny a book. 'Alice said you are good with wood, Kenny. This book has many drawings of animals and perhaps will give you ideas.' Kenny's eyes widened. He bowed to the Queen and gently carried the book back to his father.

'And for you, Peter, a box of puzzles.' She gave Peter a wooden box. 'The pieces all fit together to form a picture, and underneath are pieces to make other pictures.'

The next gift was for Wee Jeannie. It was a beautiful silver clasp, decorated with pearls. 'Alice was right, you have beautiful hair. You can tie it up with this.'

Wee Jeannie could not take her eyes from the clasp. She forgot to courtesy and rushed to show her father.

The Queen smiled up at Moira, handing her a dark blue cloak. Moira stroked it gently. 'It is beautiful, your Grace. Thank you.'

'Alice, I would like you to have this.' The Queen opened a black velvet box to reveal a gold ring, set with four small rubies. 'This ring belonged to my great grandmother. I have always loved its beautiful colour. I would like you to have it. It will please me greatly if you would wear it and perhaps when you feel it on your finger you will think of me.'

'Thank you, your Grace.' Alice took the ring and placed it on the middle finger of her right hand. 'I will not forget you. You will always be in my prayers.'

The Queen then turned to Kenneth who had joined his family after securing the boat. 'I would like you to know that we appreciate all you have done for us. Please accept this as a small token of our gratitude.' She handed him a coin pouch. Kenneth was embarrassed but managed to mutter his thanks as he accepted the pouch from the Queen.

'We must go now, Madam,' John Erskine said.

'Yes.' Marie de Guise kissed Alice on both cheeks and hugged her. 'Take care, my dear. Remember if you ever need my help get word to me.'

Alice turned to the Queen who signalled for her to come closer. Alice bent down and the child threw her arms around her neck. 'I will miss you, Alice. I will write to you from France and when I return to Scotland we can again walk on Inchmahome and look for the fairies.'

'They will always be here, waiting for you to come home.'

Michael grasped Kenneth's arm, nodded to the rest of the family then turned to Alice.

'May God guard the way for you, Alice.'

'You will be in my prayers, Father.' she said.

William finished helping the children into the carriage and then rushed over to Alice.

'You will wait for me, Alice.'

She hoped he felt her overwhelming love for him. 'Aye, William, for as long as it takes.'

Alice felt the heavy weight of sadness bear down on her heart as the two men she loved turned and followed the others. The family watched in silence as they all rode away.

The rest of the day was a happy time, despite the sadness in Alice's heart. The children talked endlessly about meeting the Queen and their presents. Alice told them about William and they were overjoyed. She was happy to again be with her family.

Life went on. Father Andrew became ill over the winter and was unable to make it to the mainland. Father Joseph asked Alice if she would teach the children. She was delighted. Although Father Andrew recovered, it seemed unlikely that he could resume his full duties. The monks seemed to know that Alice would never be returning to the island. Her family did not ask her why, and although her father still worked for the monks he never questioned Alice's decision.

Alice gave little thought to the future. She was content to teach and to heal. She was careful, very careful, when villagers came to her with an illness. She recommended herbs and suggested rest, but in doing so she would find a way to lay her hands on them. She touched a shoulder, an arm, held a hand, knowing that she was channelling the healing power of God. Folk thought the herbs had cured them, or the rest. Alice did not want them to know the truth. She guarded her secret well. She also loved teaching the children.

Alice also had moments of overpowering loneliness and ached to see Father Michael and William. When she found time to be alone in the garden or by the edge of the loch, to turn inwards and shut off the outside world, she felt Father Michael's presence. She knew that at some level he was connecting to her, letting her know he was still with her. Alice practiced what he had tried to teach her before he left. She imagined him talking to her, telling her to be calm and feel safe. Alice again heard his words of encouragement to separate her spirit from her body and allow it to be free. There were times when she felt it about to happen, but her excitement held it back. If only she could go back in time to those quiet moments in the scriptorium, or listening to Father Michael's voice at her lessons. If she could only again feel the touch of William's lips on hers.

Chapter 35

Alice was feeding the hens just after dawn when she heard horses approach. She looked up to find Lord Erskine and three others dismounting. He smiled at her and threw the reins to one of his men.

'Alice, it is good to see you again. Are you and your family well?'

'We are.'

'I have a letter for you from Michael. He reached into his saddle and brought out a folded parchment.

Alice tried to hide her excitement but knew she failed.

'I am going home to see my family and attend to some urgent matters. Michael wanted me to make sure you were safe and had come to no harm.'

'All is well. I have kept close to home.'

'Good lass.' Lord Erskine handed Alice the document. 'I do not have to tell you to keep it safe. In fact it might be better if you destroyed it.' He laughed at Alice's shocked expression. 'Well, at least keep it hidden.'

'I will, my Lord.'

'I will call back this way in three days if you wish to reply.'

'Thank you. I will have a letter ready. Is William well?'

'He is. He asked me to tell you he thinks of you often. He misses you I am sure. I often come upon him by the castle walls, looking out to the horizon. It is not difficult to know what he is thinking about. The Queen likes to have him near so he was not able to come with me. She has been very ill with measles but is recovering. That is why we have not yet left for France.'

"Will you take a letter for him too?'

'He would be most disappointed if I returned without one, my dear.'

Alice waited until John Erskine had gone and then sat down on the wooden bench her father had built under the old hawthorn tree. She carefully broke the red seal and unfolded the paper.

'My dear Alice. I have entrusted this letter to John as I wanted to be sure you received it. I hope it finds you well and also your family. We leave for France as soon as the Queen is fully recovered from her illness. She is excited about the trip and seeing her family in France but sorrowed that her mother is not accompanying her. As Queen she understands the reasons but as a child she is heartbroken. The Queen Mother has told her much about France but I heard her ask why she could not return to Inchmahome. I think she felt safe there and I know that had much to do with you.

'I will try to guide her as much as I can although I know there will be many who will want to influence her when she reaches the court of the French King. She will spend time with her future husband and my wish is that they become friends.

'Are you being careful, Alice? I hope so. John knows the circumstances and offered to send Father Feandan away but I debated greatly on whether this was the right course. He would no doubt say it was because your friends are trying to protect you. He only has to get the ear of the Queen Mother's enemies. You must promise me that if there is a need you will find a way to contact her and allow her to help you. I wish there had been more time to explore the other options we discussed.

'I know you can read my heart, so there is no need for further words. If I thought you would destroy this letter I would say more but I know you will not. Take care, Alice. My prayers are with you.'

Alice smiled. Father Michael was right. She could never destroy the letter. She carefully placed it in the front page of the Book of Hours that he had given her for her birthday. She would write back to him tomorrow but she would not tell him of the dreams that still plagued her almost nightly.

It was late on a warm May evening. Alice walked to the edge of the loch, intending to meditate for a while as she felt restless and unsettled. She turned when she hear movement behind her to find William walking towards her. Without hesitation she rushed to his arms, tears streaming down her cheeks. He scooped her up and swung her around, laughing and holding her close.

'Alice, Alice, I have missed you so.' William took her hands in his, kissing each again and again.

Alice slipped her arms around his neck. 'Oh William. I am so happy to see you? How long can you stay?'

Not long. The ship is expected any time to take us to France. Everything has been arranged. I had to see you again. I needed to look into your eyes, tell you I love you and make sure you know I will return as soon as I can.'

'I love you too and think of you constantly.'

William cupped her face and kissed her, gently at first, but then more fervently. She happily responded and every other thought faded away as they stood together in the fading light.

It was almost dark as he held her from him and smiled. 'I have a surprise for you. Let us go back to the house.'

Reluctantly she followed. She assumed Lord Erskine was there and perhaps he had another letter from Father Michael. Alice saw the tall figure standing by the house. Her heart stopped. William let go of her hand and she rushed to embrace him. He willingly opened his arms for her.

'Oh Father, I have missed you.'

Michael smiled down at her. 'And I you, Alice.'

She realized her action may have seemed inappropriate for after all he was a priest but when she looked at William, he was smiling.

'William and I decided we could not leave without seeing you again. The ship is expected any time so the Queen Mother allowed us to make this short visit. I received a letter from Father Joseph and he has growing concern about Father Feandan's state of mind. I wanted to satisfy myself you are safe and well.'

'I am, Father. I have stayed away from the island.'

'Good. Well, Moira has some food ready so I will leave you both to spend some time alone. It is good to see you again, child.'

Their visit was indeed short. Parting was painful but Alice comforted herself by thinking the quicker they went to France, the sooner they could come home.

Chapter 36

Alice walked across the lush soft grass which was sprinkled with the colours of many flowers. They reached towards the sun and the light breeze was laden with their fragrance. Two monks were on the loch in their little boat, their fishing lines hanging from rods. Life was good, she thought. At least the days were.

That night, as she lay in the darkness, the house at peace, the dream came.

Alice looks down at the loch from a high hill. She sees the Port and the surrounding area but then the picture expands. There are large towns crowded with people and small ones with only a few houses. She sees a town with a castle on top of a hill and knows it must be Stirling. Then quickly the scene changes. The towns grow before her eyes. What seems like boxes move on the roads and large objects fly in the sky. The changes are happening so fast she is unable to make out details. As she watches, fascinated, everything just stops. In the distance she sees a small black cloud as it moves towards Stirling. The darkness grows. It looks like black mud which increases in thickness as it rolls over the town and totally obscures it. It keeps moving, covering the surrounding countryside. It engulfs farms and houses. From her vantage point on the hill Alice watches it engulf the Port and Inchmahome. All she sees below her is darkness. Fear fills her heart. And then through the darkness a tiny speck of light appears. It moves towards her and she recognizes the woman in white. Still she cannot see her face clearly but she senses her usual sadness has gone. The woman's hands come to rest across her stomach. Alice sees a small ball of light there. It detaches itself and moves through her fingers. She smiles lovingly at the light and Alice joins her as they both watch it move away from them towards the darkness below. The light glows even brighter and as it grows it pushes the darkness away. Larger and larger it grows and the darkness keeps receding until it completely disappears.

Alice woke with a start. What did it mean? Her questions went unanswered as she slipped into a deep, dreamless sleep.

Alice sat on the grass by the water, allowing the stillness to engulf her. Her father, Moira and the children had gone to the next village to attend a wedding of the daughter of one of Moira's friends, Annie. They did not see each other often and Annie insisted that the family stay with them overnight. The children could hardly contain their excitement. Kenneth was not going as someone had to attend to the animals but Alice insisted on being the one to stay. She pleaded tiredness and they could see for themselves her weariness.

She sighed. How she missed Father Michael and William. She prayed for them every day and hoped that they were aware they were in her thoughts. They would surely be in France now. So far away. She looked over to the island at the silent bell tower imposed against the sky. For a moment she wondered what her life would have been like if she had not come to Menteith and met Father Michael. Almost instantly she dismissed the thought. There was no place in her thoughts for what might have been. Her life had taken a course and she was more than content with it.

Alice realized she had been watching the little boat approach without registering what she was seeing. As it came closer she recognized Father Joseph. She greeted him with a smile and was surprised to see the look of concern on his face.

'Is something wrong, Father?'

'I am afraid so. Father Andrew is gravely ill. We are not expecting him to live through the night. He knows it is his time and he wants to see you before he goes. Are you able to come with me? I will bring you back when you are ready?'

'Of course I will come. I will get my shawl.' It was not until she reached the house that she remembered Father Feandan and her promise to Father Michael never to return to the island. He will understand, she thought. She grabbed her shawl and headed back to the boat.

'We all miss you on the island, Alice.' Father Joseph said when they were on the loch. 'It was always a joy to see your happy face around the place.' He gave a little laugh and smiled. 'You and Father Michael always brought a little excitement into the lives of us old men.'

'I am sorry I was unable to finish my work.'

'There is no need for apologies. I understand why you could not return. I thought deeply about coming for you today but I know Father Andrew is very fond of you and it will bring him great comfort to see you.'

'I am glad you did.'

'I will watch out for you, Alice, and make sure you are safe.'

Alice looked at him with surprise.

'Father Feandan has also been unwell,' Father Joseph said. 'Not in body, but he has become a little...a little difficult. He has been counselled to spend more time in quiet contemplation with the Lord. I am sure he will get the help he needs.'

Father Joseph looked weary by the time he eventually tied the boat to the landing post. He walked with Alice to the room on the ground level where Father Andrew was being looked after. Father Malcolm was trying to get him to sip some fluid when Alice quietly entered. She was shocked by his thin face, devoid of colour. He seemed smaller than she remembered. The look of pleasure on his face when he saw her dispelled any discomfort she felt at returning to the island.

'Alice, my dear,' he said, waving Father Malcolm away. 'I am so glad you came. Come closer and sit beside me.'

Father Malcolm pulled the stool closer to the bed for her. 'It is good to see you again, Alice.' He winked at her. 'Perhaps your visit will cheer him up a bit. He has become very grumpy since he took to his bed.'

'I have not been grumpy,' Father Andrew said. 'Anyway, you can leave now. I have much to discuss with Alice.'

'I will see you when you are ready to go home, Alice,' Father Joseph said. They both left, closing the door quietly behind them.

'Come closer, my dear. How are you?'

'Well, Father, and how are you?'

'Well, they have probably told you it is my time to leave, although they will not say it to my face of course. It is strange, Alice, for we are men of God and we have chosen this way of life to be closer to Him, but when the time comes to actually leave this mortal existence and go to God, we say "not yet God, we are not ready". Michael and I had long discussions about dying and death, but the others, they say not to worry, I will get well again.'

'You are not afraid?' Alice asked.

'No. Why would I be? I am going home.' He took her hand. 'I miss Michael. I am sure you do too.' he said.

Alice nodded. 'Very much.'

'You two have a special bond. I could see that. It is as if you both understood so much more than the rest of us about this life and its wonders. I would sometimes overhear you talking and just listen. Your words gave me food for my soul. I even enjoyed just watching the two of you together. There was such an energy around you.'

'Others were not so understanding,' Alice said.

'I know. It is sad the things men hold in their heart. You were right not to return, Alice. When I spoke to Father Joseph about asking you to come and see me, I extracted from him his promise that he would guard you while you were here and see you safely home after your visit. Otherwise I would not have let him bring you.'

'I had to come and say goodbye to you, Father. You should not be worrying about me.'

'You are a brave girl, with a good heart.'

'What did you want to talk to me about?'

'I wanted to ask you to give me healing to help me on my journey. I want to embrace the light with joy. I know I said I was unafraid but I lack courage. Is it selfish for me to want to hold your hand when I cross? I know it is silly to think like this but perhaps I will get lost and I know if you are with me I will find the way.'

Alice smiled. 'It will be an honour, Father.'

'Thank you.' A tear slipped from his eye. 'Thank you.'

'I have heard such good things about your teaching, Alice. It is been such a relief to know the children are continuing their lessons. I could not have wanted anyone better to take over my duties.'

'I love it, Father. They are such a joy. I learn from them too.'

They talked of many things but gradually Father Andrew grew tired. Alice knew the time had come.

He sighed deeply. 'Take care of yourself, Alice. I will continue to pray for you and when I see Him I will ask Him to watch over you.'

Alice lifted Father Andrew's hand, kissed it gently and smiled. His eyelids slowly closed. Alice too closed her eyes and connected to his spirit. She had the sensation of floating on a cushion of air and she still felt Father Andrew's hand in hers. Upwards, upwards they floated and then above them she saw a spectrum of lights, so beautiful it took her breath away. They became part of the lights. She was aware of Father Andrew letting go of her hand and suddenly she was again seated by his bedside. She opened her eyes and looked at him. She knew his spirit had gone.

Behind her Alice heard the door quietly close. She laid Father Andrew's hand gently on the bed and stood up.

'Well, well, Father Michael's little playmate, returned to the scene of her indiscretions.'

Alice felt the venom in Father Feandan's voice reach out and touch her and she consciously dispersed it. She turned to him.

'And how is Father Andrew? We have been praying for his recovery. Did you think we needed your prayers too?'

'He is gone,' Alice whispered.

'Gone! What have you done to him?' Father Feandan smiled and left the room.

There were tears and sorrow for Father Andrew had been well loved. Alice told Father Joseph that she would borrow one of the boats and row herself back to the mainland. He protested but she insisted she would be fine. He looked around and saw Father Feandan with the other monks, his head bowed in prayer. 'Go quickly, child,' he said. "I will make sure we all stay together.' Alice left them to mourn their dear friend.

The sun was already descending on the horizon as Alice made her way to the boatshed. Her heart was heavy with sorrow. She felt lost and alone. Perhaps it was her sadness that blocked her usual alertness for she had no sense of danger until she felt the pain on the side of her head, and slipped into darkness.

When she opened her eyes, Alice knew something was wrong. Her head thudded painfully and her body ached. She was lying on her face on the grass. She tried to sit up but the world spun around her and she lay back down with her eyes closed.

'The witch's head hurts, does it?'

Alice fought her fear when she recognized the voice. Slowly she turned onto her back and used her hands to push herself up. The side of her face was wet and when she touched it she saw blood. She stared at Father Feandan who came to stand in front of her. She looked into his eyes and saw that the demon of madness had finally overcome him.

'You thought you would never see me again, Alice. Well, I could not let it end like that, with you just walking away and not paying for your sins. God would want you punished, Alice.'

The pounding in her head eased slightly so she tried to stand up.

'Stay where you are. I have much to say.'

'Say what you will and let me go home.'

'Not until you confess your sins to me.'

'My sins! What sins.'

'Ah. Do not pretend to be stupid, Alice. You know how you sinned. You like others to think you are a good girl but you are Father Michael's harlot—and a witch.

'How can you say that? It is not true.'

'Come now, Alice. No more pretence. I have seen you together. I do not understand how the others could not see the hunger in his eyes for your body and you so easily giving him your favour. Then there is that young stallion of Lord Erskine's. You gave him what he wanted too.'

'You can believe what you want but Father Michael is my friend and William has never laid a hand on me.'

'Alice, Alice. You must stop this lying. God will not forgive you unless you confess.'

'I will not confess to something I have not done.'

'Then I will have to force you to tell the truth"

Father Feandan suddenly grabbed her arms and dragged her to her feet. He roughly pushed her against a tree and she felt his breath on her facc.

'You are very beautiful, Alice.' He used his spare hand to stroke her cheek. 'I can destroy you, do you know that? All I have to do is tell my uncle about your secrets. I have much to tell about your impure relations with Father Michael and how you used witchcraft to seduce William. And how the devil helped you heal the young Queen when she fell in the bell tower. And now you visit Father Andrew and while you are with him he dies. Do you know what they do to witches, Alice?'

'I am no witch.'

'Oh, I think you are. I will tell them how you tried to seduce me. How you used your young body to lure me to sin.'

Alice tried to struggle out of his grip but he slapped her sharply across the face.

'You are not going anywhere, Alice, not until I exorcise the curse you put on me.' He pushed the weight of his body against her. She felt the roughness of the tree scrape her back as she struggled to free herself. He smothered her neck and cheeks with his wet lips. His panting increased and she realized her struggling was exciting him more. She stilled herself. He stopped what he was doing and stared at her in surprise. Then he smiled. He slowly released his grip on one of her arms and moved it down the curve of her body. He took hold of her skirt and began pushing it upwards.

She smiled. 'Let me help you.'

Father Feandan's eyes bulged. While he was thinking about it Alice took her chance. She sharply brought her knee up between his legs. He cried out in pain and his grip slackened as he stumbled backwards. She started to run but he made a grab for her and they both fell to the ground, his arms grasping her waist. She wriggled forward and kicked out with her foot, connecting with the middle of his face. He yelped in pain and clutched his nose. Blood streamed through his fingers. She kicked out again and dragged herself away from him. She got to her feet and ran.

'You cannot get away from me, witch.'

Despite the thudding in her head Alice kept running. She bumped into trees and bushes but still she kept going until she felt her legs start to weaken and the pain in her head made her dizzy. She craved rest but knew she could not stop. Eventually she could go not a step further and collapsed beside a large tree. She dragged herself to a sitting position and listened. Nothing. Then she heard the breaking of twigs and the sounds of heavy panting. She struggled to get up but could not. On her hands and knees she crawled as fast as she could, ignoring the pain. Then suddenly a calmness came over her and Father Michael's face swirled in front of her. She realized her fear was controlling her. She forced herself to stand and began to run again. She felt her strength return to fill the space where her fear had been.

'I will be safe. I am safe.' she repeated to herself.

She did not know how far she had ran until eventually she felt the world around her fade and she slipped into darkness.

Chapter 37

Michael lingered in the chapel at Dumbarton Castle after Mass. He could not shake the anxiety that lay heavy in the pit of his stomach. He paced back and forth in front of the altar trying to calm his mind and get some sense of the energy disturbance.

The Queen was fully recovered from the bout of measles. The ship from France that was to carry her to her new home was taking longer than expected and there was still the threat that the English ships would try to stop her. The betrothal of the Queen of Scotland to the future King of France was not something the English accepted graciously.

Marie was a strong and determined woman and capable of handling the nobles of Scotland and the English threat. Although saddened by the impending departure of her little daughter, she was convinced the only way to protect Mary's throne was to send her to France.

So, if the anxiety was not for the Queen then what was its cause? He stilled his thoughts and almost immediately fear exploded within him. His eyes shot open and his hands went to the blinding pain in his head.

He did not realize that John Erskine had entered the chapel and was by his side.

'John, something is wrong.'

'A messenger arrived from the Port,' John said. 'Father Andrew is dead and Alice is missing.'

Father Feandan prayed fervently. He kept praying after the others left the church. The words masked the fear that rose from his stomach and pounded in his head. Exhausted he eventually slumped on his seat. He had to work out a plan. What should he do? He could run, but where would he go? As much as he bragged about his noble connections, he knew he would not be welcomed by any member of his family. Stupid people! The incident with the Earl's young daughter was a misunderstanding. She had led him on with her innocent smile and fluttering lashes. How was he to know she was only eleven? It was not his fault. She encouraged him and when she struggled he knew she was just playing. It was part of the fun.

In his lust he did not hear her screams, but the others had. They rushed into the room and pulled him off the hysterical girl. He saw their looks of disgust as he stood there, his clothes undone, panting like a wild animal. They did not believe him of course, that he had been provoked. They told him to enter a monastery or they would not be responsible for his safety. Such pathetic creatures! He did as they asked and spent all these years in the drudgery of prayer and work, always cold and hungry. There was no peace for him.

And now it was happening again. That whore Alice. It was fine for her to fornicate with a priest and then that stupid boy of Lord Erskine's. She was probably doing both of them at the same time.

Why should they get all the fun? Surely she could spare some of her charms for him. How he hated Father Michael, so full of his own importance and coming and going as he pleased. Watching him talking to the Queen Mother it was obvious to those who looked hard enough that there was an unhealthy union between them. Yes. He hated Father Michael more than anyone he had ever known. And that stupid stupid Alice. Why did she resist? She had hurt him but he had retaliated. How did she have the strength to run from him? Where was she now? He was sure he hit her hard enough to cause her great injury, so perhaps she was dying in the woods. He made sure he landed the boat at an isolated area. She would not be found for a long time. No-one would know it was him. He rowed quickly back to the island, cleaned himself up and rejoined the other monks. They were too caught up in their grief over Father Andrew to notice he had left.

But what if she was alive? He could not bear that. She would accuse him. But it would be her word against his. She was a mere girl and he a man of God. They would think her delusional. The blow to the head had affected her brain. No-one could possibly believe he had done such a thing.

He was starting to feel better. If she was dead then good and well. If not, and she accused him, they would not believe her. His improved humour was short lived. There was Father Michael. He would hear of the death of Father Andrew and that Alice was missing. Would he come? Father Feandan's heart beat faster and his head thudded until he thought it would explode. Yes! He would come. Even if he managed to run away, he knew in his heart that Father Michael would hunt him to the ends of the earth.

Michael stood in perfect stillness, his black cloak wrapped around him and his cowl drawn over his head. He did not think he would see his beloved Inchmahome again so soon. He had kept his anger in check on the ride from Dumbarton Castle but now that he was here, he allowed it to surface. It trickled then poured through every cell of his body. It released the demon he had fought to keep chained since the bloody battle at Flodden. Anger was the key that opened the lock. For a little while he allowed his demon freedom to fill him with hate and the need for revenge. Then he again reined it in and imprisoned it.

Slowly his breathing returned to normal. He had work to do. He would find Alice whatever the price. He knew she was still alive—he sensed it. He promised her he would protect her with his life and he would.

He wondered if Father Feandan knew he was coming. Aye, he would know.

Chapter 38

Port of Menteith, 2010

Paul lay on the red tartan rug, his eyes closed. The warm breeze caressed his body and the sounds of chirping birds and lapping water eased his busy mind. He wanted to stay in this moment forever. Jenny was always telling him that it was the only way to be. When he worried about an impending deadline or the creative juices dried up, she would say 'Live in the moment, baby, live in the moment.' And it almost always worked. One of the many reasons he loved her—and there were many—was that she had gently shifted him from being a workaholic to being one only some of the time. She knew how absorbed he got when researching and writing a new novel. She recognized when he was particularly tired or frustrated and would gently distract him when he needed it.

Only last week, when he had been struggling to finish an important scene, she called him to dinner. He wearily dragged himself to the dining room where he found candles burning, flowers on the table, and Julio Iglesias' voice drifting in the air. She was standing in the doorway wearing a long silky black dress. She smiled and held up her left hand to display the ring he had given her on their engagement a decade before. He had seen it in the window of an antique jeweller's shop in Stirling and bought it for her on impulse. It fitted her perfectly and she loved it. She would flash it at him when she thought he needed to relax and it was her signal that she was more than willing to help him do just that.

Slowly he opened his eyes. Jenny was standing perfectly still by the water's edge. He watched her, his whole being filled with love. Her short dark hair was covered by a large straw hat and her slim tanned legs protruded from her pink shorts. Her white cotton tee-shirt came to just above her slim waist.

She must have sensed him walking towards her on the soft spongy grass for she turned and smiled at him. The smile of an angel, he thought. She returned her eyes to the hills opposite this ancient island of Inchmahome. He put his arms around her waist and rested his chin on her shoulder. She kissed him gently on the cheek.

'What are you thinking about?' he asked.

'I was just wondering what it must have been like for the monks who used to live here. It's the perfect place for a monastery. All this beauty and peace.'

'A shame there's not much left of it.'

'Enough to get a feel for the place. I think some of their spirits might have lingered. Maybe to keep guard. Or maybe they just stayed because they thought heaven couldn't be more beautiful than this.'

'You have such a wonderful imagination. You'd make a good writer.'

She laughed. 'It's not my imagination. Right at the beginning when we moved to the Port I felt drawn to the island. I feel I belong here.'

'Do you really?'

'When we went for a walk the day we came to look at the house and I saw this island across the lake, I wasn't surprised it was there. I really loved the house but when I saw this I knew we were meant to be near this place. I think if we come here just as the sun is setting and stand right where we are now, we might catch a glimpse of the monks on their way to prayer. And if we're very quiet we might even hear their singing. You think I'm silly, don't you?'

'Honey, I never think that.'

'Oh yes you do.' She turned to him and wound her arms around his waist. She hugged him tightly then looked into his eyes. 'You won't forget me ever, Paul, will you?'

'Forget you! Why are you asking that? How can I forget you?' The sadness in her eyes tugged at his heart. 'No!' he screamed. But it was too late. He felt the dream draw back and no matter how hard he tried, he could not stop it fading.

Finally he opened his eyes in the darkened room. She was gone. The sadness approached him like a giant wave and he let it drown him.

Paul sat on the wooden bench by the outdoor table, his hands around his mug of tea. Susie jumped onto the bench and then the table. Gone were the days when she could get there in a single bound. She went right up to his face and nudged his nose. She purred loudly as she curled up in front of him.

'Well girl, what are your plans for the day? A wander around the garden perhaps?' He stoked her under her chin which she lifted as high as she could. 'Maybe you'll think about chasing a bird or two but then again why would you bother. It's too warm for such antics, isn't it, sweetheart. You never catch them anyway. I'll be going for a nap later so maybe you'll join me.'

After the dream he knew sleep would evade him so he had worked through the rest of the night and was feeling a little weary. He knew that the minute he lay down Susie would be beside him or on his chest playing happy feet.

Paul turned at the sound of crunching on the gravel path.

'Hi Wilma, You're up and about early.'

'Couldn't sleep. The days I need to get up I could sleep all morning but when there's no timetable I'm wide awake at six. You been working all night?'

'How can you tell?' he said, aware of his crumpled tee-shirt and shorts.

'I wasn't sure if you were home today so I thought I'd check up on this wee darling.' Wilma went over and stroked Susie. She was rewarded with a quick lick and her increased purring. The morning peace was shattered when Wilma's two Jack Russells, Pip and Taz, came bounding around the corner, panting and jumping up his leg.

'And how are you beautiful ladies this morning,' he asked, trying to stroke both at the same time. Susie turned up her nose at the interruption.

'I need a refill,' he said, holding up his mug. 'Want one?'

'Yes please.'

Through the window Paul watched Wilma juggling between throwing the ball for the dogs and stroking Susie.

'How's Cliff doing on the trip to France?'

'They're having a ball. They're camped near the racetrack at Le Mans in the thick of it all. He said he'd phone this afternoon but he hopes to head back tomorrow.'

'Didn't you want to go this time?'

'Once was enough. I don't mind the long drive through France but all that noise. I can only take so much of screeching tyres. Still coming to dinner on Thursday? I'm trying something new.'

'You're always trying someone new. I don't think Jenny and I have had the same meal twice at your place.' Then he remembered. He gave Wilma a half smile. 'I forget sometimes.'

'I took her flowers yesterday and told her all about Cliff's trip.'

Wilma was a good friend. She never gave him that sympathetic look others did when he forgot Jenny was not there. She let him deal with the grief any way he wanted. When he did want to remember and talk about his wife, Wilma listened and often they ended up laughing about the good times they all had together.

'I'm going later,' Paul said. 'I thought I'd take some carnations from the garden. She said they remind her of her father. Wouldn't want her to think I was neglecting them.'

They sat in comfortable silence for a while, each deep in their own thoughts.

'Thanks for the tea,' Wilma said. 'I'd better get back. You try and get some rest.'

Paul watched the trio head back along the lane before heading to the bedroom.

Paul turned off the ignition but could not bring himself to move out of the car. His sadness was so profound it seemed to engulf every part of his mind and body. He had no thoughts, such was its intensity. He had spent the afternoon with Jenny. He put the flowers near her, hoping she could smell their fragrance, and talked to her as if she could hear him. He told her how the book was going, how lazy Susie was getting, and how empty his life was without her.

The sudden thud on the bonnet stirred him from his hell. Susie was staring at him through the windscreen, her tail swishing from side to side. He could not help but smile and the involuntary reaction to the sight of this beautiful cat released him from the place of darkness.

Susie rubbed against his legs as he walked towards the house. He picked her up and she nuzzled her face against his. He managed to open the front door with her still purring loudly in his ear but she instantly jumped down once inside. He followed her to the kitchen where she stood beside her empty bowl, looking alternatively from it to him.

'Hungry are you?' He opened the cupboard. 'And what would madam prefer this evening? Tuna or lamb?'

Susie stretched herself up his leg and meowed. 'Just give me food,' she seemed to be saying.

'Well, let's go for the tuna shall we? Or maybe the lamb would be better.'

Her claws dug ever so gently into his skin.

'Okay, Okay.'

Paul made himself a coffee while Susie slowly ate her meal. She followed him into the lounge and jumped up beside him on the sofa to begin her washing ritual.

If it was not for Susie's gentle ways, Paul thought he might just die of loneliness. He clung to her dependence on him as a man clings to a raft on a vast, unending ocean.

The light was fading as he sipped his third malt. Suddenly Susie jumped up, jerking him out of the quiet, still place he had been. She padded slowly towards him and nuzzled her nose beneath his chin. That was when the world came crashing in. The tears flowed freely as he cried like he had not done since he first saw Jenny lying so helpless in the hospital, attached to all those machines. Susie curled up beside him and put one of her paws on this arm. She stayed with him until he had no tears left.

'Well, Susie, what do I do now? The doctors say Jenny's body is deteriorating and that she won't come out of the coma. If she's left as she is it may take six months for her to die. They want me to consider turning off the life support. I don't know what to do. We love her so much, don't we girl?'

The cat gently laid her head on his arm. They both stayed like that for a long time until eventually Susie got up and stretched herself. She roughly nudged him under the chin, jumped down and headed to the bedroom. She slept on Jenny's side of the bed every night and when she was not outside sunning herself she would have a nap in Jenny's wardrobe.

After this fourth drink he dragged himself to the kitchen to make a coffee. While he waited for the kettle to boil he opened the patio doors and stepped outside. The full moon lit up the garden. He had never felt so alone and the pain of not being able to reach out and touch Jenny, or hear her gentle voice, was more than he could bear.

The sound of something moving in the bushes abruptly brought him back to the moment. Perhaps it was fox or a wild cat. He stood up and moved towards the sound. It stopped for a moment and then he jumped back in surprise as someone fell out of the bushes and collapsed at his feet. Paul stared at the prone figure, his heart racing. He gently bent down and touched the body. No response. His eyes adjusted to the moonlight and he saw that it was a girl. He turned her over and gasped at the state of her face which was caked in blood and dirt. Her long hair had fallen over her face. She was dressed in a long dark skirt and green blouse which were also dirty. Paul thought she must have been in a car accident and wandered off the main road into his garden. She was only slight so he gently picked her up in his arms and headed inside. He would have to get her to a doctor. He put her down on the sofa on top of the throw-over cover. Suddenly Susie jumped on top of her, purring loudly and kneading her way up the girl's body. The purring increased as she licked the girl's face and then she just lay down on top of her chest, curled her front legs under her body and rested her head. Paul could not believe what he was seeing. Susie never treated strangers like this. The girl's eyelids flickered and slowly opened. She looked directly into Susie's eyes and smiled. Then she caught sight of Paul. She pulled herself to a sitting position, her eyes scanning the area, then fixing on the door.

'It's okay. You're safe. My name's Paul. I found you in my garden. I think you may have been in an accident. You'd better stay still for a while.'

The girl stared at him, her eyes like saucers.

'Really. You're okay. Wait here. I'll get you some water.'

When Paul came back with the glass the girl was sitting on the edge of the sofa holding her head in her hands.

'Here, take this.' She drank the water in one go.

'Would you like more?'

She shook her head. Susie was rubbing her face against the girl's side.

'What's your name?'

'Alice,' she whispered.

'Well, Alice, we need to get you to a doctor.'

'No. Please, I just need to go home.'

'Okay, calm down.'

Susie stepped onto Alice's lap and sat down. Alice stroked her and then stared around the room.

'Where is this?'

'It's my home. You're in the Port of Menteith.'

'I do not know this place?'

The village is a few minutes away and if you walk up the road a bit you get to the lake.'

'Lake?'

'The Lake of Menteith.'

'Inchmahome.' Her eyes brightened.

'Yes. Do you live around here?'

'At the landing place near the village. Pa rows the boats to the island. He works for the monks.'

'Monks!'

'On the island.'

It now occurred to Paul that Alice must have had a nasty bump on the head. There had not been monks on Inchmahome since the 16th century.

'I think you should see a doctor?'

'No. Please.'

'Okay. Would you like to clean up? I'll show you where the bathroom is and I've some clothes I can give you.'

Alice nodded. She stood up but started to sway. Paul offered his arm and she took it.

'That must have been some bump you got.' He helped her down the hallway, closely followed by Susie. He opened the door and indicated for her to go through. 'You can use the shower or run a bath.'

Alice took a step back. 'Where is your well?'

'Well!' Paul was definitely getting the feeling the girl was not quite normal but he decided to humour her.

'We don't need a well. Watch.' He opened the shower door and turned on the tap. Alice jumped back. He showed her the rest of the workings of the bathroom, and laid out the soap and towels.

'The temperature is automatically set. Just turn off this tap when you finish. I'll leave you too it. I'll put some clothes outside the door for you. When you're done, come out and I'll make you something to eat.' Susie refused to leave so he gently closed the door behind them.

Paul was not sure what to make of Alice. She seemed harmless but was acting very strangely. Perhaps she had escaped from a mental hospital and somehow got lost. She obviously did not want a doctor. And Susie! Her friendly attitude towards a stranger was totally out of character. He left a pair of Jenny's cotton trousers, a tee-shirt outside the door and then started on the food. The table was set, the coffee ready and mushroom omelette in the oven when he heard the bathroom door open.

Alice's face shone and her long dark hair hung down her back. She looked so young and vulnerable in Jenny's clothes. Susie was still at her feet.

'The clothes fit okay?' Paul asked.

'Thank you. I have never seen anything like that before. The water was warm. Your house, it is very strange. You must be very wealthy.'

'Not really. But here, come and have something to eat.'

She followed him to the kitchen table and he held out a chair for her. Her eyes darted around the room, narrowing at almost everything she looked at. He put the plate of piping hot eggs in front of her and pushed the toast closer to her. He poured coffee into the cups and then sat down opposite her.

She took a sip of the coffee and screwed up her face. 'What is this?'

'Coffee. You've never had coffee?'

'No.' She took another sip. She ate all the food on her plate and three slices of toast.

'Would you like more?'

'No, thank you.'

'Are you feeling better?'

'I ache a little but my head does not hurt anymore.'

'Where did you come from, Alice? What happened to you?'

Suddenly her eyes filled with tears. 'He wanted to kill me. I saw it in his eyes. A madness came over him. I tried to fight him but he hit me. I think I hurt him and then I ran. I heard him come after me but I could not run any more. And then I woke up here.'

'Who was trying to hurt you?'

Alice stared at him. 'I cannot tell you.'

He saw the fear return to her eyes. 'You can trust me, Alice. I just want to help you.' She continued staring at him and then let out a long sigh.

'Father Feandan. He never wanted me on the island. He resented the friendship I had with Father Michael. There was such darkness around him. I promised Father Michael I would never return to the island when he left with the Queen but Father Andrew was dying. He asked to see me. Father Feandan said they would burn me as a witch.' Alice looked pleadingly at Paul. 'Will he find me here?'

Paul was stunned at her outburst. He had no idea how to handle this. The girl was obviously delusional.

'Come and sit on the sofa.' He led her into the other room and handed her a box of tissues. She looked puzzled so he took some out and handed them to her. She wiped her tears and seemed calmer especially when Susie jumped up and sat beside her.

'Alice, where did all this happen to you?'

'Inchmahome. I left the other monks to mourn Father Andrew and went to the boatshed. Everything went dark and when I woke up I was back on the mainland.'

'Okay, Alice, I just want to understand this. You talked about the Queen and the monks.'

'Little Queen Mary. They brought her to the island to keep her safe after the battle at Pinkie. Father Michael left with them to go to Dumbarton Castle. A ship was coming to take them to France. They will be there by now. She is going to marry the Dauphin. I used to work at the priory helping the monks to copy the books. Father Feandan said my friendship with Father Michael was….was unnatural. He said I was a witch and had Father Michael under a spell. We both saw him slip closer to the darkness so I left at the same time as the Queen and promised Father Michael I would not go back. I thought I was safe and Father Feandan would forget about me.'

'Alice. When was this? I mean, what year is it?'

'1548.'

He stared at her, his mouth open.

'What is wrong?'

'I don't know what happened to you but something isn't right. This is the Port of Menteith but the year is 2010.'

Alice eyes closed and she slowly slipped from the sofa.

Chapter 39

Paul sat on the chair watching Alice sleeping. Susie had not left her side and was curled across her feet. He did not know what to make of all this. She did not seem crazy but her story was. She thought she was living in a time when Mary Queen of Scots was a child and had sought sanctuary in a priory that was now ruins on an island whose only visitors where tourists.

His thought that she had escaped from a mental institution must be right but he could not think what to do about it. With four malts under his belt, driving was out of the question. He could not call an ambulance. The state Alice was in, she might become hysterical and run away. She was breathing deeply so he decided to let her rest. Eventually he fell asleep on the chair and when he woke it was daylight. He made himself coffee and went back to the chair with his laptop. Mid-morning Alice eventually stirred. Susie immediately padded to her side and licked her face. She laughed as she opened her eyes and she looked over at Paul, pulling herself up to a sitting position.

'How are you feeling?' he asked.

"Better.'

'Good. We have to talk.'

'I do not understand this. It cannot be the future. How can my body be here?'

Paul knew he had to humour her until he found out what was going on. 'But why now? It's a long way in the future.'

'I do not know.' Suddenly Alice went white and left out a low growl. Tears welled in her eyes. 'My family, Father Michael, William. They are all dead. A long time ago. I must go back. They will not know what happened to me.' She jumped to her feet. 'I must go home.'

Paul was out of his depth. He needed to get her some help. Eventually she stopped crying.

'This will not do,' she said, accepting the tissue from Paul. 'It has happened. I have to work out how to get home.' She suddenly grabbed his arm. 'Can you take me home?'

'To where you lived?'

'I need to be there. If I am there maybe I can go back. Will you take me? Please.'

'Give me time to clean up and then we can go.'

By the time he had quickly showered and changed, he had worked out a plan. He would take her to where her home used to be and over to Inchmahome so she could see the ruins. Perhaps it would bring her back to reality and it would then be safe to get her help. He did not know why he felt protective of her but he just knew he could not abandon her to strangers in her delicate state. It flashed through his mind that she might be a homicidal maniac but the thought lasted but a second. Her gentleness seemed genuine and besides, he considered Susie a good judge of character.

Paul watched her from the hallway. Alice was walking slowly around the living room, gently touching things. She jumped when she realized he was there.

'I'll get the car out.' Again that puzzled look. 'I'll be back in a minute.' How was he going to explain this mode of transport?

'Well, ready any time you are. He took some shoes out of the cupboard. 'Try these on.' The canvas shoes fitted her perfectly. Once outside she stared at the white Subaru in the driveway.

'This is a car, Alice. It'll take us to where your home was.

'Where are the horses?'

'This has an engine instead of horses and will take us wherever we want.' He knew she did not understand and even if he explained, it would mean nothing to her. He opened the passenger door. 'Sit in here. There's nothing to be afraid of.'

Alice jumped when he shut the door. He could tell she was anxious. Her curiosity seemed to take over as he fastened her safety belt but she gasped when he turned the key in the ignition and the engine purred.

'You don't need to be afraid,' he said. 'You won't come to any harm. Trust me.'

He headed down the narrow private road and turned into the main road that led to the Port of Menteith. Alice stared out of the window.

'Inchmahome,' she said pointing. They caught glimpses of the island through the trees as they travelled along the road. 'It looks different.'

'Perhaps you haven't seen it from this point before?'

'I do not know.'

They drove past the church, the Lake Hotel and the car park where the small boat took tourists back and forwards to the island. Paul wondered if he was making a mistake. If her mind was firmly set in her world of 1548, nothing would be same for her. How would she react to her family and her home not being there? Despite his doubts he could not turn back now.

'The village is just up there, Alice. We turn left?'

'It is not the same. I do not recognize anything.'

Paul could sense her rising panic and was relieved the road was almost empty of traffic as he drove slowly along it, the island now in full view to the left.

'There are so many trees but my home is over there. Here, here. 'Stop here. This is it, I am sure.'

He pulled the car onto the grass verge just along from a white cottage. He got out and went round to her side, opened the door and undid her belt. She quickly got out. He stood with her as she scanned the area leading down to the lake.

'The house, the farm. They have gone.' There was such sorrow in her voice. 'It should be down there. The road that ran by the house to the edge of the loch is not there. I used to walk down to the water and look over at the island. What will I do? It is not there. My family. Everything has gone.' Tears streamed down her face and she began to shake uncontrollably.

'You're still tired. Let's go back and you can get some rest. We can come back tomorrow. You have to think this through. Plan what you want to do. You're in too much of a state to think straight now. Please. We can come back tomorrow.'

Once home, he settled her back on the sofa with Susie for company and made some tea.

'Here, sip this. I'll make us something to eat and then we can talk.' He thought of putting on the TV but realized she might not quite be ready for another wonder of the modern world. 'I'll be back soon.'

Paul opened a large can of soup and toasted some bread. When he came to tell her it was ready he found her staring straight ahead, her hand gently stroking a purring Susie.

'You are being very kind to me,' she said, after eating the meal in silence. 'Thank you.'

She helped him clear the dishes. 'What are these?' she asked, touching the kettle and microwave. 'You do not have a fire. How did you warm the broth?'

Paul tried in the simplest way possible to explain electricity, the cooker, fridge, microwave and electric kettle. Her surprise turned to curiosity as it had done with the car. She was fascinated by everything. How could she lose such a grip on reality that she did not recognize the basics. It occurred to him that she might never have lived in the outside world. Perhaps she had read a history book and made that her world.

She accepted a glass of wine and they settled themselves in the living room. 'Do you believe what I told you?'

'I believe you believe it.'

She smiled. 'If you just appeared outside of my home I would not have believed you.'

'My wife would have though. She ....'

'Your wife! Where is she?'

It suddenly occurred to Paul that Alice had been a distraction from thinking about the difficult decision he had to make. He went over to the lamp table and brought back a framed photo.

'This is Jenny. On our wedding day. She had an accident. She's been in a coma for six months. She's very sick and is being kept alive by a breathing machine. The doctors think she's getting sicker and won't come out of the coma.'

'Oh, Paul, I am sorry.'

Just then Susie started to purr loudly, her eyes still closed in sleep. They both smiled.

'Susie is Jenny's cat really. She just puts up with me. They adore each other. She follows Jenny everywhere. It's unusual for her to be so friendly to a stranger. She always hides when we have company. Not because she's afraid. Jenny said it's just that Susie can't be bothered with anyone but us.'

'I am honoured then,' Alice said, stroking the cat. 'Have courage, Paul. God has a plan for us all. Maybe it is not Jenny's time to die. There is always hope.'

'I'm trying to believe that. I love her very much. I can't imagine my life without her.' Paul sipped his wine and tried to drag himself out of the pulling darkness. 'Have you thought any more about how you got here, and how you can get back?' He felt guilty at humouring her but he did not know how else to handle it. 'I'm not making fun of you. You believe what you believe. I just don't understand it.'

'I think Father Feandan must have rowed me to the mainland near here. It was only trees before. He must have thought they would not find me. I do not know how this happened. I remember being afraid and wanting to get away from him. But I do not know how to get back. Maybe if I go to the island and will myself home. Or where my home is, was.'

'But you don't know what you're going back to. Maybe to exactly when you left and you'd still be in danger.'

'My family went to the next village to a wedding. Father Feandan will have stopped looking for me but my Pa will be back and worried about me. Can you take me to the island tomorrow?

'Sure. We'll go early, before the crowds.'

'Crowds!'

'Lots of people visit the island.' He wondered how she would react to seeing the ruins of the priory up close. He poured them each another glass of wine.

'Tell me about you and Jenny.'

'I used to be a history lecturer at Glasgow University. Jenny's an archaeologist.'

'What is that?'

'She studies the past.' He laughed. 'We both do really. Seems appropriate, considering what's happening now. She used to travel to sites all over the world, digging up ancient artefacts, but for the last five years she's lectured at Stirling University. That's when we bought this place. We've been married 10 years. I'm a full time author. I write fiction.'

'Fiction?'

'Stories. I make a good living from it. Jenny knew writing is my passion and after the success of my first novel she convinced me to give up lecturing and take a chance at my dream.'

'I love books,' Alice said. 'I missed working in the scriptorium when I had to leave, but Father Michael gave me some books to keep. They are very precious to me.'

'You copied books on the island?'

'I started when I was 13. I was able to copy the sacred texts well. The monks were pleased with my work and they gave me schooling, just as good as I would have got at one of the universities, Father Michael said. Your books, people buy them?'

'I sold 20,000 copies of my last book in the first week of release.'

'You would need many monks to copy 20,000.'

Paul laughed. 'No-one copies books by hand these days. We have machines to do that.'

'Then I would not have work,' she said with a smile. 'You and your Jenny are happy?'

'Oh yes. That's why it's so hard to.... You mentioned William. Is he your husband?'

'Oh no. We are not wed. But I do love him very much. He works for Lord Erskine and he went to France with the Queen. I miss him. William asked me to wait for him and I will.'

Paul felt himself being pulled into her fantasy. He liked her and could feel her sincerity. Of course it would have to end—he would have to find out where she really came from and get her help, otherwise she could be a danger to herself. But for now, sipping wine and talking about a different world, was an indulgence he would allow himself.

'You talk of things as if they're happening now for you but they're events I've read about in history class at school.'

'There are books about Inchmahome and Lord Erskine and the Queen?'

'Many books. Jenny has a real interest in the island. She's friends with Lynne Gardiner who works at the information booth on the island. They studied archaeology together. They can talk for hours about local history, and love finding out new things about the island. I remember her telling me the Erskines were in charge of Inchmahome and the family lived at Alloa Tower.'

'Father Michael used to go to Alloa Tower. He told me he lived there after the battle at Flodden. He was only 16 then. That is when he first started to see the dead.'

'What?'

'He told me all about it; how he was afraid when he saw the ghosts but Maurice helped him to understand. Maurice had been a monk at Inchmahome hundreds of years before that. He was the chaplain for King Robert and was at Bannockburn. He helped Father Michael with the spirits. Father Michael does not see the spirits so much on the island. He said they keep away from there most of the time. But he sees them everywhere else. Father Michael and Lord Erskine are great friends and he goes with his Lordship often to help him because he can also tell when people are lying. I thought he could read people's minds but he said he only senses feelings.' Alice smiled. 'I believe he does read minds because he always seems to know what I am thinking.'

Alice told Paul about life on the island and at home. She talked about Henry VIII, her talks with Marie de Guise and Queen Mary. She told him all about her family, describing each of them in detail and the great love they shared. Her eyes lit up when she talked about

William and Father Michael. He felt her sadness at the death of her mother and the hatred that Father Feandan bore her.

By evening Paul's thoughts of getting Alice to a doctor had disappeared. They were replaced with thinking of ways he could help her. He realized he almost believed she was telling the truth.

'You keep Susie company while I make us some dinner. Then you can get an early night and we can go to Inchmahome in the morning.'

Paul put the casserole he had taken out of the freezer that morning in the oven. While it was heating he checked his emails. He popped his head into the lounge a couple of times but Alice was sitting on the sofa with her eyes closed so he did not disturb her until the food was ready.

It was early in the evening when he opened the door to the spare room, Alice gasped in surprise. 'It is so beautiful. How many sleep here?'

'Only one. Or two maybe. It's the room we keep for visitors. I've left a nightdress for you on the bed. I'll be in the room at the end of the passage. Call me if you need anything.'

Paul felt a twinge of jealously when Susie decided she would rather sleep with Alice. He sat in the armchair sipping a malt and thought about the day. He remembered Jenny's encouragement to always go with what feels right, to allow instinct to guide him. As much as his logical mind resisted the idea, his instinct told him Alice needed his help. He decided to go with it. At least he knew Jenny would be pleased.

Chapter 40

After breakfast they headed off in the car. Paul packed some sandwiches and fruit into his backpack as he was not sure how long they would be on the island. It was the first run of the day and there were no other cars in the car park when they arrived. Malcolm, who operated the boat, greeted them as they walked up the jetty. Paul and Jenny knew Malcolm well as they were regular visitors to the island. They often met him at the local pub and he had been to dinner a few times. Jenny thought Malcolm might have been a swashbuckling pirate or an adventurer in a past life. He was a character, well-travelled and had a story for every occasion. He even suggested that Paul include him in his next novel. He could be Malcolm, the enigmatic boatman. He was well liked by the Port people as he always had a smile and greeting for everyone. Both he and Lynne visited Jenny in hospital. Paul arrived one day to find them chatting to her about the island as if she heard every word. They were that kind of people.

Malcolm smiled when he saw them approach. 'Hi, Paul, good to see you.'

'It's been a while. Just showing Alice the sights.'

'No problem.'

Malcolm told Alice about the history of the lake on the short journey to the island. He did look a bit puzzled when she said she used to row herself to the island. Alice was silent as they disembarked at the jetty and walked towards the ruins. Paul followed behind, allowing her time to take it all in. She touched what was left of the stone walls now and then and stood silent in some places. She walked to the water's edge and stared across the lake.

Paul eventually went over to her. She turned, tears streaming down her face. 'This must be hard for you,' he said.

She wiped her face. 'There is nothing left. All the monks and the books. I thought I would get some sense of them but I cannot.'

'It's been a long time, Alice.'

'Not for me.' She wiped her tears. 'Let us walk. I will tell you how it used to be.'

'This is the scriptorium where I worked on the books. I was in a world of my own here. It was so peaceful. Father Bernard was a good teacher but I always thought my work was much better when Father Michael would come and stand behind me.'

They walked where the cloisters had been and Alice pointed to the enclosed garden where Father Malcolm grew his herbs.

'This was the warming room and the kitchen. The fire was over there. You can still see where it was. Father Callum would always have warm milk ready for Pa and me when we arrived in the morning. He told me he never wanted to leave the island. And this is where I sat when Father Michael told me about Flodden.'

They walked around the grounds. She told him about the hens and Maisie the cow, the walk she took with the little Queen and

William when they found the ladybird and where the Queen picked flowers for her mother.

They walked into the area where the church had been.

'You should have seen it then, Paul. It was so beautiful. The light would stream through the coloured glass of the windows. There were paintings and tapestries on the walls. The altar was over there and the monks sat here. We would come on Sundays and Holy Days and sit there.'

Paul was fascinated by it all. The island came alive to him as he imagined the line of monks on their way to prayers or working in the garden.

Alice tried to find the tree where she used to eat the midday meal with her father but the orchard no longer existed.

'It has all changed. Let us go this way. I want to find Father Michael's oak tree.'

Paul followed her but she became agitated when she could not find it. She asked him to leave her alone for a while. He watched her from a distance as she sat under a tree, her face in shadow. He wondered if she might just disappear. He realized how hard it must be for her because in her mind her world had gone. The people she loved, her friends, her entire life had just disappeared. She was now in a totally alien world.

Eventually Alice stood up and came to sit beside him on the bench. 'Everything looks different. I do not know what tree it is or even if I am in the right place.

'Was there something special about the tree?'

'Father Michael's spirit was able to travel to the past when he sat under it. He said it must be a sacred portal. He tried to teach me but I could not do it.'

'He was a time traveller?' Paul did not feel as surprised as he thought he should be at this new revelation.

'Only his spirit. His body stayed under the tree. He would go back to old battles and help the lost spirits move on. He said it was his way of seeking forgiveness for those he killed at Flodden. What is happening now, it is different. My body is here, and it is the future. I do not know how this happened.'

They sat together in silence and ate the sandwiches and fruit. 'What do you want to do, Alice? Try again?'

'Perhaps I need to rest more. I am confused and worried and that might be stopping it.'

'Well, let's leave it a day or two and try again.'

'I cannot expect you to take care of me. You have your work, and worries of your own.'

'You're staying with me. No argument. Take as long as you like and when you feel ready we'll come back and try again. In the meantime let me show you the world as it is now.'

Alice gasped and grabbed Paul's arm. 'Is Rosslyn far away? Alloa Tower?'

'I've been to Rosslyn. It's not too far. I'm not sure about Alloa Tower but I'll find out.'

'Father Michael went to Rosslyn often.'

'Why did he go to there?'

'He would not tell me. Said it was a secret. He told me he would take me there one day.

'Then we'll go. Tomorrow.'

'We can?'

'And Alloa Tower. I'll get on the web when we get back and find out where it is.'

'The web?'

'Maybe I'll need to show you.'

'Father Michael loved the Tower. He met the love of his life there. Her name was Kate. She died and then he became a monk.'

'You obviously care for him very much.'

'I do. My life would be so different without him. He taught me so much and made me see the world differently. Without him I would have lived in fear of the spirits. I would not have understood.'

'You see the dead too?'

'Did I not say? Father Michael and I are the same. That is how we became friends. He taught me not to fear my gifts but to use them well.'

Paul shook his head. Was this really happening?

He led Alice into the information booth and introduced her to Lynne. He told her that Alice had a special interest in Inchmahome.

'Is this your first visit to our beautiful island, Alice?'

'No. I have been here before.'

'Lynne got married on the island, didn't you?' Paul said.

'That would be very special,' Alice said.

'It certainly was. I'll never forget it. I've a photo somewhere.' She rummaged in the drawer behind the desk. 'Ah, here it is.' She handed it to Alice.

'You are so beautiful, like I would imagine a princess would look.'

'Thank you, Alice.'

With her usual kindness, Lynne answered Alice's many questions. Armed with a copy of the guidebook, and a promise to visit again, they headed to wait for Malcolm to return with the boat.

'Who lives in the castle?' Alice asked, pointing across the lake. 'It looks much bigger than I saw it from the road.'

'That's not a castle, it's the Lake Hotel,' Paul said. The hotel was nestled among a variety of old trees and its magnificent white façade, dormer windows and grey roof were reflected in the still water.

'What is a hotel?'

'It's a place people come to stay, or have a meal. Some come for a drink and just enjoy the views. Jenny and I often walked there on a summer night.'

They watched the fisherman in their boats. 'The monks fish on the loch,' she said. 'Father Callum loves to be on the water. He is in charge of the kitchen.' Suddenly she put her hand on Paul's arm. 'They do not eat the swans here, do they?'

'No. Swans are the property of the Crown. They're under the Queen's protection and no-one is allowed to harm them.'

'Queen Mary would be pleased. She loved the swans.'

Paul kept Malcolm talking on the return journey. He did not want him to ask Alice how she enjoyed the island. She was silent in the car and he left her to her thoughts. She put her hand on his arm when they turned off the main road.

'Paul, there is a spirit in your house.'

'What!'

'The woman in the portrait by the window. She is with a man and a young child. They are standing beside a river.'

'That's Jenny with her parents. Her mother's in the house? She died when Jenny was fourteen.'

'She said she is watching over her child and waiting for her to come home.'

Sadness gripped his heart. 'She's waiting for Jenny to die.' His world came crashing back. He was no longer in the world of lords and monks. His reality was that his wife was dying and he could do nothing to stop it.

As Paul pulled into the driveway Alice gasped. He followed her gaze and saw Wilma in the garden.

'It's okay, Alice. Wilma's a friend.'

As they got out the car Pip and Taz came bounding over. They headed straight for Alice who laughed and bent down to stroke them.

'Come on girls, leave the lady alone,' Wilma called to the dogs but as always they did exactly what they wanted.

'Well, here was me thinking I was their favourite. Your dogs are very fickle, Wilma.'

'Girls, girls, here's the ball.' Wilma threw it down the garden and they both raced after it.

'Alice, this is Wilma. She lives over there.' Paul pointed to the white house up the lane.

'Pleased to meet you, Alice. And those two are Pip and Taz.'

Paul wondered if Wilma might have noticed that Alice was wearing Jenny's clothes. 'Let's go inside and I'll put the kettle on,' he said.

Wilma got the cups out of the cupboard while Paul made the tea. 'I passed earlier and didn't see any sign of life so thought I'd see if Susie was okay.' As if on cue, Susie came running through the catflap and headed straight for Alice, who picked her up gently. Susie settled in her arms and purred loudly.

'I've never seen Susie do that with anyone but Jenny. I'm lucky she lets me stroke her.'

'She is being very kind to me,' Alice said.

Paul knew Wilma was too much a friend to ask any questions.

They took their tea and a plate of biscuits outside and settled themselves at the garden table. Susie followed them and sat at Alice's feet.

'She obviously doesn't want you going anywhere without her,' Wilma said.

There was an awkward silence for a while. Paul knew he had to give some explanation but did not know where to start.

'Cliff get back okay?'

'A bit later than he expected. He's really tired and still in bed.'

'Cliff is Wilma's husband, Alice. He's just back from France.'

'Does he have a car too?'

'More than one. They're his passion. He doesn't take the car everywhere though. When he goes up north for work he flies, but I'm sure he'd drive there if he had the time.'

As if on cue, a deep roar started in the distance, building to a deafening shriek a second later as two jets flew overhead. Fighter jets from the Royal Air Force station at Lossiemouth sometimes used the area on training exercises. Alice dropped the cup she was holding, a look of absolute terror on her face. She stood up and cupped her hands to her ears. The roar faded as quickly as it had come but the fear on her face did not. Paul rushed to her put an arm around her shoulders.

'There's nothing to be afraid of, Alice. It's a plane. They can't harm you. You're safe.'

Alice held on to him, burying her face in his shoulder, her body shaking. Wilma was staring at them both.

'You're probably wondering what's going on?' Paul said.

'None of my business really.'

'You've been a good friend to Jenny and me, Wilma. I owe you an explanation. Let me get Alice settled and I'll come over to your place.'

Half an hour later he was sitting at Wilma's dining table. Firstly he told her about what the doctors had said about Jenny and the decision he was going to have to make. After they both shed a few tears, he explained as well as he could everything that happened since he found Alice in the garden.

'She thinks she lives here in the 16th century?' Wilma said.

'I know it sounds ridiculous.'

'You're not telling me you actually believe her?'

'I think I do. The things she's told me, and the way she describes her life, she seems so genuine.'

'Paul, you're talking time travel here. Do you know how that sounds? Maybe she's mentally ill. She could've got all the information from books. She might believe it herself but it doesn't mean it's true.'

'I know, but if you listened to her and saw her face when she couldn't find her home and then saw the ruins on the island. I didn't at first but.... oh I know it sounds crazy, but I do believe her.'

'You're going through a hard time now. You're vulnerable.'

'I know. Please don't say anything to anyone. I have to see this through with her. I'm taking her to Rosslyn Chapel tomorrow and then she wants to go to Alloa Tower. Apparently her Father Michael spent a lot of time there with the Erskines after the Battle of Flodden. I'll need to find out how to get there.'

'Flodden! Good heavens. Look, I've been to Alloa Tower with Katie when she was over last year. You and Jenny were in Italy remember, so you didn't get to see her. Do you want me to come with you? I can show you the way.'

'Would you? I'd appreciate that. Alice is very fragile. It'd be nice to have another woman there.'

'What about Jenny?'

'To be honest, this thing with Alice is taking my mind off thinking about it. I don't want that to sound heartless but I need to stop for a while and get my head straight. I see the doctor again on Friday.'

Chapter 41

At first Alice jumped at the cars speeding by them on the motorway, but gradually she settled and gazed out the window through the light drizzle at the passing scenes.

The streets were quiet as they drove through the picturesque village of Roslin. By the time Paul parked the car, the clouds had disappeared and the sun was warm on their backs as they made their way to the entrance. Once inside the grounds, Alice stopped and stared at the majestic building before them.

'I'll be back in a minute,' Paul said, leaving her to take it all in. and headed to the shop to get the tickets.

Alice stopped for a second, took a deep breath and entered the chapel. A few visitors were milling around but otherwise it was silent. Paul followed her at a distance. She made her way to the centre aisle where she stood for a long time, gazing at the altar. Then she slowly made her way around, gently running her hand across the stonework, sometimes closing her eyes. 'I am here at last, Father,' he heard her whisper.

He left her alone and walked around. He was caught up in the beauty of the place, the intricately carved pillars, the carvings of knights on horseback, angels with musical instruments, the stained glass windows, the decorated ceiling. There were Knights Templar symbols everywhere. It had been a long time since Paul had been inside a church. Not since he made up his mind that priests would no longer dangle the keys to hell in front of him. He looked at the wall behind the altar. It had stood there for over 500 years, absorbing the prayers of people long dead, those who thought God would help them and keep them safe. Perhaps He answered their prayers, perhaps not. Not long after they met, he asked Jenny why she meditated at some point every day. Was she praying? She told him that praying was to talk to God, meditating was to listen to Him. What was she doing, he wondered, in the place she was now. Was God telling her it was time to join Him? Would He hold out His hand and take care of her? But Paul was not ready to let her go. He did not want to live his life without her.

'Can you wait God,' he asked silently. 'Will you let me have her back for a while longer?' He put all thoughts from his mind and listened. Nothing. Paul went over to the corner where there was a stand with candles and an open book beside it. He lit two candles, one for Jenny and the other for Alice. In the book he asked God to protect Jenny and to safely return Alice home.

He went the souvenir shop and bought a silver bookmark and a book on the history of Rosslyn. When Alice finally joined him outside, her face was glowing. She said not a word as she followed him down the path to the castle. A house stood in the grounds but parts of the castle still remained. For Alice, Father Michael had been here not so long ago. Just before they got into the car to leave, Alice looked back at the chapel. A tear run down her cheek. She quickly wiped it and got inside.

They stopped at the Stables pub for something to eat on the way back. Alice's initial fear at the things of this new world seemed to have disappeared and was replaced with fascination. He ordered fish and chips for the two of them, a glass of wine for her and a beer for himself.

'Well, Alice, what did you think of your first visit to Rosslyn Chapel?' he asked.

'I loved it. Thank you so much for taking me. I can see why it is a special place for Father Michael. You can feel the history in the walls. I felt close to him.'

'Well, tomorrow you'll see Alloa Tower. I hope you don't mind but I've asked Wilma to come. She's been there before. I told her your story.'

'You did? She will think I am mad.'

'She doesn't know what to think about it all but she's a kind person and Jenny and I are very fond of her, and Cliff. I trust her completely.'

Once home, Paul took Alice on a walk up the lane, past the holiday chalets, to the lake, where she was able to get a different view of the island. When they got back he left her in the garden to look over the guidebook as he paid some bills online and checked his emails. When he brought her a cup of tea later in the afternoon, he found her gazing into space, the guidebook folded on her lap.

'It must be difficult for you to look at that and know what happens in the future,' he said.

'I did not read it.'

That night Paul introduced Alice to the wonders of television. She stared at the screen as he flicked from one show to the next.

'You can see what other people are doing? They allow strangers to see them?'

'It's not quite like that. People act out stories so others can watch them. Some shows are designed to make you laugh and others tell you what's happening in the world.'

'When do they work? How do they feed their families if they are watching what other people do?'

'They still work but this is entertainment. Instead of reading a book they turn on the TV and watch a show.'

'I do not understand.'

'Here, take this. Press the button and see what happens.' He handed her the remote but soon became dizzy as she kept changing the channels, her laughter ringing through the house.

The next morning they collected Wilma and headed to Alloa Tower. Wilma pointed out different places to Alice as they went along. By the time they reached their destination, both seemed relaxed with each other.

Paul imagined the historic building to be on a hill and was a bit disappointed to find it surrounded by a shopping centre and houses. But once he walked up the long pathway and stepped through its door, the outside world seemed a long way away. He and Wilma followed Alice as she wandered around. Although parts of the Tower had been restored in later centuries, it was easy to get a feel of what it was like in the times of John Erskine and Father Michael.

On the first floor, they spoke to a lady called Joyce Reekie who was an expert on the history of the Tower.

'Alloa Tower was built not only as a home for the Erskine family but to guard the River Forth,' she said. 'The Erskines go back centuries and they have a very varied and colourful history.'

'Do you know anything about the 5th Lord Erskine?' Paul asked Joyce.

'John Erskine was also Governor of Stirling Castle,' she told them. 'He was guardian to James V when he was a child and also Mary Queen of Scots so both stayed here at some point in their lives. John lost his son Robert at the battle at Pinkie. He then went with Queen Mary to France in August of 1548.'

'August?' Alice put her hand on Joyce's arm. 'He went to France in August?'

'Yes, I'm sure it was then.'

'He is still at Dumbarton Castle, Paul. Father Michael is still there. He has not yet gone to France.'

Joyce looked at them strangely.

'Oh, Alice is writing a novel about that time,' Wilma said. 'We just needs to get the facts right.'

'Let me show you something special over here,' Joyce said, walking away.

'If Father Michael is still at Dumbarton then he will know about Father Andrew's death and that I am missing,' Alice whispered. 'He will help me. He will find a way.'

At the other end of the room, Joyce was standing beside a cradle and highchair. 'Queen Mary was ill after giving birth to her son James and she brought him to the safety of Alloa Tower,' Joyce told them.

'This is a replica of the cradle where the prince slept. The original is still owed by the Erskine Family and is kept at the museum.'

Alice tried to imagine the young Queen as a grown woman, a mother. She smiled at the thought of it. Perhaps the Queen's life would not hold the darkness she once saw as part of her future. She remained silent as they explored the rest of the Tower. So much of the original building had been uncovered or restored—the original indoor well, which meant that there would always be a water supply during any siege, the vaulting on the second floor and the solar on the top floor. Joyce told them that this would have been the private living area for the family where the windows were larger. The views were magnificent. Alice sat on one of the stone seats built into the wall and looked out at the countryside below. She spent a long time looking at the portraits. Although there was none of John Erskine, she could see the family resemblance in his descendants.

They climbed the narrow stone steps to the roof. Alice looked over towards the River Forth, tears trickling down her face.

'Are you okay?' Wilma asked, handing her a tissue.

'Father Michael told me how he and Kate spent time together on this roof; how they spoke of their love for each other and the future they hoped to have. It was here he saw her ghost after she died. I believe his heart was truly broken.'

Alice seemed reluctant to leave, but after disappearing up the stairs to say goodbye to Joyce, she joined them outside. She was silent on the way home, the guidebook clutched tightly in her hand. As with the one from Inchmahome, Paul wondered if she would read it. He had not mentioned to her the ultimate fate of Mary, Queen of Scots. Perhaps it was something she did not need to know.

Wilma came in for a cup of tea before going home. Paul noticed her watching Alice intently. Was she perhaps considering the possibility that Alice was telling the truth?

Chapter 42

Wilma put on a light jacket and locked the front door. The rain had been persistent since early morning but now the clouds had cleared and the sun was shining. The bulbs she had planted in early April provided a beautiful display of colour. Taz dropped the ball at her feet and she threw it into the field. A few seconds later the little dogs were back again, dropping the ball and waiting for her to throw it. She was sure her throwing arm was longer than the other.

Wilma walked slowly towards Paul's house. He had phoned earlier to say he wanted to go the hospital and would be gone until about noon. He asked if she would go over and keep Alice company for a while. Wilma liked Alice but could not bring herself to believe her story. And if it was true? Was she really stranded in a time not her own, in a world that was strange and overwhelming? What could be done about it? How could she go back to a place that existed over 400 years in the past? What if she could not go back?

Wilma put it out of her mind. She picked up the ball and threw it along the path. The little dogs ran like the wind after it. She wished she had some of their energy. She had been like this since the bout of pneumonia she had in the winter and the doctors were not sure why.

Sometimes she was fine and then all of a sudden the tiredness returned. She was due to see the specialist again next week and hoped he could come up with some relief for her.

Wilma knocked on the door and let herself in. Taz and Pip stayed to sniff out the garden. She could not see Alice and wondered if she was asleep. She hung up her jacket and quietly walked to the kitchen to switch on the kettle. It was then that she saw Alice standing perfectly still outside under the porch. Something stopped her calling out and she just watched her. She was wearing a pair of jeans and a red jumper. Her long hair lay down her back. Wilma wondered where her thoughts were. If Alice believed her own story then she must be lonely so far from her home and those she loved. Suddenly Alice turned around and looked directly at Wilma, a gentle smile on her face. She came inside.

'I am glad you came,' Alice said. 'I was thinking about you. You are sick?'

Wilma stared at her. 'How did you know that? I do have a problem. It wears me down a bit but I'm hoping it'll get better. What were you doing outside? You seemed far away.'

'I was praying.'

'What for?'

'For you. That God would heal you.'

Wilma smiled. 'Thanks. I need all the help I can get.'

Alice walked over and took Wilma's hands. 'Close your eyes. Think of the good things in your life, and be grateful for them.'

Wilma did as Alice asked. No harm in humouring her. She felt grateful for Cliff and the life they had together, Taz and Pip, their beautiful home, her family. It seemed as if for a short time the world slipped away. She suddenly felt a surge of energy through her body and when she opened her eyes Alice was smiling. She let out a deep sigh.

'You will be well now,' Alice said. 'God took away your illness.'

'What do you mean, took it away? It won't come back?'

'No. It will not come back.'

'What did you do?'

'I am able to channel God's healing power. Father Michael showed me. It is what he does too. It is something we have to keep secret as others would think me a witch. I would be sent to the fire if anyone found out.'

Was this girl real? 'Thank you, Alice. It's very kind of you to help me.'

'Let me make you a cup of tea,' Alice said. 'I know how to do that now.'

Paul stood in front of the mirror, the reflection of the bed behind him. He loved the warm colours of this room. Jenny had chosen them. She had insisted on buying all the bedsheets and curtains and the rest of the soft furnishings. He had gone into Glasgow for the day to see his publisher and when he returned Jenny made him close his eyes as she led him into their bedroom. When she excitedly told him to look, he was delighted at the sight before him. The deep red colour of the bed quilt fitted perfectly with the polished floorboards as did the patterned red curtains. The new bedside lamps gave out a warm glow. Now, it was only a room, an empty lifeless space without Jenny. Often at night he would awake from sleep and forget she was gone. His smile would quickly fade when he remembered and the loneliness would engulf him. Susie would sense his sadness and move closer to him.

Quickly he pulled on his dark grey jumper, switched out the light and closed the door behind him. Alice was standing by the window looking out into the garden. He watched her from the doorway and thought how her presence in this house seemed so natural. She was virtually a stranger, someone whose story was too fantastic to be true but yet he did believe her. He invited her to stay in his house, gave her Jenny's clothes to wear and spent hours listening to her talking about her life. It was as if some alien being had come to stay. She knew nothing of television and fridges, washing machines and phones. She was not afraid of anything, just curious.

'Are you ready Alice? Here, take this jacket just in case it gets a bit chilly later.

She turned and smiled at him. 'Thank you, Paul.' She gently stroked the fabric as she did with almost everything. He held open the jacket and she slipped her arms into the sleeves. Paul could smell the shampoo, Jenny's shampoo, and for a moment he wanted to put his arms around her and pretend.

They were greeted in the driveway by Pip and Taz. Cliff came out and threw their ball well into the garden to divert their attention from the new arrivals.

'Hi Cliff. This is Alice.'

'Pleased to meet you, Alice.'

Paul knew Wilma would have told Cliff about Alice but he could not get any indication of what Cliff thought of it all.

'Come in and I'll get you a drink.' he said.

Wilma greeted them both with a kiss on the cheek.

'Beer for you, Paul,' Cliff asked, 'or would you like a wine?'

'Beer would be great, thanks.'

'Alice, would you like a glass of wine?'

'Thank you. I like wine.'

They all laughed.

'Katie phoned earlier,' Wilma said. 'She said to send her regards. She hopes to come over again next year. Says she still has some research to do for the new novel. Katie is my sister, Alice. She lives in Australia and is a writer like Paul.'

'Australia,' Alice repeated the name slowly. 'Where is Australia?'

'It wouldn't have been discovered in your time, Alice,' Paul said, 'so no-one would've heard of it.'

'This world is such a big place,' Alice said. 'You must miss your sister,' Alice said.

'I do,' Wilma said. 'But I speak to her on the phone all the time and she comes home every few years.'

'Paul told me about the phone but I do not understand.'

'I don't either,' Wilma said. 'I just pick it up and use it.'

During the meal, Alice watched everyone carefully and copied what they did. Her enjoyment of the food was obvious. Alice asked Wilma and Cliff many questions about their lives and seemed fascinated by their trips to France and other places in the world. She did not mention her own situation and the others did not bring it up.

Chapter 43

Alice drifted in the space between wakefulness and sleep. Her heartbeat was the only sound in the silence that surrounded her. She could not answer the question that burned in her mind. Her thoughts were a myriad of images and memory. Although she had seen some of the wonders of a world she was not born to, she knew she did not want to stay here. She wanted to go home. But why was she here?

As Alice moved further towards the darkness, she sensed she was not alone. Father Michael? No. She turned when she felt a hand on her shoulder.

'Hello, Alice.' The woman's short dark hair framed her beautiful face. She was wearing a long green dress that matched the colour of her eyes. Alice recognized her instantly from the photograph Paul had shown her.

"Jenny. You are the woman in my dreams.'

'I was lost in the darkness and I saw a light. When I moved towards it I found you.'

They talked together of many things and then the vision slowly faded.

Paul found Alice staring out of the window when he went into the living room the next morning.

'I think the reason I am here is for Jenny,' Alice said.

'What!'

'I think I have to help her get back to you.'

Paul's legs started to give way under him. He sat down on the chair and held his head in his hands. When he looked up the tears flowed freely down his face. 'Do you know how long I've prayed for a miracle, the hours I've spent talking to her, hoping that somehow she could hear me. I didn't want her to be lonely and afraid. That's how I imagine her to be, held in her silent, empty world.'

'Jenny has not been lonely or afraid. Your love kept her safe. She heard every word you said to her. She felt every thought of love.'

'How do you know this?'

'Somehow she connected with me. Before I came here I had visions of someone wrapped in white. I felt her reach out to me. I heard her in my head, asking for help. I did not know who it was or why I had the visions. I know now. Last night she came to me again. She was wearing the same dress in the likeness you showed me. We talked. There is a reason I am here and it has to do with Jenny. When I was confronted with fear and had nowhere to run, I somehow came up here. Of all the places it could have been, I was brought here. I can help her, Paul. I know I can.'

'It's taken me so long to get to this stage. The doctors tried to warn me that her body was deteriorating, but I wouldn't listen. I've seen it myself. I can't pretend any longer it isn't happening. I thought I'd go crazy just thinking about it. I've told the doctors I'd give them a decision soon. You really think it's possible to save her?' There was a pleading in Paul's voice.

'I do.'

He stared at her for a long time. 'I'll phone the hospital and tell them we're coming. I'll see if Wilma can come too.'

Sadness gripped Paul's heart as they approached the hospital. He parked next to Wilma who had driven her own car. Wilma slipped her arm through Alice's as they walked to the building. Paul was allowed access to Jenny's room whenever he wanted and the nurses nodded briefly to him as they passed.

The room was as in most hospitals—stark, the smell of antiseptic. Vases of flowers covered the table next to the small window that looked onto the street. Machines and monitors stood on either side of Jenny's bed, displaying readings that showed her body was not dead. Some beeped gently, others flashed their displays silently.

Paul approached the bed first and gave Jenny a gentle kiss on the cheek. He took her hand and sat down in the chair beside the bed. 'Maybe she's dead already and you saw her ghost, Alice. Maybe the doctors are right. It's the machines keeping her alive.' His deep sadness touched both women in the room. 'You said you might be able to help her. Maybe you're here to help her die peacefully. Do whatever you can and if it's to help her move on then that's alright too.'

Wilma went to stand behind Paul. Alice walked around to the other side of the bed and gazed down at Jenny. She reached out and took her hand from under the edge of the cover. She let out a gasp and nearly let it fall. She stared at the ring on the third finger of Jenny's left hand. It was a gold band with four rubies side by side.

'The ring,' she whispered.

'It's her engagement ring. She calls it her forever ring. I bought it for her in an antique shop in Stirling. She isn't supposed to wear jewellery in the hospital but they let her because…'

'It is my ring,' Alice said.

'Your ring?' Paul and Wilma said at the same time.

'Queen Mary gave it to me when she left the island. I would know it anywhere. It has a crown engraved on the inside.'

'My God!' Paul stood up and stared at Alice. 'It does have a crown. It's a bit faded but you can still see it. I cannot believe this. The dream, and now the ring.'

'It must all mean something, Paul,' Wilma said. 'There are too many coincidences here.'

Alice gently stroked Jenny's hand then held it in both of hers. She closed her eyes. The room was still. The sound of the machines faded into the distance. Alice was standing at the water's edge on Inchmahome. It was just before dawn and the sky was tinged with white. She could hear the monks singing. She felt at peace. She was home. She turned when she sensed she was not alone. Jenny was beside her.

'Thank you for coming, Alice. I've been waiting for you. When I first saw Inchmahome, I felt a sense of belonging. Perhaps the island and the ring connect us somehow. I don't think it's my time to die but if it is, then you will help me get to wherever I'm going. Whatever happens, will you tell Paul he must do what he feels is right. Tell him it's okay and that I'll love him always.'

They stood together as the light fully embraced the darkness. Alice felt the energy surge through her body into Jenny. Suddenly the wind sucked her upwards. She gasped and found herself again in Jenny's hospital room. She blinked to steady herself. Wilma gently sat her down on the chair.

'Are you okay?'

'Aye.'

'What happened?' Paul asked. 'You were out of it for about 15 minutes.

'I was with Jenny.'

'Oh God.' Paul's eyes filled with tears.

'You talked to her? Is she going to...?'

'I do not know, Paul. I am sorry.'

'No need to be. You did what you could. I'm grateful.'

'She said to tell you she loves you and you need to do what you must.'

They all turned around as the door opened. 'Paul.' The tall blond man nodded a greeting.

'Dr Graham. You know Wilma. This is another friend, Alice.'

'Sister told me you were here. Have you made your decision?'

Paul took a deep breath. 'Yes. You can turn off the machines.'

'I know this must be difficult for you, Paul. When would you like to do it?'

'Now.'

'Now! If that's what you want, certainly we can do it now. I just need you to sign some papers.'

Paul followed the doctor out of the room. Wilma leaned over Jenny, tears streaming down her face. 'I'll miss you, Jenny. I'll miss the good times we had and seeing your smiling face. But remember all the things we talked about. This isn't the end. We'll see each other again one day, I just know we will. You take care on your travels. Let me know if you can when you get where you're going. Love you.'

Paul returned with Dr Graham and some nurses. They gently detached Jenny from the machines and wheeled them away from the bed. Jenny looked as if she was just sleeping.

Alice sat with her arm around Wilma in the hospital corridor. Eventually Dr Graham came out and closed the door quietly behind him.

'She isn't breathing on her own,' he said.

And so they waited while Paul had his final conversation with his wife. The minutes ticked by as they sat in silence, holding hands, and praying.

Suddenly the door flew open.

'Get Dr Graham. I think she's breathing. Dear God, I think she's breathing.'

Dr Graham and one of the nurses rushed along the corridor into the room. Paul joined Wilma and Jenny in the doorway.

'I saw her chest rise. I know I did. Oh God, please let her live.'

Dr Graham looked up from his examination. 'Paul, I don't know what to say. There are signs of life. We're going to check to see if there's any brain function. Sometimes this happens. Please don't get your hopes up. Have a seat and I'll let you know as soon as I can.'

After what seemed like an age Dr Graham came out. 'We're registering brain function but we won't know how much until she comes around. I can't even tell you how long that will be. All we can do is leave her and hope she gains consciousness.'

'I'll stay with her.'

'Yes, of course.'

'Wilma, will you take Alice home with you. I'll phone you if anything changes.'

'I'll look after her. Call me.'

'I promise. Pray for her.' He kissed them both and went to sit by his wife.

Wilma and Alice were silent on the way home. 'You'll stay with me until we hear,' Wilma said. 'We'll have a cup of tea and then we can walk over and feed Susie.'

They sat on the decking, taking no pleasure from the warmth of the afternoon sun.

'Are you alright, Alice?'

'I am just sad, and confused.'

'You did what you could.'

'I do not know why I am still in this time. If I did not come to help Jenny then why am I here?'

'You must be afraid too, so far from your family.'

'I do not know how I am going to get back. I need to go home. I do not belong here.'

'When Paul comes we'll talk it all through. There must be a way and we'll help you find it.'

'Thank you, Wilma. I am glad we met.'

'Me too.'

They walked with the dogs to Paul's house. They found Susie sound asleep on the sofa. She opened one eye, and then jumped down to greet them. She ate the food Wilma gave her and then returned to her position on the sofa.

'We'll come back later if Paul doesn't get home before dark.'

They headed along the path to the lake and stood gazing over at the island.

'There are so many trees,' Alice said.

'What was it like in your time?

'Just as beautiful. There is a peace there. It makes everything seem in place. Father Michael says there are many sacred places in the world where people can feel close to their God.'

'Cliff and I aren't religious but I know what you mean. We visited the Rennes-le-chateau in the Languedoc region in south west France. It had connections to the Knights Templar. We were the only people there but it felt as if there were others. It made the hairs on the back of our necks stand up.'

Alice laughed.

'What is it?'

'Father Michael knew the Templars. They came with him to the island one day with books from Rosslyn Castle.'

'Good heavens.'

'You and Cliff have travelled to different places, like Father Michael?'

'It's easier now I suppose than in your time. Do you want to travel Alice? Are there places you want to go?'

'I got to see Rosslyn Chapel. I always wanted to go there and Father Michael said that I would one day. And Alloa Tower. Now, I just want to go home.'

'Tell me about your family.'

Alice's sadness lifted as she told Wilma about her family and William. She glowed in the telling. For her it was only yesterday.

'And Father Michael. How did you first meet him?'

'We went to Mass on the island with Aunty Moira. They had been friends for a long time. He had been away for a while with Lord Erskine. He was with Queen Marie when little Queen Mary was born, and with King James when he died. Before I met him I was always afraid. I saw ghosts and heard voices. I sometimes knew things were going to happen. Granny was the same. That is why we came here. They spread gossip that she was a witch but she only ever helped people. I never saw her again after we left. I knew there was something strange the first time Father Michael looked at me. He knew my secrets but that was because he was the same as me. He stopped me being afraid. He helped me accept who I am and taught me so much. I miss him.'

'He sounds a very special person.'

'He is.'

Chapter 44

Wilma and Alice reached Paul's house when they saw his car coming along the road. They waited anxiously in the driveway. He was smiling.

'She's still alive, not conscious, but alive.'

'Thank God,' Wilma said.

'They still can't say how much damage has been done. They've stabilized her. No drugs or machines. She just seems to be sleeping. I've come to shower and change. They told me to come back tomorrow but I want to be there in case she wakes up.'

'You go do what you have to, Paul. I'll make you something to eat.'

It was a much happier Paul who joined them at the kitchen table.

'I've made some poached eggs and lots of toast. I didn't think you'd eat a big meal.'

'This is perfect. Thanks.'

They took their tea into the living room. Susie merely looked up at them, stretched, and contently went back to sleep.

'Susie would know if Jenny wasn't coming back, I know she would,' Paul said. 'You said her mother's ghost is in the house, Alice, waiting for her. I thought it meant waiting for her to die but she means waiting for her to come home here. I know she's going to be alright. I just know it. She'll wake up soon and she'll be back to normal. Dr Graham says they don't know how she'll be until she comes round, but he sounds hopeful. I know this is down to you. Alice. I have no words to thank you enough for what you've done for us. You didn't choose to come here but I'm glad you did. You've lost everything and I'm so sorry for that.'

Alice smiled. 'It was meant to be. I do not understand it but God must know what He is doing.'

'Let's talk about getting you home. Do you have any idea what we can do to make it happen? I was thinking on the way back from the hospital that if it's possible to get you from 1548 then it must be possible to get back. We just have to work out how. Should we go back to the island or where your home was? You've done what you came here to do so maybe it's time to try.'

'Sunset and sunrise are Father Michael's favourite times of the day. I think he will try at those times. At sunset I will go to where I must have landed? I will try to get a sense of him. I know you want to go back to Jenny.'

'It's not long to sunset now. I won't let you do this on your own. We'll go together and try. Do you want to come, Wilma?'

'Cliff is due home soon and I think it's something you should do together.'

The three of them walked to the door, Wilma linking her arm with Alice.

'When I get home, Wilma, I will bury something for you beside that big old tree in your garden. Perhaps it will still be there.'

'Wouldn't that be fantastic? I'll wait until Cliff gets home, otherwise I'll have to explain the holes in the garden. I'm so glad I got to meet you, Alice.'

'I will pray for you every day, Wilma.'

'You take care of yourself. I wish you and your William a happy life together. Let me know how things are going, Paul.'

'Will do. Thanks, Wilma. We'll talk soon.'

Both woman were crying as Wilma gave Alice one last hug.

Paul made them more tea and they sat on the sofa with Susie between them. The cat laid her head on Alice's leg and purred loudly as Alice stroked her gently.

'She'll miss you.'

'I do not think so. She knows she will see her Jenny soon. Cats know these things. And there is something I did not tell you. When Jenny and I talked in my dream that last time we realized I came here not just for her. I came for your daughter.'

'My daughter? We don't have any children.'

'But you will.'

Paul sighed. 'No. We tried before the accident but the doctor said he didn't think Jenny could conceive. It was hard but we accepted it and got on with our lives.'

'No, Paul, you and Jenny will have a daughter.'

'And you came for her. Why?'

'It is Jenny's destiny and yours to guide your daughter to where she needs to be.'

'And where's that?'

'She will bring light to a darkness that is coming. I do not know what it is, but she has something special to do with her life.'

'Oh Alice, I don't know what to say. How can I not believe you after all that's happened?

They walked arm in arm along the path to the lake. Paul thought how vulnerable Alice looked dressed in one of Jenny's woollen coats. He insisted she wear it as he did not know how long they would have to wait. They stood among the trees gazing over at the island.

'Perhaps I'll write a book about you, Alice,' Paul said. 'It'll have to be fiction of course. No-one will believe it's true.'

She smiled. 'But we will know it is.'

'You didn't bring the guidebooks from Alloa or Rosslyn,' Paul said.

'I was tempted to read them and to bring them but I do not want to know what happens. I just want to be with the people I love and live in the time I have on this earth.'

'You really have to go? What am I saying? Of course you do. Back to your family. I'll miss you, Alice, and there are no words to describe how grateful I am.'

'I will miss you too, and Wilma. She has such a strong and giving spirit.'

'You don't know what you're going back to?'

'I am going home, that is all that matters. Whatever awaits me there, I know God will give me the courage to face it.'

'You won't forget us?'

'No. When I look to where your house will one day be, and on the island, I will think of you all. Perhaps if we remember at the same time we will connect again.'

'I hope so. We'll come here with our child.' He took her hands, drew them to his lips and kissed them.

Alice put her arms around his neck and held him close. When she pulled away he saw her tears. He wiped them gently with his hand.

Paul did not take his eyes from her as she walked slowly towards the water. As the sun began to disappear behind the hills, he struggled to keep her in view. Time passed but still he watched. Then something caught his eye. He saw movement near the tree. It was hazy but then Paul clearly saw the tall figure in a dark cloak with the hood drawn up. Alice rushed forward into his waiting arms. They stood there for a moment, holding each other tightly, and then they were gone.

Father Michael had come to take Alice home.

THE END

Epilogue

Michael stood on the roof of Alloa Tower, his eyes fixed on the path of moonlight that led to the river. As he always did in this place, he thought of his beloved Kate. His memory of her never faded. To see her smiling face and feel her breath on his cheek, all he had to do was close his eyes.

He was happy to be finally home in Scotland. He still worried about young Queen Mary but for now she was safe and happy in France.

Father Feandan's disappearance from the island was never discussed. Michael still found great joy in the times he spent in the company of Marie de Guise. She was to arrive tomorrow when he would conduct the marriage service for Alice and William. True to her word Alice had waited for William's return and their love blossomed. With Michael's consent, John gifted the land where he and Kate were to build their home to the young couple. He knew Kate would be pleased.

Michael wondered what the future held for him. He knew it was possible for his spirit to travel to the future as well as the past but for now he was content not to explore any new adventures. Whatever lay ahead, he hoped it would not lead him too far from his beloved Inchmahome.

Author's Notes

INCHMAHOME

The island of Inchmahome is both beautiful and mystical. It is situated on the Lake of Menteith which in the 16th century was referred to as a loch. The priory is now mostly ruins but great effort has been made to keep it a place for visitors who will appreciate its place in the history of Scotland.

PORT OF MENTEITH

The Port of Menteith was established as a burgh of barony in 1457 by King James III of Scotland. It is situated on the north-east shore of the Lake of Menteith.

ALLOA TOWER

This magnificent medieval tower was built by the Erskine family around 1368. I found it easy to imagine Michael sitting with John Erskine by the fire in one of its elegant rooms, and Michael and Kate on its roof. Alloa Tower is under the care of the National Trust of Scotland.

STIRLING CASTLE

Once home to the kings and queens of Scotland, Stirling Castle engulfs you in its history and beauty.

MAURICE, Michael's mentor and friend, was the Prior of Inchmahome between 1927 and 1309 and was present at the Battle of Bannockburn.

JACQUES DE MOLAY was the last Grand Master of the Knights Templar. The Order was betrayed by the Pope and the King of France on 13 October 1307. Many Templars died and after seven years of prison and torture, Jacques de Molay was finally burned alive in 1314. There has always been speculation that the Templars' treasure is somewhere in Scotland and that the Stroud of Turin was in fact the cloth wrapped around the Grand Master, not Jesus. The presence of the Knights Templars in Scotland is widely recorded.

ABOUT THE AUTHOR

Cathy M. Donnelly was born and lived most of her life in Scotland, which she considers to be one of the most beautiful and magical places on earth. This ancient land, with its endless stories of battles and alliances, villains and warriors, instilled in Cathy a love of reading and writing about history and the people who made it.

Cathy's interests include Norse mythology, the Knights Templar, secret societies and the supernatural. She enjoys incorporating these themes into her writing. Cathy researches any real historical characters and events thoroughly in the hope the reader is swept into a believable world that has a touch of magic. She likes to set her novels in a point in history and flow into the past and future using reincarnation, flashbacks and time-travel elements.

Cathy now lives by the coast in Australia and her favourite part of any day is the time she spends with her two cats.

Contact details:

Website: www.cathymdonnelly.com
Email: catherinemdonnelly@hotmail.com

NOVELS BY CATHY M. DONNELLY

DISTANT WHISPERS

Rachel is a powerful healer and for her the veil that separates the living and the dead does not exist. She experiences extraordinary challenges in her many lifetimes and faces each with unwavering courage and the determination to fulfil the destiny that awaits her.

In the year 1665, Rachel escapes the cruelty of King Louis XIV of France and seeks sanctuary in a village in England. She is here for a reason but realizes it is not for Edward, even though she loved him from that first moment. She sees the doubt in his eyes when she is accused of witchcraft, but it matters not, for as she flees to London, where a devastating plague is spreading rapidly across the city, she knows they will meet again.

Centuries later, Rachel encounters both friends and enemies from her past.

Available from Amazon in paperback and Kindle, and from the author - www.cathymdonnelly.com

Read the first chapter and reviews - www.cathymdonnelly.com

59151663R00191

Made in the USA
Charleston, SC
28 July 2016